ARCANIST FABLES

FRITH CHRONICLES SHORT STORY COLLECTION

SHAMI STOVALL

ARCANIST FABLES

FRITH CHRONICLES SHORT STORY COLLECTION

SHAMI STOVALL

Published by
CS BOOKS, LLC

Cover Design: Darko Paganus

IF YOU WANT TO BE NOTIFIED WHEN SHAMI STOVALL'S NEXT BOOK RELEASES, PLEASE VISIT HER WEBSITE OR CONTACT HER DIRECTLY AT

s.adelle.s@gmail.com

ISBN: 978-1-7347587-9-5

CONTENTS

I don't usually write long dedications, but this time I'll make an exception.

Several months ago, it felt as though I had a hole in my chest—the kind of painful void that only loss can bring. And during the roughest moments, I just wasn't myself. I'm a night owl, but I didn't want to be left alone in the dark. I enjoy cold weather, but even the slightest chill brought dark thoughts. And while I'm known to have relentless nightmares, during this timeframe, I would wake in tears, unable to sleep.

Thankfully, I have a man named John in my life.

When I told him that I was afraid of the darkness, he kept all the lights on in the house, 24/7.

When I told him the cold messed with my thoughts, he kept the heater on, no matter the temperature outside.

When I woke in tears, he pulled me close and whispered beautiful nothings.

When I couldn't sleep, he held my hand until I did.

It wasn't just the loss of people, but a future I had hoped for as well. So, when I told John I had imagined a life with a dog, fun events, cooking, and lots of story discussions and book writing, he got us a puppy (which he named Pierce, after a character from one of my books), planned tons of future gaming events, agreed to cook with me, and then said, "You don't have to worry—I'll be whatever person you need in any situation."

So, John decided that on top of being an attorney (who has now won several appellate decisions and is recognized in his field) he would also become an author. He joined my writer's group. He studied grammar and punctuation. He learned the nuances of dialogue and exposition. He even had long talks with me about the benefits of 3-act structures over 6-act structures.

He gave up all his free time to work two fulltime jobs—an attorney during the day and a hardworking author at night.

And when I asked him, "Why do all this?" He replied, "Because when I went through something similar, you were there for me. And if I needed it again, you'd be there. That's who you are. And that's why we're soulmates."

At the time of this book release, John is officially done with his novel. He wrote it in less than two months (a feat most authors struggle with). It's a great story (fantasy, dungeons, epic adventure), and it'll hit shelves in the near future. It's a labor of love, and John even admitted it was one of the most rewarding experiences of his life.

The most memorable and uplifting moment I can remember was when John said, "Doing all this is a small price to pay to have you in my life, Shami. You're worth it. And I'll be here for you until the darkness is your friend once again."

I'm happy to say that John's efforts were successful.

Which is why Arcanist Fables is dedicated to him, and him alone.

Thank you, Johns. You're a cut above the rest and talented beyond words.

I love you so much and always will.

THE FABLE OF THE TRUE SHALE RUNESTONE

ILLIA SAVAN

During the events of World Serpent Arcanist *(Book 5)*

I made an art of stealth.

When I had been younger, I had mastered crawling through every dark alley on the Isle of Ruma. Moving without making much noise became my hobby—Volke was busy memorizing the phrases on the Pillar, so I had to occupy myself with *something*. And now that I had finally become an arcanist, my ability to slip by undetected had become legendary. Or at least, it felt that way.

Rizzel magic was all about uninhibited movement. With teleportation, walls no longer posed a deterrent. With gravity manipulation, even heights became trite. And if I found something I couldn't get around—somehow—I could destroy it with my disintegration flames.

Which meant the back alleys of Millatin weren't obstacles. The Second Ascension was here. King Rishan had arrived on his vessel, the *Black Throne*, and ever since then, Volke had become tense and distant.

He had been distant for some time, actually, but he didn't need my worries on his mind while he dealt with so many other problems, so I kept them to myself. We needed to find the world serpent, and Volke has so much invested in the search... It made me invested as well, a fact I didn't know how to deal with.

I shook my head, dispelling the odd thoughts.

"You were thinking about Volke again, weren't you?" Nicholin whispered in my ear.

"Of course not," I muttered.

Nicholin wrapped his silky fur body under my hair and across the back of my neck. He was still small enough to do the motion without much effort, but I could tell he had grown over the years. His back paws now rested on my right shoulder while his front paws rested on my left shoulder. He hadn't been able to do that before.

I slipped through a narrow alleyway, keeping the hood of my cloak up over my head. Nicholin poked his head out of my cloak from time to time, glancing around with his bright blue eyes, wiggling his ferret-like nose as though he had caught a whiff of our target.

"The docks are close," he said, a smile in his voice. "You can smell the salt from here."

I nodded as we rounded a corner onto the main street. The gates of the dock weren't far. The tall, looming rocks in the bay broke the incoming waves, creating a song of tides. I had lived on an island my entire life—the song soothed me. After a few minutes of walking, I arrived at the gates, and instead of checking in with the city guard, I concentrated on my magic and teleported from one side of the barrier to the other.

The teleportation process happened in a fraction of a second, but the sensation of being ripped from one location to another felt... jarring. It rocked me enough that the process seemed to take longer in my thoughts. It wasn't painful, but I could feel my insides twist, and my limbs shake, right before the magic whisked me to a new location.

I shook away the odd sensations and glanced around the docks. The midnight hour kept everything shrouded in darkness, but the lanterns provided enough illumination to identify the ships.

The *Black Throne* wasn't difficult to find. It was a massive galleon—the extravagant kind with three masts and eight sails. Knowing that it was for a king, I suspected they were silk sails, because why not? The priorities of kings and queens always confused me.

Three nautical flags waved from the center mast. Every ship had to have three flags for communication—one was for the ship's nation, one signified if they had arcanists aboard, and the last one was to communicate the state of emergency. Obviously, the *Black Throne* flew a flag with a red rose and black dragon intertwined. It was the symbol of the Argo Empire, but the ship was so damn famous, it could've been the empire's national animal—it didn't need a flag.

The *Black Throne's* arcanist flag fluttered a bright gold, which meant there were, in fact, arcanists aboard the ship. I considered them *obstacles* rather than people who could wield magic, but that probably wasn't considered polite.

And finally, the last flag was a dull gray, which meant *nothing to report*. If I did my job correctly, they'd never have a reason to change that flag.

"I'm so excited," Nicholin whispered into my ear, a slight giggle at the edge of his words.

"Shh," I replied. "We need to keep a low profile."

"The *Black Throne* will be a challenge unlike any we've ever faced." Nicholin shuddered and offered a quiet squeak.

"That means we need to be extra quiet."

"We won't be able to use our magic—not with all that nullstone wood."

"I remember," I drawled.

"We'll have to do all the sneaking the old-fashioned way. Like, uh, *expert assassins!* Doesn't that excite you?"

My heart beat faster than before as Nicholin's words soaked into my thoughts. Volke used to read hundreds of tales involving legendary arcanists and their larger-than-life adventures. I had always enjoyed the assassins and spies Volke spoke about. While other arcanists had just been *powerful* or *well equipped*, the assassins and spies had a clever wit about them. They had plans. They had cunning and guile.

I wanted to be *that* kind of arcanist.

A man dressed in a heavy cloak wandered the dock at a slow pace. He kept his hood up, hiding his face and forehead, but I didn't need either of those to identify him. His brawn and bulk gave him away in an instant—Zaxis had a distinct look about him.

But why was he here?

I observed him from a shadowy corner on the dock, tucked between two empty barrels, my own hood over my head. When Zaxis ambled closer, his gaze darting from one pier to the next, I hustled out from my inconspicuous location and grabbed his muscular arm.

"What're you doing here?" I asked in a harsh whisper.

He tensed as he struggled to get a good look at me in the dim light of the nearby lantern. The moment recognition flashed in his green eyes, he relaxed. "Illia," Zaxis muttered under his breath. "I knew this was where you'd be."

I yanked him back to my barrels, glancing up and down the docks as I did so. It didn't appear as though anyone was watching us. Zaxis allowed me to pull him along—if he had wanted, he could've dug his heels in and stopped us dead.

"Zaxis," Nicholin said with a huff and a squeak. "We're on a secret mission. Get back to the atlas turtle right this instant."

"I'm here to help," he growled through clenched teeth. "I figured you two would be up to something the moment I saw King Rishan's fancy vessel."

Nicholin fluffed his fur. "We're stealthy. Like deadly owls at night. You're... a seagull. At best."

I knew where this exchange was going. I placed my hand on Nicholin's face and then tapped Zaxis's shoulder. He quirked an eyebrow, and I narrowed my one eye back at him. Now wasn't the time for their comical bickering.

"Nicholin has a point," I whispered. "You're tumultuous." I motioned to his body. "And large."

Zaxis gave me half a smirk as he gently ran his knuckles along the edge of my jaw. "Nothing wrong with that, right?"

"You're not supposed to leave the atlas turtle until we've confirmed or denied you have the plague."

"I don't have it. You saw. Vethica used her magic."

Technically, everyone in the Frith Guild was supposed to be searching for an arcanist from the Huntsman Guild— they had trinkets that detected the plague. But Vethica had already used her khepera magic on Zaxis... He was likely okay, but until we had the confirmation, it was still up in the air.

Nicholin ducked under my hand and then stuck out his tongue.

"Watch it, *weasel*," Zaxis growled.

"We can't risk getting caught," I said. "Who knows what King Rishan would do if he caught us?"

"What's so important that you'd risk yourself to get it?"

"The shale runestone," I whispered.

Zaxis's eyebrows shot to his hairline. "Oh, yeah? How can you be so sure?"

"I overheard Fain talking to Volke about it. King Rishan and his betrothed are gathering people to the third god-creature—the fenris wolf. They have the shale runestone with them."

Finding the Huntsman Guild was supposed to be our top priority, but the shale runestone was more important. Volke and Fain had said they would investigate the *Black Throne*, but they weren't as good at infiltrating places as I was. If I managed to get the runestone and bring it back to the guild, it would be a major win—and a major loss for our enemy.

"How does Volke get himself wrapped up in all the significant stuff?" Zaxis asked, rolling his eyes. "And shouldn't we just tell Master Zelfree or any other master arcanists here?"

"They're either searching the town or recruiting people for the guild," I said.

And we were running out of time. This was a race. The Second Ascension was rushing to find god-creatures, and so were we. I didn't know when Master Zelfree, Guildmaster Eventide, or even the Grand Apothecary would return from their assignments. Waiting for them was a waste. I could do this—and I was a journeyman arcanist now. I knew our ultimate goal, and if I was going to be more of a "team player," like Zelfree wanted, returning with the shale runestone seemed appropriate.

"We have to retrieve the runestone," Zaxis said, practically parroting my thoughts. "We don't have time to wait for everyone. What if the *Black Throne* leaves? They could do so at any time." He tugged on my shoulder and pulled me into a one-armed embrace. "And I'm going to help you. There's no discussing it."

Nicholin huffed. Then he glanced around, his tiny eyes narrowed. "Where's your eldrin, Forsythe? He's the one with all the brains. He needs to talk you out of this."

"I left him back at the atlas turtle to cover for me. Also, his bright, fiery body isn't suited for stealth." Zaxis motioned to his dark cloak. "I came prepared."

A pair of sailors ambled down the dock, each carrying a sack of vegetables over one shoulder. They mumbled things to each other, too soft to distinguish the words. The slur on their voices betrayed their drunkenness. I placed a hand over Zaxis's mouth as the men passed by our barrels. Neither glanced over, but I didn't release Zaxis until they had turned and headed for the dock gate.

"You can come with," I whispered. "But you have to do as I say."

Zaxis nodded.

"I mean it." I stared at him, his green eyes shifting back and forth, as though both trying to focus in on my one eye. "We can't afford any mistakes."

Again, he nodded.

Nicholin sighed. "I guess I'm going to have to work *extra* hard to make sure Zaxis doesn't get into any trouble." He teleported from my shoulders and into Zaxis's cloak.

Zaxis flinched as Nicholin slid around the back of his neck. "Hey," Zaxis growled, though he kept his voice low. "Careful."

"Pay attention," I said. "We'll need to avoid everyone on, and around, the ship."

I motioned to the *Black Throne* and then pointed to the guards around the gangplank.

We *could* board the vessel the normal way, but I knew that would definitely get us caught. None of us had the magic of disguise, and while ongoing magical effects wouldn't necessarily be interrupted by the nullstone wood, it would prevent any activation of new powers—no teleporting away if we got into trouble. Which meant we needed a secure way to get on and off the *Black Throne*.

"We're going to climb our way on," I whispered.

Zaxis snorted. "Seriously? Have you ever tried to do that? Scaling the side of a ship is difficult. And it's not like the sailors will have just left a rope ladder dangling off the side for potential stowaways. What're you planning? To climb the anchor chain?"

I shook my head. Then I grabbed Zaxis's arm. "I also came prepared. Hang on. We're going to teleport."

Before he could answer, I activated my teleportation and yanked us through space. A second later, we popped and appeared under one of the piers, landing in a dinghy I had secured to the dock hours prior. It was a tiny vessel—one meant for a max of three people—and it already felt cramped with just me and Zaxis. I had tucked a rope, a hook, and a jug of water under the sole seat.

"Nicholin will secure this to the bow of the ship," I said as I knelt and withdrew the rope and hook.

"Oh, we're going to do a classic *cutting out* maneuver," Zaxis said as he stumbled around, trying to regain his bearings after the teleport. The dinghy rocked with his weight but not enough to capsize us. He took a seat and sighed. "I read a story about the successful cutting out of the *White Eagle*. Pirates took the whole ship by surprise."

If Volke had been here, he would've immediately gone

on and on about the cutting out boarding maneuver. He knew entirely too much about sailing and boats. I never understood why the maritime folks needed their own special word for everything. *Stern* meant *back*. *Bow* meant *front*. *Port* meant *left*. *Starboard* meant *right*.

It was its own damn language and *cutting out* basically translated to *stealthily boarding an anchored ship at night*. Why did that need its own special phrase? Nautical people always made things difficult. On the other hand, all the odd terminology had made me think of Volke. So, I guess I didn't mind the extra words and phrases.

"What's that look for?" Zaxis asked, pulling me from my thoughts.

I shook my head. "Nothing."

"You get like that sometimes, ya know. Quiet and distant."

"I'm fine."

I untied the dinghy and pushed it away from the pier post. The little boat rocked in the wakes of larger ships as it slid atop the water. I grabbed an oar and paddled our dinghy toward the middle of the bay. We wouldn't approach the *Black Throne* from the docks, so instead, I'd go out, then circle back around so I could approach the vessel from behind.

Zaxis took a seat and leaned back. "You want me to do that?"

I glared at him.

He smirked. "I'm damn good at it."

"But I'm quieter. I'll handle it."

"Suit yourself."

With the darkness of night as our ally, we traveled out into the bay and slowly turned around. The water was as black as the sky, and it appeared as though we were gliding over oil.

Nicholin leapt off Zaxis's shoulders and darted around the dinghy, constantly looking over the edge and staring at the water. He claimed he liked looking at his own reflection, but I knew he was searching for "treasure." That was what Nicholin called all the junk he found in the ocean that people had accidentally dropped overboard.

Volke had occasionally done the same thing when we had been younger. He would set off to the beach and scour the sands for "buried treasure." It had been a stupid game—no one would bury valuable treasure on the beaches of Ruma—but that hadn't stopped Volke from talking about adventure and arcanists of old.

From time to time, Gravekeeper William and I would sneak out at night and bury things in the sand for Volke to find. Nothing important—just small boxes of knickknacks and crudely drawn maps of the island, with little Xs to represent more buried treasure.

Volke probably knew it had been us burying the objects, but he had never mentioned it—and the reality of the situation had never dulled his excitement when he found a new box under the white sands of the beach.

It was Volke's enthusiasm that I had loved most as a child. And because of his love for treasure, I felt it occasionally as well—a deep-seated excitement to find valuable things just out of view.

Nicholin teleported to my shoulders with a soft pop. He pushed his nose into my ear and whispered, "You're taking us in the wrong direction. Are you paying attention?"

"I am," I snapped. "I'm just... tired."

Nicholin drew back and crossed his little front paws. "Hmm."

I used the oar to correct my path—angling the dinghy toward the *Black Throne*. Although it was night, men still clattered around the dock, most of whom had been drinking or were still working a long shift. We could hear it all the way out in the bay.

"You okay?" Zaxis asked. He leaned forward and placed his elbows on his knees. "Is this an instance where you wished Volke were here with us?"

I gritted my teeth and forced out a quick exhale. "No. I don't wish Volke were with us." I shot him a glower. "And don't ever say that again. I don't like it."

"Why?" He shrugged. "He's your brother. I get it."

The water from an incoming ship sent tiny waves our way. They splashed against the side of the boat, but it didn't bother me. Even if we fell into the water, I could easily swim or teleport to safety.

"I'm my own person," I said, rowing with more strength and power than I had before. "Okay?"

"Yeah, of course you are."

I took in a deep breath, allowing the salt water to calm my nerves. "You say that so easily, but…"

Nicholin perked up. "But what? You think you're not your own person?"

I took Nicholin off my shoulders and placed him on the bottom of the dinghy. "It's not that. I just…" The memories of Volke, the Isle of Ruma, and Gravekeeper William swirled in my head. "It's nothing important. We don't need to discuss it."

Zaxis motioned to the *Black Throne*, and then to the distance between us and the ship. "We have a few minutes. Try me. What's bothering you?" He scooted to the edge of the seat and smiled. "C'mon. We've told each other all sorts of things. Why would this be different?"

"I'm sometimes afraid I just like things because other people do," I blurted out, wanting this over as quickly as possible. I continued to row, faster and faster. "Okay? Sometimes I think, *Illia, why do you like old tales of heroic arcanists*? And the only answer I can come up with is *because Volke liked them*. Other times I think, *Illia, why do you always prepare your fish the same way*? And it's because that was how Gravekeeper William used to prepare it. Am I even me if I keep doing and liking things that other people do?"

Zaxis and Nicholin remained quiet.

I had known they wouldn't understand.

I turned away from them, my shoulders bunched at the base of my neck. "Forget about it. I just get wrapped up in my own thoughts, thinking they're not even my own."

Zaxis reached out and caressed my upper arm with his knuckles. "Don't worry about it. All of that is normal. I still make soup the exact same way my mother made it because it reminds me of her."

"It's not about the *food prep*," I said with a sigh. "It's deeper than that." I pulled away from his touch.

"No, I get it. I swear."

I didn't reply.

Zaxis forced a laugh, his tone distant and melancholy. "When I was eight, I was smitten with a girl back on our home island. One day, she made me try these sweet rice cakes her grandmother made, despite my protests. Now, I love those damn sweet rice cakes, and it's not even because they're good, it's because they remind me of the happy memories with her."

Silence stretched between us. We had almost reached the *Black Throne*.

"I never had much of an opinion about eyepatches,"

Zaxis muttered as he leaned back on the dinghy. "But now I think every woman would look better with one."

I touched the eyepatch with a shaky hand, my fingers grazing the spot where my eyeball should've been. It was a crater in my face—I could feel my skull just beneath the black cloth of the patch—and I had always considered it hideous.

Zaxis liked my eyepatch?

He sat forward and caressed my upper arm again. "When you think about it, we're all just a mosaic of everyone we've ever cared about, ya know?"

"Wow," Nicholin whispered, his whiskers fluttering in the bay winds. "What did you sacrifice to the abyssal hells to become that sappy? Because that's not within normal human parameters."

Zaxis glared. "That was all me, weasel. And it was profound."

"Pfft. Maybe in the dreams Adelgis weaves for you, but not reality."

"I liked it," I whispered. "It was... exactly what I needed." I leaned over to Zaxis and kissed him—not quick, but not intimately either. A thorough *thank you* for helping me with inner turmoil.

Zaxis straightened his posture. "Hear that?" He poked Nicholin in the ribs. "This is why you don't have a lady-rat in your life. You're not poetic, like me."

With another quick teleportation, Nicholin appeared on Zaxis's shoulder and squeaked angrily into his ear. Zaxis swatted him away, a chuckle on his breath. The two fought each other like brothers, rowdy enough to rock the dinghy.

I didn't mind. My thoughts remained on Zaxis's statement. I was a mosaic—taking parts of everyone I had ever cared for with me and leaving a piece of myself with them.

Gravekeeper William, Master Zelfree, Volke, Zaxis... Perhaps others I had yet to realize. The fond memories bolstered me.

Zaxis grabbed Nicholin around his body and then threw Nicholin over the side of the dinghy, Zaxis's strength enough that Nicholin twirled in the air for a good ten feet before descending. As he spun, Nicholin chittered out several curses.

My eldrin teleported before he touched the water and then reappeared on my shoulder with a pop.

"Illia," he said with a squeak. "Zaxis threw me! Did you see that? Tell him that's not allowed."

"What's wrong with you two?" I said, keeping my voice low. I motioned to our surroundings, drawing attention to our proximity to the *Black Throne*. We were less than a minute away from reaching the stern, and yet they were acting like bickering children.

Both Zaxis and Nicholin gave me sheepish, and whispered, apologies. I glanced around, fearful someone had spotted us. Thankfully, it appeared as though the guards weren't keeping watch out into the cold bay. And the crew members of the *Black Throne* were either on shore, sleeping, or milling about the ship, cleaning and reorganizing.

I picked up Nicholin and set him in Zaxis's lap. "Play nice," I muttered.

They remained still and quiet until we reached the enemy's ship. I lifted the oar out of the water and placed the paddle against the side of the ship, steadying us and preventing the dinghy from crashing into the *Black Throne*.

Ten feet above us was the captain's quarters. Giant glass windows were built into the back of the ship, but the thick glass and paneling made it difficult to see anything.

"Is that where we're going?" Zaxis asked.

I shook my head.

"Why not?" He furrowed his brow. "I think they'd probably keep the runestone in the captain's quarters. It makes sense."

"No, it doesn't." I glanced over my shoulder, my eye half-lidded. "You think Prince Rishan would leave something as valuable and as important as the runestone in the *captain's quarters* of the ship? He doesn't want the *captain* to have access to his precious magical object."

Zaxis nodded along with my words. "Okay. Yeah. That makes sense. So where is it?"

"It's either in Rishan's quarters or he's carrying it on his person at all times." I glanced back at the *Black Throne*. "That's what I would do if I had a runestone. I'd never let it leave my possession."

"Then how're we gonna get it? Do we need keys?"

"I know how to pick a lock." Then I pointed up to the quarterdeck—the portion of the ship directly above the captain's quarters. "We're going to get up there and then sneak over to Rishan's quarters. If all goes well, I'll find the runestone, we'll return to the dinghy, and then we'll row away."

"What about the soldiers of the Argo Empire?" Zaxis motioned to the bow of the ship, where men in armor—some with unicorns—stood around and drank rum from tin cups. "They'll be all over the place."

"We're going to avoid them. The knight arcanists of the Argo Empire are typically bonded with unicorns or pegasi, and neither of them are creatures of *finding*. If we're good, we probably won't get caught."

Nicholin bounced around Zaxis's lap and then glanced up at him. "Any questions, Dunce-Cap?"

Zaxis stared at the black wood of the gigantic ship. "We won't be able to activate any magic."

It wasn't a question, but I nodded regardless.

He slipped on a pair of metal knuckles. "Why not just manipulate gravity and lift us up there?"

"It's... difficult," I muttered.

It had taken me much longer than everyone else to discover my manipulation—a fact that still embarrassed me to this day. And while I could do it, and had used it in crucial situations, it wasn't my best magical skill. Volke and I had practiced for hours, and it still felt foreign.

Zaxis pointed to the ship. "If we leave the dinghy, it'll bump into the ship from time to time, making noise. But if you used your gravity manipulation, it wouldn't be a problem."

I sighed. People didn't understand the difficulties of my power. Gravity was a force that pulled—as if there were something below the ground that was constantly trying to drag everything toward it. When I manipulated gravity, I wasn't *taking it away*. I lessened the pull, or even reserved it —but there was *always* a force in play.

Everyone just assumed I was levitating things, and that wasn't how it worked. I'd never be able to maintain my gravity manipulation while on the *Black Throne*. I'd be too distracted, and my magic wasn't precise enough.

"We'll use some of the rope to secure the dinghy to the anchor buoy," I whispered as I glanced around. The dock had enough ambient light for me to spot the anchor chain on the side of the *Black Throne*. Floating in the water a short distance away was a waterproofed barrel—the anchor buoy. It was tethered to the anchor itself, and if we lashed the dinghy to it, our tiny vessel wouldn't float away or bash against the ship.

We rowed over to the barrel, threw a rope around it, and tied our vessel. Once secure, I motioned for Nicholin to do his thing. He grabbed the other rope and hook and teleported away with a soft *pop*. Several tense seconds passed in relative silence. Then a rope fell down from the quarterdeck, and Nicholin waved to us from the ship.

Since he was now on the *Black Throne*, he could no longer teleport. I could still teleport Zaxis and myself, however.

"Once I teleport us aboard, there's no going back," I whispered.

Zaxis nodded. "I understand."

I touched his shoulder and concentrated on my power. The jarring sensation of being ripped through space still bothered me, but my accuracy had improved, and I no longer disoriented myself. We appeared half a foot above the quarterdeck and plunked down—louder than I had wanted. Teleporting onto the nullstone wood was impossible, which was why I'd had to teleport into an odd point above.

Zaxis and I wildly glanced around. My heart hammered against my ribs, but I didn't see anyone nearby. The quarterdeck, like most ships, had sand barrels, ropes, a cable, a whipstaff, and a place for the helmsman to help steer the ship. Fortunately, since we were in port, no one was here, and the barrels functioned as convenient hideaways.

I hid behind one, and Zaxis followed suit. His dark cloak allowed him to blend with the shadows. The creaking of the wood, and the low murmurs of sails, drifted to us on the winds. The nullstone caused a terrible suffocating feeling—the suppression of magic never felt right.

"The luxury quarters should be just below the captain's quarters," I muttered.

Zaxis nodded. "Let's get below deck, then."

After a few seconds, to make sure no one was coming our way, we snuck out from behind the barrels and headed for the stairs down to the large main deck. There were sailors about, but they were preoccupied with their own business. Unfortunately, the unicorn arcanists near the bow were heading our way, their armor clinking as they ambled across the deck.

Had they heard us arrive?

Before I could even make it a few steps down the stairs, I placed a hand on Zaxis's chest and pointed to the opposite end of the quarterdeck. There were always two sets of stairs—one on the port side, and one on the starboard side—and we'd have to hurry to the other one.

Nicholin ran up my pants, and then my shirt, clawing his way to my shoulder. Zaxis and I hustled, half-crouched, over to the second set of stairs and quietly waited until the unicorn arcanists were ascending the other side. Their armor was loud enough to hide our footsteps. As the knights clanked their way up to the quarterdeck, Zaxis and I made our way down to the main deck.

The hatch for the hold was only ten feet away, out in the open. The sailor swabbing the deck hummed a sea shanty as he worked, his head down and his movements slow. There was nothing between me and the hatch. Nothing. I had to walk over there—no way around it.

With all the confidence of someone who *belonged*, I walked over, opened up the hatch, and slid down the ladder. I hoped—due to the low light, and my demeanor—that no one would identify me as an intruder. The humming sailor never stopped his tune. I exhaled in relief and Nicholin did the same.

Zaxis followed suit and joined me a moment later,

surprisingly quiet. His clothing—both the cloth and his fire-proof scale armor underneath—wasn't the type to make much noise, so he slipped around with relative ease.

I slid to the bottom of the ladder and glanced around, spotting the cannons lined up against the bulkheads. This was the gun deck. There were doors leading toward the bow, and others leading toward the stern. We wanted the stern direction—the personal quarters would be in that direction—and we'd just have to search each one until we came across Rishan's.

And the searching would be unnecessarily difficult. The blackish wood made it difficult to see, even with the lanterns hanging off the bulkheads. Everything seemed soaked in shadows, and with only one eye, visibility was at an all-time low. The large crates and piles of cannonballs didn't help anything, either. What if someone else was here and I just hadn't seen them yet?

Zaxis nudged my shoulder and then motioned to the room. It took me a moment for my vision to adjust, but I eventually noticed the two armor stands in the corner of the large room, both filled with half-plate armor. The metal was stamped with the crest of the Argo Empire's national symbol, and I suspected each suit of armor was a magical trinket.

"We could take a couple of those," Zaxis murmured. "These dastards don't need them anyway."

"*Shh*," I hissed. "We might have company."

Zaxis glanced around. "I haven't seen anyone. I don't see anything, either."

The gun deck wasn't needed when the ship was just sitting in port. Perhaps we'd reach Rishan's quarters without much hassle.

One of the doors leading to the stern of the ship opened.

The ship strained as a dragon squeezed through the wide opening. The black and scarlet-red scales gave away the identity of our new friend—it was Crimthand the sovereign dragon, eldrin to Prince Rishan.

I ducked behind the nearest pile of cannonballs, unable to breathe. Nicholin gripped my cloak and made not even the slightest of peeps.

Zaxis—why did he do this to me?—jumped behind the crates, separating us.

The sovereign dragon's true form made its horns form together as though they were a crown on its massive lizard head. Crimthand stomped forward, his weight substantial enough to shake the deck. When he snorted, the whole area smelled of sulfur and copper.

Despite his large size, he fit perfectly. The ship had been designed to accommodate bulky mystical creatures—the roof was tall enough, the planks of wood didn't give under his weight, and the support beams were placed wide, to allow for more room. It all made sense—the rulers of the Argo Empire had sovereign dragons, so why wouldn't their flagship have the build to support young dragons traveling with them? Crimthand wasn't yet two years old, but he was still large enough to eat a man, which made him dangerous beyond belief.

Crimthand stopped near one of the cannons and sniffed the air. The slits of his reptilian eyes thinned until they were barely visible lines.

"Delicious..." he said, his gruff voice a thing of nightmares.

Delicious? What was this wyrm-brain talking about?

My heart stopped and it felt as though someone had dumped cold water over my head. I knew what the dragon smelled. It was a rizzel. It was *Nicholin*. Rizzels were small creatures that acted as lures for other mystical creatures—their ferret-like bodies oozed a mouth-watering scent.

Zaxis must've realized what was happening as well. He shot me a glance from behind his crates, his eyes wide. Then he beckoned with a *come here* motion of his hand.

Did he want me to rush over to him? Or did he want Nicholin to do so?

Fighting Crimthand in the depths of the *Black Throne* was a terrible idea. We couldn't use our magic, and the knights a deck above us would definitely get involved. Not only that, but dragons were immune to the effects of null-stone. Which meant we absolutely could not get caught.

"I'm sorry," Nicholin whispered as he tapped his front paws together. "I... didn't mean to—"

"It wasn't your fault," I interjected. "It's mine. I should've remembered."

Crimthand slowly made his way to the center of the gun deck, his nostrils flaring as he took deep breaths through his nose. The poor ventilation in ships, coupled with the oil from the cannons and lanterns, was likely hindering Crimthand's ability to track. I thanked our lucky stars he hadn't immediately detected our location, but he *had* smelled Nicholin from the nearby corridor, so I knew we didn't have that much extra time.

Zaxis beckoned a second time.

I hesitated a second too long—Nicholin jumped from my shoulder and scampered over to Zaxis, his little claws softly scratching across the nullstone wood.

Although the scurrying had been barely audible, Crimthand turned his head at the sound and sniffed again. "I know you're here," he said in a playful and taunting voice. "There's no escape for you. Come out now, and I promise I won't hurt you."

His claws extended a bit as he moved, his body tense with coiled muscles. The moment he saw anything, he would pounce.

Nicholin and Zaxis whispered to each other for just a moment. Then Zaxis ripped a tuft of white-and-silver fur off of Nicholin's little body. Nicholin almost squeaked, but he held his own mouth shut during the painful process. The chunk of fluff was larger than most coins, and even in the dim light, I noted the red splotches of blood.

Zaxis placed the fur between two of the crates and then tucked Nicholin's squirming body into his cloak, right under his armpit. He glanced over at me and pointed to the door Crimthand had walked through.

The sovereign dragon was almost to Zaxis's location. If we moved now, they would surely get caught. What was I to do? I had to act. Anything was better than just watching two of my favorite individuals dying.

I pantomimed to Zaxis—gesturing for him to take off one of his metal knuckles and throw it. He grimaced but did as I instructed. He removed one of his knuckles and then tossed it, underhand, across the gun deck. The weapon struck a cannon in the far corner, clanging off the metal and then ricocheting off into the armor stands, slamming into the half-plate and creating another round of clatters and clangs.

Crimthand rushed for the cannons and armor, but he didn't *run*—he remained vigilant as he rocked the whole ship with his massive weight. The ruckus and rumble would alert the whole damn crew!

But there was nothing to do about that now. I just had to roll with what fate dealt me.

I snuck out from my hiding spot the moment Crimthand moved past me. Zaxis rushed over to me, half-crouching the whole way, and we made our way to the door Crimthand had emerged from. The three of us ran through, and I shut the door with as much precision, speed, and care as possible, trying not to make a single sound. Fortunately, Crimthand was still focused on the cannon and armor racks—the clanging gave it away.

If Zaxis's impromptu plan worked, the dragon would eventually sniff out the tuft of fur and blood between the crates. It would buy us time, but then Crimthand would *eventually* come for us.

"We have to hurry," I said.

"We have to find a porthole to leap out of," Zaxis said. "Did you see that dragon? Curse the abyssal hells, woman— that monster must weigh at least a thousand pounds! Maybe two thousand, damn."

Nicholin squirmed in Zaxis's cloak. "Why are you sweaty?" he whined. The moment he poked his head out of Zaxis's hood, he snorted. "It stinks... so bad."

"You're welcome," Zaxis quipped.

"Eh. I just hope the eulogy at my funeral doesn't involve the words *soaked in man sweat*."

Zaxis turned to stare down the corridor. "Forget about that. Let's just find a way out."

"No," I said. "We have to find the runestone." I grabbed his arm and pulled him to the nearest door. "Listen—Crimthand must have come from Rishan's quarters. It has to be close." I pointed to the two styles of doors in the corridor— some were wide, some were narrow. "It has to be a room with a larger door. Hurry. We have to check them."

Unlike other ships I had ridden on, the corridor was devoid of random supplies. Typically, ships had ropes and chains around, just in case of storms, in order to secure down loose objects and doors. But this corridor had nothing. It was also much wider than normal, and I wondered if they kept it clear to allow Crimthand to move around.

Before we went to the first door, one of the narrow doors opened, revealing a sailor who stepped into our corridor. Without magic, I hesitated, unsure of how to handle the situation.

Fortunately for me, Zaxis didn't usually think before he acted.

Zaxis—with his last pair of metal knuckles—punched the sailor across the face in a quick, yet powerful, jab. The man stumbled backward and then collapsed to the floor, his leg twitching. A weird gurgle escaped him as his head fell to the side.

"Now pee on the man to finish establishing your dominance," Nicholin said, tugging on Zaxis's cloak.

"Stop joking around," Zaxis growled. "That seadog will wake up shortly." He effortlessly hefted the limp body up onto his shoulder and then opened one of the narrow doors. With little care, Zaxis stuffed the man into what appeared to be a storage space. He shut the door afterward, making sure it latched.

I jogged over to the first wide door. We didn't have time for caution. I knelt and withdrew my lock-picking tools from the depths of my deep pockets. The locks of ships were my specialty—when I had been younger, I had been a prisoner on a pirate ship, and I promised myself then that I'd develop the skills to escape so that I would never be held in the hold ever again.

The lock unlatched and I pushed open the door.

The first room was someone's personal quarters. The lavish bed with silk sheets told me it was someone important, but I knew it wasn't Rishan's room when I spotted three mirrors, two brushes, six dresses hanging on the bulkhead, and net gloves worn by some ladies who hailed from the far east.

Rishan was arrogant, but the man wasn't obsessed with fashion.

"Not here," I said.

Zaxis ran to the next room with Nicholin clinging to his shoulder. Zaxis threw open the door—it wasn't locked?—and lifted his fists, as though he might have to knock another man out. Fortunately, there was no one inside.

"This is it," Zaxis muttered. He motioned with a jerk of his head. "C'mon."

All three of us entered, and I understood why Zaxis was so certain this was Rishan's room. There was a "bed" made of stone and ash built into the bulkhead of the ship. It was a place for dragons, and the whole room stank of rotten egg sulfur. A normal bed—with the same lavish sheets as the other room—was set up opposite the dragon bed.

To both my curiosity and horror, seven chests littered the room, each with its own lock hanging from the latch. No doubt the prince had brought personal trinkets and arti-facts, but we weren't here for those. The runestone had to be in one—and if not, it was on his person.

We closed the door behind us, but the echoed crashes on the gun deck were dying down. Soon, Crimthand would give up his search and return to this room, or perhaps he would just smell that Nicholin wasn't there and eventually follow the trail to us regardless.

"We don't have much time," Zaxis said, his thoughts obviously on the same problem.

Nicholin puffed out his chest. "You two search the room. I'll distract the dragon."

"What?" I asked. "No. That's too risky."

"I'm small and quick. The dragon isn't. I'll avoid him by

running around the hold of the ship, and when I think I can't anymore, I'll just jump into the bay and then teleport. I'll be fine!"

While I wanted to argue, I knew I couldn't. It was a sound plan, even if it put Nicholin in danger. We didn't have many options.

"All right," I whispered. "Go."

Nicholin gave me his best salute and then dashed for the door. Zaxis opened it for him, and Nicholin scurried into the corridor, his tiny claws making the same soft scratching noise as before.

I already missed him. Nicholin and I didn't typically separate, and if we did, it was never for long. They say eldrin grow to become more like their arcanists, but I had never felt Nicholin reflected my stoic personality. When I thought deeply on the matter, I sometimes wondered if Nicholin was the person I would've been had Calisto not killed my family and taken my eye—that the world had changed me, but my soul had remained someone who loved life, humor, and all things that made someone smile.

But I didn't have time to analyze any of that.

I returned my attention to the seven chests. I hustled over to the first one at the foot of the opulent bed and knelt to examine the lock. Door locks typically had a single latch that needed to be unhooked. A padlock—the kind used on most chests—had a lock body, a steel spring, and several locking pins. It required more work to open them, and if I was too forceful, I could bend the spring in the process, which would then prevent me from opening the damn thing.

If we could use our magic, Zaxis might've been able to burn through the outside of the chest—or I could've disintegrated the lock itself. I had become too accustomed to my magic. Not having it, even for an hour, bothered me more than it should have.

I set to work picking the lock. It was a heavy device—all the padlocks were—and Zaxis hovered close by, watching me work, fidgeting the entire time. It took me three times as long to undo the lock as it had with the door, but I eventually unlatched the device and unhooked it from the chest. I threw open the lid and cursed when I found clothing and jewelry.

Zaxis grabbed a necklace and bracelet, shoved them in his pocket, and then rummaged through the rest of the contents. When he reached the bottom, he cursed under his breath.

"It's not here," he said.

I stood and moved over to another chest—this one near the head of the bed. Loud stomps echoed in the corridor.

Both Zaxis and I froze in place, me half-kneeling, and Zaxis mid-walk. I held my breath as the sovereign dragon drew nearer and nearer, coming closer to the door with each passing second.

"Maybe we should hide under the bed?" Zaxis asked, his voice barely audible.

"He'll smell us," I whispered, my heart in my throat.

Could he smell us right now? What if he could? What would we do? There was a single porthole on the far bulkhead, but otherwise, there were no exits from the room.

The knots forming in my gut didn't unwind until after the sovereign dragon stomped by our door. His pace picked up, and I wondered if Nicholin had distracted him for us. More than anything, I wanted Nicholin to make it through this.

"Is there anything I can do to speed this up?" Zaxis asked, urgency in his tone.

I forced myself to breathe. "Uh... Yes. Gather all the chests. Line them up."

"Right."

Chests were typically heavy, but Zaxis was a man with excessive muscle. He grabbed a nearby chest sitting in the corner of the room and grunted as he lifted it up. Then he walked over and set it down, careful not to make much noise.

While he rushed off to get another, I picked the lock of the second. In the distance, I heard the shattering of glass, and I wondered if Nicholin were in trouble. It caused a bit of delay, but I eventually got the lock undone.

I opened the chest—books. Lots of books.

I was about to shut the chest, but I caught sight of an unusual cover. It was leatherbound and the title was hand-written in ink: *The Remains of the God-Creatures*. Without much thought, I scooped up the book and shoved it into the pocket of my cloak. Then I shut the chest and picked the padlock of the third.

Zaxis gathered all seven chests together before I had finished picking the lock of the fourth. Fortunately, once I had mastered these heavy padlocks, the rest went faster. In the fifth chest, I found exactly what I was looking for.

The shale runestone.

It was wrapped in a velvet cloth and bound in place with a leather strap. Once freed of its holdings, the runestone was no bigger than my palm and weighed less than a pound. On one side was the carving of a regal wolf, and on the other side were runes. I had no idea what they said or repre-sented, but the longer I stared, the more transfixed I became.

Zaxis grabbed my wrist and jerked me out of my trance.

"We found it," he said with a pant. "Let's get out of here."

"Okay," I muttered as I tucked the runestone into the pocket of my trousers.

I stood, and we hurried to the door. Zaxis pressed his ear to the wood, and after a moment, he opened the door and ushered me out.

I glanced back. The seven chests—all lined up in a row on the floor—were a clear indication that someone had been in Rishan's quarters. Did I care? I ultimately decided *no*. They would figure out what we had done the moment they realized the runestone was gone, and even if we put the whole room back together, I doubted it would change the timeline of that discovery.

Zaxis yanked me into the corridor. After a few quick glances, he rushed for the gun deck. He opened the door, but he stopped dead in his tracks the moment we both heard voices. A pair of deckhands were chatting near the crates. Had the dragon summoned them to investigate?

I ripped my hand from Zaxis and pulled back my hair into a tight ponytail. My cloak hid my feminine body, and the eyepatch gave me a *pirate* look. Or at least someone who sailed on a ship regularly. I motioned for Zaxis to keep his hood up—red hair wasn't too common in the Argo Empire —and then gestured for him to follow.

We walked to the ladder that led to the main deck. As we made our way there—slow and calm—I could hear the conversation the deckhands were having.

"Glass everywhere," one man said with a huff.

"Was the whole window wrecked?" a younger man asked, his voice slurred with liquor.

"That's right. Grim reaper chasin' somethin'."

"The whole ship has been weird tonight, I tell you."

"Ghosts, maybe?"

"Death Lords from the abyssal hells, I bet." The younger

man gathered snot in his mouth and then spat. "I heard those Death Lords come for people to add to their ranks. Rishan seems like the *Death Lord* type."

"Nah."

I climbed the rungs of the ladder, my heart beating fast as I opened the hatch to the main deck. The two deckhands either didn't notice us or didn't care. They were engrossed in their conversation, and it seemed something was happening somewhere else on the ship.

The broken glass... I had heard it as well.

I leapt up to the main deck and headed straight for the railing of the *Black Throne*. It probably would've been smarter for me to head up to the quarterdeck and climb down the rope to my dinghy, but I didn't want to risk any more time on the nullstone wood.

Zaxis followed close behind, and when we both reached the railing, I pointed to the waters below.

"You want us to jump off?" he whispered, indignant.

Three deckhands and five knight arcanists rushed across the deck of the ship, all with pistols and swords at the ready.

"Help the grim reaper search the streets," one of the Pegasus knights shouted. "All hands! Help the grim reaper search the streets for the intruders!"

I turned to Zaxis and glared with my one eye. "Yup. We're jumping off."

The instant the men ran by, I jumped onto the railing and then dove into the black waters below. The chill of the evening currents shocked me the moment I became submerged, but I expected it. The waters around the Isle of Ruma would frequently get chilly.

I swam to the surface and threw back my head to make sure my hair didn't stick to my face. Zaxis leapt into the water as well. He kept his body straight and didn't make much of a splash as he entered the bay.

My heart missed a beat as I jammed a hand into the pocket of my trousers.

Did I still have my runestone?

I breathed a sigh of relief when I realized I still had it. Thank all the good stars and all the ships at sea. The shale runestone—and the path to the fenris wolf—were now in our possession.

Once a few feet from the boat, I swam next to Zaxis and touched his back. I teleported both of us, the jarring sensation knocking away all the tension I'd had a moment prior. When we appeared on the dinghy with a pop, the night wind whipped by, washing me with another round of cold.

Nicholin ran out from under the sole seat, his white-and-silver fur clumped with water.

"You two made it!" he said with a happy squeak.

Zaxis rotated his shoulders and flashed him a smirk. "Of course. We're an amazing duo." He threw an arm around me and pulled me into a tight embrace. Hugging him was like hugging a skin wrapped around rocks. His muscles sometimes made it difficult for me to get comfortable, but in the heat of celebration, I squeezed tightly. This would be another thing I would come to love, even if it didn't make any sense. Another piece of the mosaic.

"We did it," I said with a laugh. "I can't wait to tell the others."

Zaxis kissed my forehead. "I can't wait to see the look on their faces."

"Hey," Nicholin barked. He tapped one of his feet on the bottom of the dinghy. "Aren't you going to ask what happened to me? I had an amazing adventure, too, ya know.

I looked death straight in the eye and said, *Come get me, you dastard.*"

"Uh-huh," Zaxis muttered.

"I did! I even bit the sovereign dragon right on the tip of the nose. *That's* how close to death I was. It's an epic story that'll rival the legends of history." He turned around and arched his back. "But I guess you two don't want to hear it!"

I picked up the oar, but Zaxis snatched it from me.

"My turn," he said. "Because we don't need stealth, we need speed."

As he pushed us away from the anchor buoy, my attention went to the *Black Throne.* The windows of the captain's quarters had been smashed outward, as though something had been thrown through them. I glanced out over the bay and squinted as I stared at the docks, but I couldn't tell what had happened.

The farther we got from the ship, the more my confidence rose. Somehow, I hadn't heard Zaxis and Nicholin bickering until my thoughts returned to here and now.

"—and then there were twenty soldiers," Nicholin said. "And I had to dash by them all!"

"That didn't happen," Zaxis said with a scoff.

"It did. You weren't there."

"Yeah, and Illia and I fought King Rishan. And also the entire Second Ascension. On the moon."

Nicholin huffed and stomped all four feet. "Just you wait and see what I say about you in my memoirs."

<hr>

With the morning sunlight as my sole companion, I met Guildmaster Eventide out on the shell of her atlas turtle. The pond and tree and grassy field were all too familiar. It almost felt like walking into one of Aldegis's handcrafted dreams.

The city of Millatin was a gloomy location, but the radiance of the new day pierced through the fog to light up the area with pillars of sunshine. Eventide stood in one such pillar, her long coat fluttering in the morning breeze. Phoenix and griffin feathers on her tricorn cap rustled about.

She stared off toward the head of the turtle, and I wondered if she was engaged in a telepathic conversation with her eldrin. Did atlas turtles have telepathy? I didn't know. Perhaps she had a trinket that granted her the use of telepathy?

When I approached, I cleared my throat. Eventide turned around, a slight smile already in place. Her silver-white hair, always tied back, had a few loose strands. That wasn't like her. The dark rings under her eyes weren't like her, either.

"Guildmaster," I said and then bowed my head. "Good morning. Thank you for meeting me out here."

"Of course," she said. "I assume it's important, since you didn't want anyone else involved."

Instead of adding words to the conversation, I withdrew the runestone from the safety of my trouser pocket. I handed it over. The guildmaster took it, examined both sides, and then chortled.

"Well, it looks like you found another fake," she said. "Just like the one Fain and Volke brought me."

I caught my breath, my mind buzzing with a hundred thoughts. "What?" I asked. "It's... fake?"

A moment passed in silence, and then Guildmaster Eventide laughed, her mirth enough to momentarily mask her exhaustion. She twirled the runestone around in one hand. "No, I was just having a good time, my girl. This is the real runestone. You've done a great thing to bring it to the Frith Guild."

A long second passed where I wasn't sure if I was angry or happy. I settled for something in between and offered a few genuine chuckles before straightening my posture. "Yes, well, I couldn't let the Second Ascension just *have* it." Then I processed the rest of Eventide's statement. "Wait, *Volke* brought you a fake?"

"That's right."

It hurt to think he did so many things without consulting me these days. Then again, he was a man now, and why would he constantly rely on his adopted sister to accomplish tasks? It made sense that he would go off to write his own great adventure.

"How did you find this runestone?" Guildmaster Eventide asked, drawing me out of my thoughts.

"I searched the *Black Throne*. I figured it would be with King Rishan, and I figured correctly."

"I'm glad you brought it to me, and only me." Eventide lifted an eyebrow. "Unless one of your peers already knows?"

"Just Zaxis. And my eldrin."

"Not Volke?" she asked.

I shook my head. "Not yet."

"Actually, let's keep it between us. The fewer people who know, the better. I'll inform Zaxis to do the same." Eventide tucked the runestone away into her coat. The patchwork design—as though her garment had been made from ten different materials—was an odd choice, but I knew it had to be an artifact of some significance. She never left the turtle without it.

"We need to hide this from Volke?" I asked.

"For the time being. He retrieved a fake runestone from the boat and was caught while doing so. If any of the Second Ascension comes for him—or has some ability to read thoughts—I'd rather they think Volke had failed completely in his mission."

"Are you afraid someone will steal it back from us?"

"I want to feign ignorance on many things," Eventide stated, no hesitation. "And I want the Second Ascension to assume that there are more guilds and arcanists working against them than in reality. At least currently."

"So you're not going to tell *anyone* we have it?"

She shook her head and then tipped the edge of her cap. "I'll act as though we don't have it until the moment arrives when we find whoever should be the fenris wolf god-arcanist. I'm afraid some individuals could be swayed against us, and I don't want to give anyone the leverage they need to jump ship, if that makes sense."

I nodded along with her words, absorbing them into my core. I'd had no idea that Eventide occasionally did things in a grander or more manipulative manner. It gave me a new perspective on her.

Guildmaster Eventide stepped close and placed a hand on my shoulder. "Shall we head to the guild house? I hear breakfast will be biscuits with sausage and gravy. It's one of my favorites."

I half-smiled. "Thank you, Guildmaster."

Although I couldn't tell him the truth, I still wanted to speak with Volke. He had brought back a fake runestone? I was curious to see how he was holding up.

I waited in Volke's room as the sun continued to travel the sky. Who slept till noon? I glanced over at Volke, his black hair so messy, it covered half his face as he rolled from one side to the other. He had never been the type of person to sleep late, but I suspected he hadn't gone to bed until late.

A chorus of gulls squawked beyond the window, their hunger evident in each pained note they sang. Nicholin sat in my lap, curled into a tight O-shape. He was sleepy after the hundreds of soldiers he fought, and the dragon he almost managed to defeat.

I smiled just recalling the hyperbole.

Volke opened his eyes and stared on the light streaming through the window. It took him a moment to focus, but the instant he spotted me, he smiled.

"What're you doing here?" he asked as he sat up.

He hadn't been wearing any clothes—which I knew and didn't mind—but Volke clutched his blankets close, careful not to expose more of himself. He was a gentleman like that.

"Good morning to you, too," I quipped.

"Sorry." Volke rubbed at the back of his neck—an odd tic he did whenever he got nervous. "I just didn't expect you here."

"You're my brother. Of course I'd come to see you."

I still couldn't believe he had attempted to get the rune-stone without my assistance, but I supposed I couldn't blame him. He had done exactly what I had: rushed in and attempted to get the stone before our enemies left port.

"Fair enough." Volke relaxed and exhaled. "You seem happier than last we spoke."

I touched my eyepatch and smiled. "We found people from the Huntsman Guild. They checked all the arcanists of the Frith Guild for signs of the arcane plague."

I hadn't been part of the group that found the Huntsman

Guild, but Volke didn't need to know that. All he needed to know was that we now had a cure for the arcane plague. It was news worth celebrating, after all.

"And?" Volke asked.

"And none of them are infected," I said. "Vethica cured them with her khepera magic."

Volke's expressions always made me smile wider. He was so genuine, and his look of relief and happiness was enough to make me forget most of my worries. I leaned forward and hugged him tightly, thankful to have him in my life—as part of my mosaic. I sometimes felt I was a better person just because of him.

"*Hey, hey, hey,*" Nicholin shouted, his voice muffled and his body squirming between us. "I was sleeping here!"

Volke and I broke apart, both of us chuckling—it was good to see him in a jovial mood.

"I can't believe it," Volke said with a smile that wouldn't fade. "That's such a relief."

"Zaxis is thrilled as well." I ran both my hands through my wavy brown hair. "He said he's never felt so good."

Even though Volke's smile remained, something dimmed in his eyes, and I could tell doubt dwelled in his thoughts. "Illia," he said. "Has Karna returned to the guild house?"

I shook my head. "She went out last night, according to the other journeymen, and she hasn't returned."

Volke's eyebrows knitted. "At all?"

"No one has seen her."

"She *is* a doppelgänger arcanist. Maybe she's here?"

"Perhaps," I said, shaking my head. "But she hasn't made her presence known, let's say that." I furrowed my brow. "Master Zelfree left last night as well. No one has seen him, though I'm a lot less concerned if he manages to find trouble."

Volke bit his thumbnail, his gaze unfocused. I knew the expression well, though I had never seen it consume him so.

"What about the shale runestone?" he asked. "Did Fain manage to bring it to Guildmaster Eventide?"

This was what I had been waiting for. While I didn't enjoy lying to Volke, I had done it in the past, especially in moments when I had thought it would help. Now was that time.

I shook my head. "I'm sorry, Volke. According to Eventide, the runestone you brought back was a fake. She suspected the real one is with Rishan at all times, and this was just a decoy for would-be thieves."

Volke's effervescent smile finally faded. I almost wanted to lean back over and hug him again, but I held back. We had the runestone—there was no need for him to fret.

After a long yawn, Nicholin stretched and then arched his back. "Okay. I'm awake. The real work and conversations can begin." He glanced between Volke and me. "Are we heading to the world serpent yet?"

"Almost." I stroked his elegant white-and-silver fur, thankful the tuft Zaxis had ripped off had grown back. "First, we have to wait for Master Zelfree and Karna to return."

"We're leaving already?" Volke asked.

I nodded. "Eventide has all the supplies and materials she needs, and she's gathered star shards and a handful of mercenary arcanists to help us on the last leg of this trek. We can go at any time."

"Is Ryker okay?"

"He is," I said with a nod. "And he said he's finally ready to bond with the world serpent."

"So, when will Zelfree and Karna return, do you think?"

It seemed last night had been the Night of Mischief. Everyone and their mother had gone out on a mini-adventure worthy of the storybooks. I wanted to ask Volke for the details of his story, but I knew I'd get a good picture if I spoke to Fain—and I wouldn't feel guilty at all if I lied to that ex-pirate about my own evening exploits.

"No one knows where they went," I muttered. "It's really odd. If they're gone for much longer, we might have to search for them."

As long as we left the port of Millatin soon, no one would discover our extra runestone. I hoped beyond words that Master Zelfree and Karna wouldn't take *too* long with their own personal mini-adventures.

2

———

THE FABLE OF THE DREAMWEAVER
(PART 1)

ADELGIS "MOONBEAM" VENROVER

During the events of World Serpent Arcanist *(Book 5)*

Although most of the airship crew was asleep, their raucous voices kept me wide awake. Not audible voices—not the kind I could hear with my ears—it was their ever-shifting thoughts that filtered into my mind like a river flowing into a lake. No matter what I tried to dam the stream, it continued regardless. Thoughts. Dreams. Nightmares.

Constantly.

... Where did I leave my jerky?...

... Everyone snores so damn loud...

... I wonder if fish enjoy the act of lovemaking...

... I wish my wife hadn't left me...

I stared at the ceiling of the tiny storage room, swaying back and forth on a ratty hammock. The ropes dug into my narrow shoulders, and I tried to focus on the discomfort to take my mind off the thoughts, but it was no use. I closed my

40

eyes, pictured my old room in the ivory city of Ellios, and thought of my sister. I hadn't seen Cinna in quite some time. After everything I had learned of my father, I imagined our next meeting would be bittersweet.

Should I even refer to Theasin Venrover as my father now that I knew? He was a man of treachery and deceit. He had murdered, destroyed, and betrayed his way into power, and now he was poised to rip the world asunder with the aid of the Second Ascension...

Mystical creatures were sometimes born of specific events or emotions. Could my father's autocratic behavior have been so intense that a new type of creature would be created from his lust for power? It was an interesting thought, but one I didn't want to dwell on for long.

A soft knocking at the door drew me out of my vortex of depression. I glanced at the porthole. Clouds whipped by the small, circular window, and occasionally I spotted the glorious full moon and twinkle of stars far beyond. Who would come calling at this midnight hour?

It wasn't like I needed to ask. I glanced at the door and focused my attention on the space. The inner thoughts of the person knocking went straight to my mind.

... I hope he's still awake... I don't want to fail as the cabin girl... Captain Devlin is relying on me...

Biyu. The young girl under the captain's protection. I had met her the first day I had stepped foot on the *Sun Chaser*. Why was she here now?

"Come in," I said.

The door softly creaked open, and Biyu stuck her head in first. She glanced around with one wide eye—her other eye had been cut out by pirates, and now she wore a simple black eyepatch—but the injury didn't seem to have much effect on her exuberant cheer. The instant she spotted me, she smiled widely, teeth and all.

"Adelgis," she said as she hustled to me. Her long coat, which included several oversized pockets, hung loosely on her small body, swinging back and forth as she made her way over. "There you are. I need to ask you some questions!"

... I hope he's not mad at me... Please, please, don't be mad...

Her thoughts assaulted me whether I wanted to hear them or not. Her fear—well-hidden beyond her bright smile—agitated me more than her entrance into my room, but I didn't want to indicate I was upset. Especially not now.

I forced a smile and sat up on my hammock. "Good evening, Biyu," I said as I combed my long, black hair with my fingers. "It's a pleasure to see you."

... He's not mad!... Thank goodness...

"It's good to see you, too," Biyu said in a sing-song tone, her inner thoughts completely masked by her forced charisma.

She grabbed a leather strap on her shoulder and swung it around until her cabin girl journal was in front of her, instead of resting on her back. The book—or tome, rather—looked like it weighed close to ten pounds, but Biyu hefted it without hesitation. She was only eight or nine years of age, but she loved that journal so much that she refused to part with it, no matter how heavy it became.

Biyu withdrew a quill from one of her many coat pockets and somehow managed to smile wider. The gray peacock feather was black at the tip, and I recognized the ever-quill for the magical trinket that it was. It would never run dry— the perfect tool for a cabin girl with a penchant for writing copious notes.

Then she opened her journal and placed it on top of a nearby rum barrel. "Okay," she said, the cheer in her voice never waning. "Captain Devlin said he wanted information…" She tapped at her chin with the fluff of the peacock feather. "And he said all the arcanists with *rare* eldrin need to be *super* questioned."

"I'm aware," I said.

I had heard the captain's thoughts and the thoughts of the other arcanists when they had been questioned. I knew I would be questioned as well, I just hadn't expected Biyu to be my interviewer. The quartermaster, Karna, or the boatswain, Vethica, were the ones handling the assignment. They were taking stock of our capabilities. That way, Captain Devlin would know the strengths and weaknesses of everyone onboard the *Sun Chaser*.

Why was Biyu, a child, questioning me?

"Okay, are you ready?" Biyu asked as she positioned her ever-quill over a blank page. "Because Biyu the Greatest Cabin Girl Ever doesn't mess around!"

I chuckled as I stood from my hammock. "Of course."

… Captain Devlin said this would be easy… Adelgis doesn't have many magical powers… I can do this… I won't fail him…

A twist of pain knotted my chest.

Ah. *That* was why Biyu was questioning me. Because I was an "easy" assignment to give her—to make Biyu feel important. Because my magic was deemed *simple, unimpressive,* and… *worthless.*

I exhaled, allowing my breath to take some of my depression. The worst part of hearing thoughts—besides the fact that they were never-ending—was the sheer amount of negativity. People kept their judgments and vile criticisms to themselves for the most part, which I attributed to polite society, but I no longer had the luxury of obliviousness. The ceaseless stream of disapproval, petty slurs, and condescension wore at my optimism.

Biyu stared at me with her one eye wide. Then she frowned slightly. "Are you okay?"

I straightened my shoulders and glanced down at her. I wasn't too tall. Five foot, ten inches. Biyu was four feet, and it surprised me. She seemed... short. Even for a girl her age.

"You needn't worry about me," I said. "Please, ask your questions. I'm sure the captain is eagerly awaiting your report."

Biyu's frown disappeared in an instant. "Right? I need to get back to him as soon as I'm done!"

"Then what's your first question?"

She glanced down at her journal and narrowed her eyes. "What's your strongest magical power?" She placed the tip of the quill on the blank page. A dot of ink spread from the point as she awaited my answer.

"Strong in what way?" I asked.

Biyu furrowed her brow. "Hm?"

... Strong in what way?... I don't get it...

"Strong for combat?" I asked. "Strong for utility? Strong in nature? There are many ways to define strength." I shrugged. "I can read the mind of anyone within a few hundred feet—that's an extraordinary ability that no other ethereal whelk arcanists report having—but if the task is *killing someone*, I'm not sure mindreading would fall in the *strong* category."

Biyu wrote down my mindreading with the speed of a starving cheetah. Her handwriting flowed, creating an almost unbroken line. Most people knew of my mindreading, but I hadn't told everyone on the *Sun Chaser*. There were some who became offended at the thought of me hearing their inner musings. I didn't blame them... I just couldn't control the power.

"I don't know what the captain wants," Biyu muttered as she wrote. "So I'm just going to write down *everything*."

... I have to do a good job... I don't want to be worthless...

Struck with sympathetic agony, I caught my breath.

"You're not worthless," I blurted out before I even knew I had spoken.

Biyu stopped writing and glanced up at me. She was mid-word as her hand became unsteady. "Can you... hear my thoughts? Even right now?"

I nodded once. "I apologize."

... Does he know?... Does he realize I'm lowly and terrible?...

Her one eye glazed over with fresh tears. For a brief moment, I didn't know what to do. I glanced around the storage room as though I would find someone to help me with this dilemma, but all I found were crates and barrels. I would've given anything to be a barrel at this moment. What would Volke have done? He always managed to put people at ease.

... What if he tells everyone else?... Then they'll all know...

Biyu turned away from me, her lip quavering. Her thoughts shifted from dread to a chant—one that repeated on a loop as though brought on by a trance.

... Look forward, not behind... Have hope, not regret... Look forward, not behind... Have hope, not regret... Look forward, not behind...

I gently placed my hand on her shoulder, though I knew I did it with the awkward grace of a marionette. I always felt as though I were imitating human interaction, rather than following my natural instincts. My touch probably exuded hesitation.

Biyu flinched and then whipped her attention back to me, a line of tears running down one side of her face.

"You're not worthless," I repeated again, this time firm

and slow. Another imitation. Confident people spoke firm and slow.

"But..." she muttered, her voice unsteady.

"You're the cabin girl, right?"

Biyu nodded as she wiped her cheek.

"It's an important position here on the airship," I said. "I can read minds, remember? The captain is depending on you—he thinks of you all the time. You're far from worthless."

She took a breath and then exhaled. It calmed her trembling.

... The captain needs me... He needs me...

I wasn't lying. Captain Devlin thought of Biyu often. He wondered where she had scurried off to, or whether she was warm and fed—he wondered if he could surprise her with toys whenever we stopped at port, or if she had done her studies for the day. He needed her, but not because she was the cabin girl. Because he was—for all intents and purposes—her father.

I wasn't sure if I could say that to Biyu. She seemed more obsessed with the *usefulness* part. As though losing an eye somehow diminished her own self-worth.

"I have another strong power," I said, trying to distract from the situation.

Biyu took a moment to reorient herself to the room. She glanced at the journal, then her quill, and then to me. After another exhale, she placed the tip of the quillback on the page and gave me a curt nod.

"Okay," she said. "I'm ready."

"I weave dreams."

... Weave... dreams?...

Her confusion spread from her thoughts to her expression. I almost chuckled, but I kept the mirth to myself.

"I can manipulate people's dreams with my magic," I said. "While they sleep, I can see the images in their mind and shape them to my desire. I can alter them to anything."

"Really?" Biyu gasped.

I smiled and nodded.

"Can you change my dreams?"

I lifted an eyebrow. "Is there something you want specifically?"

... Unicorns!...

She had the thought as fast as she shouted, "Unicorns!" Then she took hold of my arm and stared up at me with a pleading look. "I've always wanted to bond with a unicorn and become a unicorn arcanist! Can you please give me that dream? Something amazing and wonderful?"

I stared at her holding my arm for a long moment. It seemed odd to have contact with anyone. I eventually shook myself free and took a step back, my skin crawling under my robes. Everything felt weird since the abyssal leech in my body had been removed. Nothing felt right. Not the hammock. Not my clothes. Not the girl's affections.

Nothing.

"Uh," I said, trying to regain my composure. "Yes. I can manipulate your dreams to include unicorns." I smiled to myself as I thought over the many possibilities. "You can go through a bonding ceremony and everything."

Biyu gasped—cute and playful—and then grabbed her journal. She flew through the pages until she reached the last few. They weren't blank, like half the tome. These pages were filled with drawings. Crude drawings, nothing fancy, but skilled enough that I had no trouble identifying the subject matter.

Unicorns. And girls in dresses. A giant castle. A full moon. And... a giant spider.

"Is that spider attacking everyone?" I asked, pointing to the black arachnid.

Biyu gave me a harsh frown.

... Why doesn't anyone love spiders?... Peter the Spider would never hurt anyone!... He's really useful, and he eats all the disgusting bugs...

"Never mind," I said, holding up both my hands. "Peter the Spider is obviously a friend of all the girls."

Biyu poked her finger on the page. "Those aren't *girls*. They're *princesses*. This is my picture of Thronehold. See? They have white hair. Like the princesses of Thronehold."

"That one has black hair," I said, pointing to the third girl off to the side.

"That's me." Biyu's face flushed into a slight pink. "I'm also a princess here. And, uh, we're going to attend a ball. And, also, I'm a unicorn arcanist. I bonded with a super rare black unicorn, just like Knight Captain Rendell." She pointed to the many aspects of her fictional story, all drawn out like only a child could muster.

"I see," I said.

I hadn't grown up with many friends. I had stayed home, and my brothers had pursued different interests—most of which had involved swords and pistols. I had stayed in the library, either by myself or with my sister, studying my father's writings on mystical creatures. The loneliness had never bothered me, but I knew it had eaten at my sister. She had longed to escape and run wild. If only she hadn't become so ill...

And Biyu reminded me of Cinna.

"Tonight you'll have that as your dream," I said. "All of it. Even Peter the Spider."

... I can be a unicorn arcanist?... And be a princess at a ball?... And be with Peter the Spider?...

Her thoughts grew in intensity as she imagined all the possibilities. I couldn't help but chuckle.

Even if the rest of the crew thought of me as *simple* and *unimpressive* when it came to my magical talents, at least I could still help individuals through their dreamscapes. Perhaps—eventually, and with enough practice—I could alter my own and finally get some peaceful sleep.

3

THE FABLE OF THE SOUL FORGE GOD-ARCANIST

THE DREAD PIRATE CALISTO

During the events of World Serpent Arcanist *(Book 5)*

Humanity was vile.

They could all be gutted and thrown into the abyssal hells for all I cared.

Well, perhaps not all... but *most*. Certainly enough to clog the hells with bodies, and stain the oceans a permanent shade of crimson. The majority of people were too cruel, and greedy, and callous beyond the pale. They wouldn't admit it, of course, but I had sailed these waters for decades, stopping at every port and town—I knew the truth of human nature.

I crossed my arms and dug my fingers into my biceps. The pressure of my grip returned my focus to the immediate. I stood at the edge of a twisted woodland, men slowly carving a path through. Or was it considered a jungle? I wasn't sure, nor did I care. The trees had gnarled trunks as thick as a damn battleship, and their branches grew in clusters so dense I couldn't see a sliver of the sky through their canopy. The roots jutted in and out of the ground in multiple locations, like dolphins leaping through the waves.

The whole place smelled of wood rot. The bark of those massive trunks fell off at an interesting rate, and the rustling of the waxy leaves sounded more like metal than plant.

Men from the Second Ascension hacked their way through the undergrowth and roots. They were sturdy enough, but the accursed woodland was sturdier. The men struggled, even with masterwork swords, and the two salamander arcanists in the group had to do most of the heavy lifting. Their flames weakened the vegetation—the smoke had nowhere to escape, however. The canopy kept it lingering.

My men—my pirates on the *Third Abyss*—weren't involved in finding us a path. Why would I risk them? This place was obviously designed to keep the wretched at bay, and I hadn't been paid to *clear a path*. The Second Ascension had hired me to provide a ride to Theasin, and then protect him while he bonded with a *god-creature*. Nothing else.

Normal men wouldn't have taken on such an insane request, I knew. But their leader had promised me magical trinkets and artifacts from the lair of the god-creature, and I was greedy enough to take the deal. It wasn't like I was saving my life for something or someone, so what did it matter if I put myself in danger? Might as well get as much pleasure out of life as I could.

The clanking of metal, glass, and ceramics caught my attention. It sounded as though a whole house was slowly rolling its broken carcass up the beaten path and straight for the woodland. I knew the sound well enough. It was that damn relickeeper—a dragon made of *objects* rather than flesh.

Sure enough, when I glanced over my shoulder, I spotted the relickeeper. A massive beast of twisted iron, stained glass, and bits of brass, all held together with translucent threads of magic. I hated everything about the creature—anything that couldn't bleed wasn't to be trusted. Relickeepers especially. Those *dragons* treated everything as objects because they themselves were nothing but junk.

The monster's arcanist, Theasin Venrover, walked beside it. Theasin's smug expression was a cornerstone of his personality, and I hated him more than his relickeeper eldrin. If I had my way, they'd both be at the bottom of an ocean trench, bloated from salt water and covered in barnacles.

Theasin stopped at my side, his black boots too shiny for my liking. *Everything* on him was too clean for my liking. His ebony cloak, tied tight around the waist, didn't have a smudge anywhere on it. His hair—cut short—had the same black shine as his boots. Men who valued appearances over practicality irritated me. Did the fool think he could keep himself clean out here in the wilderness? We were likely to get muddy and bloody, but perhaps Theasin intended to have *some boy* clean his boots for him between every brisk jaunt out into the wilds.

I loathed this man. What a wagon wheel.

Theasin lifted an eyebrow with oddly perfect precision and then tugged at his gloves, securing them in place. His hands seemed strangled by the apparel. What sadistic tailor made gloves that tight? A Death Lord from the abyssal hells?

"Captain Calisto," Theasin said with a bored tone. "How have the men been doing?"

He watched the men struggle with the woodland, their swords and fire barely enough to tame the wilderness. It was almost amusing, in a pathetic way. The roots had more fight than most blackhearts I had met at sea.

"This place isn't right," I said, staring at a piece of bark that curled in on itself, blackened, and then tumbled to the dirt. "It's all a damn warning. The woodland wants us to turn back."

"You aren't getting paid to offer your advice," Theasin drawled. "Just stay alert and follow my lead. The god-creatures hide themselves in perilous lairs. Only the worthy make it through."

I stared at the overgrown woodland, taking note of how the gargantuan trees grew only a few feet apart, leaving little room for carriages or large mystical creatures. Making this trek would be like traveling to the abyssal hells and back. Agonizing the entire way.

"You think you're worthy?" I asked, knowing full well this pompous blowhard would say *yes*.

Theasin shot me a sideways glance, a smirk creeping onto his smug expression. "I am the only one who can bond with the soul forge. No other person alive has the knowledge, intelligence, and skill to impress the god-creature."

Normally, I liked a man with a mix of arrogance and brains. It reminded me of Everett Zelfree. But Everett wasn't an insufferable blackheart who loved his own reflection. Everett was clever. Cunning. A man with charm enough to work through any social situation, if he gave enough of a damn.

Theasin's relickeeper shifted on its four patchwork feet, its odd body of floating metal and glass clinking with even the slightest of movements. What did *it* think of that statement? Was Theasin's old eldrin going to remain bonded? Would Theasin kill it? I didn't know—I didn't really care, either.

I offered Theasin half a smile, though I knew it wasn't anything friendly. "I guess it won't be long until we see if you're worthy or not, will it?" Then I patted him on his twig-like arm and headed for the tree line.

I wanted this over with. The faster it happened, the better.

Four days of hacking, sawing, and burning the trees. That was what it took. I didn't trust the villains of the Second Ascension, but at least they weren't slackers. After all that work, most of them looked like they had been caught in a tornado and dragged—upside-down and screaming—through fifty trees and a mud pit. The smoke from the fires didn't help with their breathing. Every one of them had a terrible cough by the end, like their lungs had filled with ash.

It amused me every time they broke out into fits of wheezing. Not because I thought men with broken lungs were funny, but because any one of these dastards would happily watch me fall off a cliff to my death. They weren't my allies. They were fanatics of that fool they called *the Autarch*. And if that Autarch lunatic said I needed to die, every person in the Second Ascension would make it their personal mission to skin and gut me. And they would prob-ably delight in it, like the vile sadists all of mankind were at their core.

I ambled down the charred and narrow path, taking note of the continual rot on the vegetation. A younger man, leaning against one of the colossal trees, coughed and then spat a gob of black saliva onto the dirt near his boot. He had no arcanist star on his forehead, but he wore fine clothing of smooth leather, wool, and brass buckles. Even with the mud stains, I could tell his outfit cost him a few shiny coins.

I stopped and gave him the once over.

His scowl told me he didn't like that.

"You could've helped us more," the man said, his tone bordering on *way too prissy*. "I know you have a reputation as a scoundrel, but you're still a manticore arcanist. Why hasn't your eldrin been out here with us? It could've—"

"What was that?" I asked, cutting him off with a half-smile. "I couldn't make out your words over all that whining."

The man straightened his posture and squared his shoulders, but his eyes shifted from mine to the ground and then to mine again. A telltale sign of fear. Yet the man hardened his brow regardless, preparing to speak. He had a spine—too bad he didn't have the wisdom to match it.

"I'm Markus, the second son of Hippogriff Arcanist Mark Anthony," he said. "My father won't tolerate such rude behavior from sellswords and..." The young man clenched his jaw and swallowed the rest of his words. Perhaps his common sense had finally caught up with his mouth.

"Who can't I be rude to?" I sarcastically held a hand to my ear. I frowned as I said, "Damn. I keep forgetting the *Pirate Handbook of Etiquette* in my quarters. Pirates are well known for being rule-following tryhards, after all. I'd hate to ruin that reputation." I dropped my hand and chuckled at the man's increasingly red face.

Then I spotted something interesting. The skin on the back of Markus's hand flaked and peeled away, much like the bark on the nearby trees. The little crybaby scratched at his arm without any concern or consideration for his skin, and I suspected he was too wrapped up in his own delusional world to grasp the ever-evolving situation around us.

Instead of informing him of the potential danger, I dismissively waved my hand. "Maybe *you* should be careful who you're talkin' to, boy. Next time I might not be in a good mood." I strode off into the woodland, the pompous man already forgotten. All I could think about was his damaged skin, and the ever-increasing speed at which the trees were dying all around us.

I knew something was wrong with this damn area. We couldn't stay here long.

What a load of shit. It took us another *two days* to find the door we were looking for. And to make matters worse, most of the Second Ascension thugs had dark patches on their skin, and more and more of them reported their bodies feeling sluggish or had nightmares of *falling apart*. The woods were killing everyone, I was certain of it.

Theasin had insisted we continue, and *I* never had any problems, so I didn't concern myself too much. But I did wonder what the ultimate cost of this would be.

Fortunately, we found some giant circular stone thing in the middle of the overgrown woodland. The door was flat on the ground, which was a shock to Theasin, apparently. He had expected a building. Nah, that likely wasn't true—he had probably expected a castle and a damn parade to welcome his arrival. Instead, all he got was some freakish entrance with a slug or something carved into the stone surface.

Theasin stood at the edge of the door, his smirk replaced with a prominent frown.

That amused me a bit.

His men stood around in the nearby forest, resting by

the trunks of the trees or playing lookout by climbing the thick branches and observing the surroundings with a spyglass. They awaited directions, and the longer the silence stretched, the more my patience wore thin.

"So?" I asked. "What now?"

"Open the door," Theasin commanded.

I glanced down at the circular slab of stone. There wasn't a handle, just a split down the middle. The Second Ascension goons had tried to dig around it, but all they had found were thick rocks with rough surfaces.

"You don't have some sort of magic for this?" I asked with a sigh.

"I'd rather not waste any of my energy or resources if I can avoid it."

I should've known.

"*Hellion*," I shouted. "To me!"

The heavy beats of leather wings echoed in the distance. Manticores were large—they had the bodies of lions, after all—and Hellion was a champion among his breed. Ever since Hellion had gained his true form, he had practically doubled in size, which included his wingspan. When he flew over the woodland, *everyone* had to stop and notice. His white fur glistened in the afternoon light, and his black scorpion tail had a sleek shimmer that seemed equal parts beautiful and terrifying.

When Hellion flew through an opening of the leaf canopy and landed, the ground shuddered under his weight. The members of the Second Ascension hid away behind the trees or cowered in the cover of ferns and undergrowth.

Hellion's black bat-like wings cast large shadows until he furled them against the side of his mighty lion torso. He "stared" at me with his face mask—a hilariously freakish getup that looked like a human face, and even contorted to reflect his mood. It was ivory, like his fur coat, and the eyes and mouth were currently curved to represent a simple smile. Most fools got unsettled when Hellion glanced their way—he had no eyes, just a mask—which was probably the most amusing part of his true form. Normal manticores had the faces of lions.

"You think you can open this?" I asked, gesturing to the circular stone door.

Hellion's smile tilted downward into a slight frown as he examined the entrance. He stepped closer and reached out with a "paw." Well, more like a human hand. His front paws had the five fingers of any normal human hand, just furred and padded, like a cat's. He could operate tools as well as the next person, including writing with a quill—manticores were freakishly human in a lot of ways. But I liked to think of manticores as just visual representations of humanity. Twisted and warped. *Pretending* to be decent more than half the time.

Hellion reached out with his human hands and grazed the stone door. He extended his claws from the tips of his fingers as he traced the etching of the slug. Well, maybe it was a slug, I wasn't certain. It looked like a fat, shell-less snail with tiny whiskers—or arms?—sprouting from its back. The monstrosity reminded me of the deep-ocean-dwelling sea creatures that occasionally plagued ships out in uncharted waters.

"What is that?" I asked, pointing to the carved picture. "It can't be the *soul forge*."

Theasin sneered. "It is, in fact, the soul forge, you cretin."

"Why is it called a *forge*?" I glared at the disgusting

artwork. "It sure as hell doesn't look like it's forging anything other than a slime trail."

"Your complete lack of an education betrays you. The word *forge* means 'to create.' '*To mold.*'"

"Heh," I said. "And *slugs* are master crafters of souls, apparently?"

"Historians of ancient civilization have taught us that all life started in the darkest depths of the ocean, near the first level of the abyssal hells. And since you can't put these facts together yourself, I'll continue." Theasin cleared his throat. "The soul forge has taken the shape of proto-life—it is a beginning. A vessel with which new life will be shaped and created."

Proto... life?

I bit back a chuckle. Not the most *intimidating* of creatures.

The funniest part was that Theasin had said every word as though it were a prophecy of unimaginable importance. His megalomania was on full display, and I tensed. Men like Theasin were *never* to be trusted. Sure, he could be talented, but I could already tell that he detested speaking to me. It was beneath him. *I* was his lesser. Someone to disregard and step on until he had all the power he needed.

With a snort and a grunt, Hellion placed both his hands on the door and attempted to pry it open. He strained and hunkered down, exerting himself to the fullest. Manticores were known for their extreme strength. They were unrivaled for their size, possessing power ten times anything they should have had.

And it was a magical benefit I enjoyed as well. As a manticore arcanist, I could rip a man down the middle without breaking a sweat.

I wasn't going to mess with the door, though. The

accursed area still had me on edge. Hellion was more than sturdy enough to handle any initial problems.

But the door wouldn't budge. Hellion struggled with it for three straight minutes, gritting his fangs until his mask had a frustrated face on it. He stopped and stepped away from the door.

"It's sealed with powerful magics," Hellion said, his voice half-muffled by his mask. "No amount of raw strength will open it."

I turned to Theasin and shrugged one shoulder. "Guess you'll have to use up some energy after all."

Theasin regarded the door with a narrowed glare before snapping his fingers. "Essellian!"

His odd eldrin, the pile of broken windows and religious buildings, shifted among the trees. Apparently, the relickeeper had been in its "garbage form" and just *lying around* as fragments. When Theasin called its name, the junk came together, tied in place through magic threads. It formed into its dragon shape, its eyeless head rising a good fifteen feet into the air. It had to duck to avoid hitting the leaf canopy, but the creature didn't seem to mind.

Essellian headed our way, its jagged body cutting up the plants and ground. Those glass shards and metal pieces were pointed in every direction.

"Give me the rose quartz runestone," Theasin commanded. He held out his hand, palm up. "Quickly now."

His relickeeper nodded its head and then sat on its back legs. His chest had bits of brass and copper, and the metal shifted around until the "insides" of the dragon became apparent. A pink runestone emerged from the depths of the beast, and Essellian grabbed the magical object and handed it over to Theasin.

"Finally," Theasin said as he held the runestone tight

and close to his chest. "I thought this would be the key required for the chamber of the god-creature, but perhaps it is merely to enter the lair. Stand back."

Although I stood semi-close to the door, and perhaps in the range of potential traps, I didn't budge. I wanted to see this.

Theasin sauntered to the edge of the stone circle and then gently placed the rose quartz runestone against the door. A bright light filled the etching of the soul forge, and then the whole damn door. It grew in intensity, shining with such radiance that I had to shield my eyes. Hellion—protected by his mask—didn't seem bothered. He stood close to me, protective, and watched the event unravel.

The glowing light vanished a moment later, and the door opened, revealing a tunnel with a sixteen-foot diameter. It was slanted—like a slide—and dark enough that I suspected it led to the depths of the abyssal hells. The "walls" were smoothed stone, each slab carved with pictures of mystical creatures in various stages of life. Some babes, some eggs, some giant and grown. Even a few dead ones, which amused me.

There were so many...

Dragons, manticores, unicorns, phoenixes...

And the tunnel *reeked* of rotting flesh. Coincidence? I didn't think so.

"Smells lovely," Hellion said with a purr on the edge of his gruff voice.

I chuckled, mostly because Theasin gagged and leapt away like a frightened bird. I had to admit, it was an unpleasant scent, but I had enough intestinal fortitude to stomach the stench. Men like Theasin—who never left the comfort of civilization—couldn't handle rank odors.

Pathetic.

"You want me and Hellion to take care of this?" I asked with a raised eyebrow. "For an extra cut of the loot, of course."

Theasin shot me a sneer. "*Fool*—the god-creature is *mine*. I will complete its trial of worth. You will simply protect me from unexpected problems and get paid in magics no more than we agreed upon."

I glanced at the ominous tunnel. "That's the trial of worth?"

Hellion leaned over the edge and inhaled deeply.

"Essellian and I will handle this," Theasin said, snapping his fingers. "You and the others will just accompany us."

"Because you suspect there will be plenty of trouble?" I asked with a laugh.

Theasin frowned. "I'm uncertain. So, you'll follow close behind and deal with any troubles of a physical or gory nature as they arise."

Every time this man opened his damn mouth, I was rewarded with another reason to laugh. He wanted us to handle the dirty work. Of course he did. These Second Ascension zealots were worse than pirates—each of them reeked of self-importance and elitism, as though they had been chosen for a greater purpose above the *filth*. They were mostly from noble houses—minor ones, but that was beside the point.

Pirates at least acknowledged they were sea thieves. These Second Ascension fools thought their thievin', murderin' treachery was somehow justified because they were *so* superior when compared to the *bumbling nincompoops* who stumbled around them.

Theasin was the exact same. He had a runestone that had been stolen for him, to find a creature in a location handed to him by the Autarch. He hadn't done jack shit to earn this *trial of worth*, yet here he was, demanding more from everyone else because he was *so exceptional.*

It made me sick. More than the foul odor in the tunnel.

But did it matter? Not really. I was here for the magical items and nothing more. Anything to make me stronger. Anything to protect myself from the world's many cutthroats out to steal everything I had, from my coins to my life.

"Come, Essellian," Theasin said as he grabbed an odd bar of metal on the relickeeper's shoulder. He pulled himself onto his eldrin, standing with one boot half-inside the creature, careful not to touch the sharp and jagged bits. Then he motioned for the tunnel. "Take us down."

I snorted and glanced at Hellion. My eldrin knelt on his front leg and lowered his head. I pulled myself onto his back by using his white mane as a handhold. His muscular back wasn't the most comfortable, but his silky fur had the lush quality of rabbit pelts. Few people understood the beauty of manticores. None knew them like I did.

Hellion turned his head like a freakish owl, practically all the way around, to look at me with his happy-face mask. "I'm excited." His voice had an edge of hunger.

I chuckled. "Don't worry. We're sure to see something good."

"Excellent."

Before I could jump into the tunnel, Theasin motioned to the men between the trees. They scurried out, each one more hesitant than the last. They probably weren't prepared for whatever horrors were in this lair, which would make their shock all the more delicious.

Hellion stepped to the edge and slid down the side of the tunnel at a slow and steady rate. His claws couldn't seem to damage the carved walls of the bizarre entrance. Fortunately, the tunnel was wide enough that I didn't need to duck my head. I just held on to Hellion's mane, my fingers twisted into his fur.

The darker it grew, the tenser Hellion became. When the darkness became overbearing, Hellion braced himself against the walls and halted our descent. He couldn't see, but I could. My first mate had crafted me a kappa trinket—a necklace made of the silver bones of elves—that allowed me to see through fog, haze, smoke, and darkness.

"No one is gonna be able to see a damn thing," I called out, my voice echoing up to the entrance.

"I will handle it," Theasin replied.

His garbage eldrin entered the tunnel, heralded by a cacophony of clacking glass, bashing metal, and clattering brass. The relickeeper steadied his pace, and once he nearly reached us, another part of his multi-faceted body opened up to reveal illumination from a small collection of glow-stones. The light reflected off the glass and smooth metal of Essellian's body—some of it colorful and radiant. Rainbows speckled the walls of the tunnel, creating a bizarre contrast to the smell of decay.

"Aren't we fancy now?" I muttered.

Hellion chuckled. "We're the champions of light, here to save the world."

His sarcasm got me laughing along with him.

With Essellian's light, we continued down the tunnel. Occasionally, I stared at the wall, examining the carvings as we went deeper. The pictures became increasingly... disturbing. At first, there was life at all stages, but the farther we traveled, the more the pictures involved children— mystical animals, normal animals, *people*—infants, basically. Some creatures were so young, their eyes weren't open. And to make things more confusing, all these babes were held up by hands that seemingly sprouted from the ground, each child cradled in a palm.

What in the abyssal hells was going on?

"Hellion?" I asked under my breath.

My manticore laughed—he knew exactly what had gotten under my skin. "The meat of babes is the most tender and delicious."

I half-smirked. "You think the lair will be filled with helpless whelps?"

"One can hope."

I wasn't so sure. I liked to pretend I had seen the worst of life, and thus had nothing left to fear, but that was a lie. I feared men's twisted desires, and the dark depths to which humanity could descend. And I didn't mean the desire for wealth, fame, love, or power—those dwelled in the hearts of all men—I meant the perverse desires that drove individuals to torture animals or bed children.

This tunnel seemed like a shrine to a desire I couldn't name. Theasin had said this god-creature *created*, so maybe it was a monument to that, but something in my gut told me these carvings weren't harmless.

It took us nearly two minutes of careful sliding to finally reach the bottom. The clatter of the relickeeper made our entrance noisy, which I disliked, but that didn't worry me too much. *I* was the thing most people were afraid of. *I* was the monster in the dark—the villain of children's stories and a scourge of the seas. The beasts in this lair were nothing but obstacles. If they knew what was best, they'd stay hidden in their shadowy holes.

Theasin and his eldrin joined us a moment later. The lights shining from Essellian provided enough illumination for anyone to examine the wide-open room we had landed in. I took a deep breath and then gagged. Something smelled of powerful death, more than before. Fresh, soiled death. Like the stench of a corpse that, as its last act, had evacuated its bowels.

I steeled myself before asking, "Shall we be on our way?"

Theasin covered his nose and mouth with the collar of his robes. "We'll wait for the others." He coughed afterward, his honeyed skin growing paler with each passing moment.

I gritted my teeth and waited. The sound of the Second Ascension goons tumbling toward us made for an amusing distraction, but it was another couple of minutes before everyone had landed inside the lair. The two salamander arcanists lit fires in their hands to help light up the dungeon we were all in.

"What is this?" someone whispered.

"How do we get out when we're done?" another person asked.

One goon didn't have the stomach for the odor. He vomited, adding yet another pleasant aroma to our surroundings. A few of his friends barked and yelled at him.

What comradery.

But I wasn't surprised. That was how most of humanity acted.

"I will solve the puzzles of the soul forge," Theasin declared. "I will go first, and you will wait until I call for you."

He had the voice of someone brimming with confidence, so I sarcastically waved him forward and gave a little bow as he passed. I knew he'd be callin' for help soon enough, but for now, he could have the delusion of *fearless leader*. He walked to the opposite end of the room and discovered yet another tunnel—this one more a hallway than a slide—and continued forward.

The men of the Second Ascension withdrew their

cutlasses and flintlock pistols. They held them at the ready, and I briefly wondered if I could rely on their combat prowess in the middle of a life-or-death fight.

Probably not.

The wide-open room we were in was circular in shape. Unlike in the entrance tunnel, the walls here had no markings or pictures. They were smoothed stone, as far as I could tell. I wasn't an expert on rocks. Or architecture. Or ancient god-lairs, for that matter. So it could probably be something else.

Fortunately, I knew it wasn't an illusion. I had yet another trinket—made from the eyeball of a griffin, since they had the ability to see through deception—and it allowed me to know when illusions were nearby. With the trinket, illusions shimmered, much like a heat mirage in the desert.

But this place didn't shimmer. It was as real as death and taxes.

"What should we be, ugh, doin'?" a man asked through a gag.

"Just answer to me when I give the orders, and—"

"*Calisto!*" Theasin barked.

The commanding edge to his voice irritated me faster than when the rum went dry. I yanked on Hellion's mane and pointed him toward the second tunnel. He sauntered in Theasin's direction and didn't stop until we had traveled the length of the corridor and entered another room. Hellion's feet crunched down on something, however. It sounded like... dried leaves and brittle twigs that had been placed over sacs of liquid. There was a crunch and a pop with each one of Hellion's steps.

I glanced down and almost regretted it.

Almost.

Instead, I just stared, tense and unmoving, as my mind slowly came to terms with the *objects* covering the floor.

Little bodies.

Dead little bodies.

Mystical creatures—babes, all of them—dead and scattered around the floor. It was like an adorable battlefield of kittens and puppies, each one freshly deceased.

Hellion yelped and then leapt backward, clear away from the bodies.

"They're dead," I said.

"No," Hellion growled. "They... attacked me."

"What? How?"

I leaned over Hellion's side and glared at his body, as well as the bizarre massacre. Hellion's paws were rotted in patches, much like the bark on the trees above—like he had aged quickly in small locations around his feet. To my shock, the damn corpses that Hellion had squished were now moving. They were stitching themselves back together, similar to how arcanists healed from damage. But how?

"It felt like... they were suckling from me," Hellion said, his voice tinted with rage. "Feeding from my life."

The young mystical creatures stood on wobbly legs, like newborn foals. Their mouths hung slack-jawed, and their eyes remained unfocused. Had they fed from Hellion's life? Maybe his magic?

I didn't give a damn.

"Destroy them," I commanded.

"*No*," Theasin hissed.

I snapped my attention upward, glancing around until I spotted Theasin near a stone door on the opposite end of the room. His relickeeper had clearly walked across the bloody floor—the shredded corpses of pups and cubs were left in Essellian's wake—but the relickeeper wasn't harmed.

Was it because the garbage dragon wasn't a being of flesh? The corpses had attacked Hellion because he could bleed and decay?

Theasin, still riding his eldrin, high above the creepy floor, pointed to the moving corpses.

"This is a test," he said. "These are the creations of the soul forge. We must help them."

Help them? I hoped Theasin meant *help them die a second time.*

Hellion took a few steps backward as the shambling zombie creatures hobbled forward. They were small—babes, of course—but what if they continued to drain Hellion of his life? There were hundreds of these cadavers in the room. Could they swarm us? Like bees?

"I'm seconds away from burning this place to the ground," I said as I gripped my pistol. "What's your damn plan?"

Theasin stared at the floor, his eyes narrowing. "Bring me living beings," he eventually commanded.

I lifted an eyebrow. "You mean *the men*?"

"I don't care what you bring. Just bring me beings made of flesh."

We were in the middle of a bizarre, rotting woodland —one devoid of random animals. The only thing to bring him was the men. His own men. His own damn men.

"Interesting," Hellion growled as he turned his masked face around to stare at me.

"They aren't *my* men," I muttered with a shrug. "They're all dastards, anyway."

"True."

I had done some terrible things over the course of my lifetime, so who was I to judge? If Theasin wanted to drain his men dry in the pursuit of power, I might as well let him. It wasn't my business.

Hellion turned around, and we ambled back to the main room. The death stench made sense now, though the knowledge didn't comfort me. When I reached the main room, the only light came from the two salamander arcanists, their flames flickering with enough intensity to chase the darkness to the walls.

"You four," I said, motioning to a small group sitting on the stone floor. "Theasin needs you."

Three of them got to their feet, but one had enough of an indignant attitude to sigh and roll his eyes. The others didn't question me, or volunteer to accompany the group of four, or even look in our direction. They avoided glancing at me whenever possible—like the cowards they were.

I motioned for the four men to walk ahead of me. They complied, though their pace was slower than I liked. To my surprise, I recognized one of the men. Markus, the son of Hippogriff Arcanist Mark Anthony, blended in well with the others—he had no tattoos, no scars, no distinguishing marks of any kind—and his fancy clothing had long since lost its luster. The scruff on his chin made him seem more like an approachable man from the streets, rather than the fancy noble I knew him to be. Despite that, I recognized him. I had an uncanny ability to remember people and faces.

When we reached the room of corpse infants, I noticed that Essellian's lights had been enclosed within his body. The darkness prevented the four men from seeing anything —though not me.

Theasin cleared his throat. "Calisto, have you brought what I requested?"

Even he couldn't see.

"I got you some men, yeah," I said as I scratched at my chin.

"Bring them inside. And don't allow them to leave."

"Wait, what?" Markus asked.

Hellion didn't wait for my command. He shoved the four men into the room with his massive body and strength, practically hurtling them into the center of the wide-open space. The four men crushed some of the baby corpses, each one popping and exploding with coagulated blood.

Unfortunately, all it took was for something to *touch* the monsters for their hideous magic to take effect. The next few moments disturbed me to the point that I couldn't look away. The four men rotted—falling apart as though aging at a rapid rate. Their skin flaked, black spots blossomed across their bodies, and each one attempted to run from the room, but they couldn't see, and they became weaker with each passing moment. With all the grace of comedy theater, the four men stumbled and fell over, landing on more corpses and adding to the intensity of the life-draining magic.

"Help!" one yelled.

"What's happening?" another screamed. "What is this?"

"It hurts! It hurts so much!"

Their cries didn't unnerve me. I had heard worse when I had served under the Dread Pirate Redbeard. That monster had boiled members of his crew alive. Those screams still haunted my nightmares... These didn't compare.

But at the rate they were decaying, it would take a full minute of their shrieking before they died, which was unfortunate. I exhaled and brushed my fingers through Hellion's mane, trying not to allow the horror to seep into my thoughts. If I concentrated, I could detach myself from the present and get lost in a few pleasant memories that kept me sane.

"Calisto! *Help me!*"

The last man calling out—none other than Markus—finally broke my apathy. I hated it when people called out to me specifically. If they used my name, even my alias, *Calisto*, it somehow felt... too personal to ignore. My skin crawled, and my veins filled with ice. I wasn't a passive observer anymore. What would Everett think if he saw me now?

"Please!" Markus shouted, his voice weaker by the end of the word.

I gritted my teeth, removed my kappa trinket, and placed it on Hellion, allowing him to see in the darkness. Then I commanded, "Get him. *Now.*"

Hellion didn't need any further instruction. He turned around—careful not to touch the undead creatures or the ones that were "waking up" and moving about—and then used his long scorpion tail to reach out to the center of the room. Although I couldn't see, I heard the hooked stinger on the end of Hellion's tail pierce through Markus's shirt. Hellion lifted him above the deadly floor, saving him from the accelerated rot.

I took back my trinket, nervous about being blind in this lair of undead babes.

Markus took deep and shaky breaths as Hellion brought him out of the disgusting bodies. That didn't reverse the damage done—Markus still had welts, black spots, and lesions—but he wasn't dead.

Unlike the other three.

They flailed for a few more moments, but it wasn't long before their strength failed them, and they could no longer cry out. When they eventually perished, the baby creatures around them sprang to life—no longer zombies or undead, but *alive*. A griffin cub, a unicorn foal, and a caladrius chick all regained their fur, coat, and feathers, each one cuter than the last.

"Thank you," Markus rasped as Hellion set him down on the floor of the corridor. He was too weak to get up. "Thank you," Markus whispered again.

The other shambling corpses ignored the newly "born" creatures and instead hobbled in my direction, though at a slow and unsteady pace. They'd be easy to avoid, but it was clear now that if I fell into this trap, they'd suck out my energy in a heartbeat. Could I last longer because I was an arcanist? Probably, but I didn't want to test the theory.

Theasin's relickeeper opened a compartment of his chest and revealed the glowstones once more. The rainbow illumination sparkled across the writhing floor, but the bits of light that hit the unicorn, griffin, and majestic caladrius highlighted the natural beauty of the newborn creatures.

The mystical creatures didn't seem very old, though. None of them spoke, and the griffin's wings didn't have enough feathers for it to fly.

The corpses of the three men... they were another story. They appeared blackened and half-ash. Their clothes rested over their skeletal bodies, as though someone with a sense of humor had tried to dress a pile of burn victims.

No, they weren't burned. They were old. Decayed. Lost to time.

"Fascinating," Theasin said, his attention focused on the newly born creatures. "Just as I expected. The soul forge can manipulate life itself."

I glanced over to Markus and then to the three unlucky blackhearts in the middle of the room. Then I returned my attention to Theasin. "So, this was the outcome you wanted?"

"It's an outcome I had expected." Theasin snapped his fingers.

Essellian reached out with his glass and metal claws and scooped up the three infant mystical creatures. He didn't have a soft touch—the creatures practically rattled around in his palm as he brought them over to the door on the other side of the room. Theasin motioned with a flick of his wrist, and his relickeeper touched the babes to the door itself.

Another flash of light, similar to the one outside, and the way forward was revealed.

"Now we continue onward," Theasin said, no hint of remorse or reflection.

I wondered if those three goons had had families? Did Theasin even know their names?

I exhaled, dispelling the chilling thoughts. If no one else cared about the dastards, why should I?

"Thank you," Markus wheezed again. "Thank you."

"Shut up," I growled. "You're making me regret what I've done. At least corpses are quiet."

Markus trembled as he tried to stand, but it was futile. His skin flaked off, leaving small bloody patches across his body. He glanced up at me, his eyes sunken, and his hands veined with age.

He looked a good twenty years older, in his late thirties now.

Theasin exited the room, seemingly unable to see anything happening before him. His relickeeper even dropped the three young mystical creatures from a height that looked like it hurt. What was that lunatic thinking? Young creatures were worth plenty of coin! If Theasin wasn't gonna take 'em, I would.

I urged Hellion to continue—perhaps we could leap

over the room with a few powerful wing flaps—but before we could get far, Markus held up an unsteady hand.

"Wait," he pleaded. "Don't leave me. Please... don't leave me."

I glanced over my shoulder and frowned. "*Hey,*" I barked, my voice carrying down the corridor to the front room. "Come get an injured man!"

Markus whimpered. "No. No, not them. I want to stay with you..."

Me, eh?

I hesitated for a moment, uncertain of what I was going to do about this. On the one hand, why should I have cared? On the other, the screaming of his buddies had been loud enough for the neighboring nations to hear, yet none of the other Second Ascension cutthroats had come rushing in to help, even though they could have.

The sound of footfalls told me the men had heard my command and were on their way.

"Wait there," I called out. "Forget my last order."

The footfalls stopped. Perhaps they were more than happy to comply.

I pointed to Markus and Hellion groaned as he lifted the broken man up. With less-than-gentle movements, Hellion placed Markus on his back, between his wings. Markus reached forward and grabbed my coat, using it as a balance. I almost shoved him off Hellion, but I held back the urge.

"Don't touch me," I said through gritted teeth.

Markus kept hold of the edge of my coat, but he didn't do anything further. He replied with a weak nod. "Thank you," he murmured.

"If I hear that again, I'll throw you from my manticore."

"O-of course."

"Let's move, Hellion."

Although the room wasn't large enough to accommodate all of Hellion's wingspan, it did allow him to make an assisted jump. He half-flapped twice and then leapt over the undead monsters. Most of them, anyway. He crunched down on a pile near the far door, splattering bits of them around. Parts of his back paws were rotted by the time he ran into the next corridor, but it wasn't enough to spawn more mystical creatures.

We passed the unicorn, griffin, and caladrius, all of which were mewing and crying. I wanted to stop for them, but there would be time on the way out.

Hopefully.

Markus had almost lost his balance in all the movement and had to wrap one arm around my waist. I remained tense as nightmarish memories of Redbeard haunted my thoughts. My previous captain had hurt everything he had touched, and he had left me with scars on my back, sides, and chest. They no longer hurt—physically—but I remembered the agony with shocking clarity whenever someone touched them.

Once Hellion steadied his walk, I glanced back at Markus. "What the hell did I tell you about touching me?"

Markus leaned away, his whole body shaking.

"This hall goes on for some way," Hellion said. "And I still haven't eaten."

I snorted a sarcastic laugh. "Neither have I."

"I hear griffins are delectable."

"He's worth money. Forget it."

Hellion turned his whole head around to show me his unhappy face mask.

Instead of answering my ever-starving eldrin, my curiosity got the better of me. I gave Markus a sideways glance. I still had goosebumps across my skin from his touch, but I didn't want to focus on that.

"What in the name of the abyssal hells did the Autarch promise you, huh? What's gonna be worth all this sufferin'? Coin? Women? Artifacts and trinkets?"

Markus took in a shallow breath. "He promised.... He promised me I'd become an arcanist. He said that... once he had bonded with multiple god-creatures, he would be able to ensure all his loyal followers were bonded with powerful creatures."

"Let me guess—you failed a trial of worth when you were younger, didn't you?"

Markus didn't reply, but his sunken-in gaze told me everything I needed to know.

He had failed. He had probably failed several, actually. I could see the whole story in my mind's eye. Mark Anthony the Hippogriff Arcanist had probably arranged several trials of worth for all of his children—but Markus had failed each. And then the Autarch had come along, with his fancy *golden kirin*, an eldrin so powerful and rare that even kings felt the painful touch of jealousy. If the Autarch promised these lackeys and second sons the chance to be powerful arcanists, who wouldn't support him?

"He said I would bond with a dragon," Markus murmured, his voice soaked in both hope and doubt. "That the dragons would listen to him... and do as he commanded."

Dragons were some of the most powerful eldrin around. Their trials of worth were said to be deadly—sovereign dragons required duels to the death—so there was no way a man as pitiful as Markus could bond with one.

Again, I could see the appeal of the Autarch. He could, in theory, eliminate the need for the trial of worth. Why wouldn't someone like Markus—who thought they were entitled to be an arcanist—jump at the opportunity, even if it meant he might face peril?

"Why are *you* here?" Markus whispered. "You're already an arcanist."

I ground my teeth. "I'm here for the magical items. Nothing more."

Dead silence followed my statement.

My answer seemed to be all he needed. Or perhaps he had no more energy for conversation. I didn't care. I didn't feel like talkin' regardless.

Hellion stopped once we reached the next room. My heart pounded hard—I figured we'd be beset by undead creatures beyond our imagining—but the room had nothing of the sort. Death still tainted the smell of the place, but this room was circular, wide, and clean.

The door on the opposite end was already open. From what I could see, gemstones of various colors had been placed into an intricate lock. Had it been some sort of puzzle? Had Theasin solved it in the time it had taken Hellion to saunter down the corridor? Interesting. I supposed the man was damn smart, though I was loath to admit it.

The bright lights of Essellian's glowstones shimmered in the next corridor. I urged Hellion to catch up, and my manticore jogged forward. A slight chuckle on his breath betrayed his excitement. I liked that about Hellion. He was never afraid. Every room, every path, every enemy—it was one more thing for him to conquer and devour. I loved the attitude.

The path angled downward and twisted to the side. We maintained a short distance behind Theasin—only fifteen feet or so—but the farther we traveled, the more the air became stagnant. Almost unbreathable.

Markus coughed and wheezed.

I ignored him. There was nothing for me to do. My manticore magics didn't allow me to heal others.

When we finally reached another room, it was much larger than the others, perhaps five times as wide and tall. It was still circular, and there was still another door on the opposite end of the room, but the impressive size made it seem intimidating.

A single pedestal sat in the center of the room, sized for a human and not a massive giant. Theasin climbed down off his eldrin and approached the pedestal with giddy movements. When he reached the pedestal, he placed his hands on either side, gripped hard, and then stared down.

Hellion walked over, and I finally got a good view. The pedestal was carved from bone and covered in writing. It wasn't a language I recognized—I knew how to read the northern languages of the countries that surrounded the Shard Sea—but that wasn't an impressive repertoire. I was certain Everett would be disappointed.

Theasin read over the pedestal, his excitement fading as his frown deepened. Whatever was written there was bad news, apparently.

"Is there a problem?" I asked.

"No," Theasin snapped.

"Can you use your runestone for this?"

"Unfortunately, this is yet another test I must overcome."

I patted Hellion's mane. "Uh-huh. A test of smarts?"

"Determination."

That sounded ominous. But it wasn't my damn test.

"Let me know when you're done," I said. "Or if you need me to rough something up."

Theasin didn't reply. He just glared at the pedestal, his concentration unwavering. I urged Hellion away by tugging on his mane, and we went to stand by one of the far walls. Markus grew weaker—his grip on my coat loosening—and I wondered if he'd make it through this entire ordeal. I was half-tempted to take him up to the surface, but I shrugged and chased the thought from my mind. Worrying about someone else's wellbeing was a fool's errand.

To my fascination, Theasin reached into his robes and withdrew a dagger.

Ha! Who was I kidding? Theasin pulled out a butter knife, at best. It was a dinky thing, barely more than the size of a man's finger. Perhaps it was a trinket imbued with power, but even then, Theasin should have been ashamed.

He pulled off one of his tight, black gloves. Even from over ten feet away, I could see something was wrong with Theasin's hands. They were scarred from the tips of his fingers to his wrist, and it was only then that I realized he seemed to have a limited range of motion. Nothing horrible —he could still grip, hold, and snap his fingers—but without the gloves, it seemed his hand wasn't as dexterous as it should have been, like he couldn't close his fingers entirely or bend his thumb. Perhaps the gloves themselves were trinkets used to help him?

Relickeepers were difficult to bond with, or so I was told. They required all potential arcanists to sift through moving piles of broken glass, metal, and junk in order to find the valuables hidden within. Such a task would likely leave someone's hands broken and bloody...

Theasin cut his palm and splashed crimson on top of the pedestal.

At first, nothing happened, but then the room trembled, and the pedestal glowed a soft white. Would the door open?

I kept my eyes on it, waiting and listening for what felt like a full minute. Then a low growling emanated from the ceiling.

I snapped my attention upward, just in time to catch sight of *something* oozing downward, as though the substance were melting into the room and slowly falling to the floor. It appeared like sap—or tar—and it molded as it fell, coalescing into solid shapes as it went. I held my breath as I drew my blade, certain this was a beast meant to kill us.

Theasin glanced upward and frowned. "Why has this happened?"

The ooze formed into a relickeeper, of all things, before slamming into the floor. The clatter of its junk insides echoed off the walls, hurting my ears for a short moment. The enemy relickeeper appeared as large as Essellian and towered over everyone except for Hellion himself.

What in the abyssal hells was going on?

"I must have failed," Theasin muttered, anger in his voice, but no panic.

Relickeepers had no vocals—which was why they couldn't speak—so when the enemy creature opened its mouth and revealed its broken metal fangs, no roar issued. Instead, it lashed out at Theasin, striking him in the shoulder and carving a chunk from his robes and flesh. The frail man hit the floor, and his own relickeeper rushed to shield him from the monster.

Without the need for my instruction, Hellion used his tail to hook Markus and place him on the ground. Then he lunged forward and struck the fake relickeeper with a powerful slam. I held on for the ride, never dismounting. We'd fight together until I found an opportunity to strike.

Unfortunately, relickeepers were perhaps the worst creature for a manticore and its arcanist to fight. True form manticores could remove their face masks and paralyze their enemies upon meeting their gazes—but relickeepers had no eyes. Manticores also had a potent venom in their stinger that, once injected in the victim's body, prevented an arcanist or their eldrin from using their magic—but relickeepers had no blood or veins.

And when anything touched a relickeeper, they were punished for it. Hellion knocked over the enemy, but he was slashed up everywhere he had made contact. It was like rolling around on a pile of broken glass.

"*Fool*," Theasin shouted. "Relickeepers are only killed when their hearts are separated from their bodies!"

I wasn't too familiar with relickeepers, but I did remember Redbeard killing one while I had served on his ship. That sadist had known how to murder *all kinds* of mystical creatures, and it was a knowledge that, for better or worse, had been passed down to me. Redbeard had ripped something out of the chest of the garbage monster...

The enemy relickeeper got to its feet and then lashed out with its tail. The beast had a wrought-iron fence that formed spines, and Hellion leapt backward, but not enough. I used my cutlass to block the tip of its tail from striking us, but the relickeeper had hit so hard that my blade flew from my hand.

Instead of continuing to fight from my eldrin's back, I jumped off and headed toward the monster.

Theasin was useless. He and Essellian backed away from the conflict with all the courage of a spineless jellyfish.

The relickeeper swiped at me with glass-shard claws, but I had a surprise for him. Instead of dodging, I stepped into the shadows—falling into the darkness as though it were a bottomless pool of water. Sensing the environment outside of the darkness, I shadow-stepped to the other side of the relickeeper and emerged from the void.

I smirked to myself, pleased I had managed to get a hold of a knightmare trinket: a pair of black boots that allowed me to shadow-step. The ability to slip into the darkness and move with impunity was a tactical godsend.

Before the enemy relickeeper could turn around, Hellion bashed into it again, hurting himself but also keeping the beast's attention. Thankfully, manticores healed much faster than other mystical creatures, and the slashes to Hellion's white pelt were already stitching themselves back together.

While the damn monster had its claws and fangs directed at Hellion, I clenched my jaw and rushed for its side.

"The relickeeper's heart is the source of its magical tethers," Theasin called out, his tone bordering on bored. "It's located at the center of their chests."

I huffed and held back choice words. The heart was located in the chest—past the hazards of jagged edges and razor points. Which meant I wasn't walking away from this unscathed.

With my unparalleled strength, I bashed at the creature's patchwork ribs with a tight fist. I broke the bones in my hand, cut up my arm, and shredded my coat, but the two ribs I struck had shattered. Bits of the creature clattered to the floor, no longer held together by its magic.

Hellion lashed out with his stinger tail, hoping to penetrate the hole I had created, but the enemy relickeeper stepped away just in time. Hellion's stinger impacted on a series of brass scales, dealing little injury.

Despite the burning pain of my injuries, I leapt forward and thrust my arm into the monster's chest. It jerked to the side and took me with it, nearly ripping my limb from my body. I ground out a curse, swearing I'd kill every last relickeeper I ever came across in the future, and then refocused myself. My body also healed at incredible rates, and soon I wouldn't be injured at all.

"The relickeeper's heart should be warm," Theasin said.

Although I hated the fact he was sitting on the sidelines, the information was at least useful. I reached in deep until my fingers grazed the heat. Fueled by unmitigated rage, I gripped the monster's core—the source of his magical tethers. The relickeeper thrashed again, this time slashing Hellion and nearly striking me with its elbow.

Hellion locked up, his body shaking as he half-fell to his side. He didn't seem to be capable of movement, almost like he had become a statue.

Theasin held up a hand. "Relickeepers can paralyze their victims and keep them in stasis."

That would've been nice to know sooner.

The enemy relickeeper opened part of its body and seemingly evoked a mist of glass shards. It gushed outward, and I suspected breathing the mist would rip my insides up like a shark ripped up helpless seals.

"Watch for that," Theasin called out.

If I lived through this, I would gut the man.

I yanked back on the relickeeper's heart and leapt away. The core of the monster was much like a ripe avocado—firm, while still being rather soft. Threads of magic clung to the heart like melted strings of cheese unwilling to release food.

If the monster could roar, it would've. The beast flailed and lashed out with its tail. It swiped at me, but I shadow-stepped out of range, finally cutting the last of the magic threads. The moment they detached, the beast crumpled into a pile of junk—a marionette that no longer had its strings. The crash and ensuing noise once again stung my ears, but the high of victory masked all of that.

Even the glass dust seemed to settle, which was a relief. Hellion also managed to get to his feet, the paralysis fading.

With blood running in rivulets down my arm and side, I sauntered over to the pile of broken materials and smiled. "Was that all, freak?"

The heart of the mystical creature disappeared from my hand. Then its whole damn body vanished, and for half a second, I thought it would reform again from the ceiling, just because I had taunted it.

Instead, silence settled over the room.

I glanced over at Theasin.

"Now what?" I asked. "Now that you've messed this up, how can we fix it?"

With a shaky hand, Theasin grazed his injured shoulder. He took in a deep breath and then exhaled. A cold and calculating demeanor settled into place. Theasin met my stare and sneered.

"My relickeeper magic allows me to identify magical objects, whether they're trinkets, artifacts, or even powerful fixtures," he stated matter-of-factly. "The pedestal is a magical fixture that requires an offering of the body to activate. But clearly, *blood* wasn't the correct offering."

"Is that what happened?" I snorted. "You had to fight your own eldrin if you got it wrong?"

"That's obviously what I'm saying, you cretin." Theasin strode over to the pedestal, his injuries still noticeable, even though mine had mostly healed. "I'll just need to determine what the soul forge wants as an offering in order to bond."

I laughed once and shrugged my uninjured shoulder. "An arm, probably."

Theasin caught his breath.

I almost laughed louder. Had Theasin not thought of that? All the walls were lined with weird hands and arms holding babes and mystical creatures—the soul forge even had hands and arms growing off of him, for crying out loud. If there was any part of the body the soul forge wanted, it was *definitely* a damn arm.

Theasin ran his blood-stained hand through his black hair, half-slicking the locks with his own vital fluid. It gave him an edge of *madman*, especially when he smiled afterward.

"Yes," he muttered, his gaze falling to the pedestal. "Yes... You're right... How had I not thought of that?"

I walked over and retrieved my weapon from the floor, irritated I had lost it in the fight. I hadn't expected the enemy relickeeper to be strong enough to disarm me. I wouldn't allow it to happen again.

"Perfect," Theasin said. "We will need a blade."

My cutlass was a step above most other swords. It was curved, like all cutlasses, but it had been made from the metal bones of iron dragons. It wouldn't shatter, and the magic imbued within prevented the blade from ever dulling.

I walked over to Hellion—to make sure his injuries weren't too grievous—and caught him returning Markus to his back. Although Hellion's fur was marred with blood, he still looked majestic. I patted his side and whispered encouragement for his efforts. Then I gave Markus an odd glance. The man returned my stare with a single nod.

"You really handled that situation," he muttered.

"I didn't become a *dread pirate* by sitting on my ass," I quipped.

"The stories make you out to be..."

But Markus never finished his thought. Perhaps his common sense had finally taken hold.

I exhaled and then returned to Theasin's side. To my amusement, he had already used his little knife to cut the left sleeve off his robe, exposing his arm. He had also removed his left glove, exposing his scarred and half-functional hand. The man wasn't as weak as I had initially imagined. The tone of his muscular arm told me he had been putting in work to maintain himself.

Interesting.

Theasin held out his arm. "Cut it off," he commanded, no hesitation.

I lifted both eyebrows and smiled. "What? No ceremony?"

"Fool—this isn't the time for sarcasm. We're in the midst of making history."

I loved how Theasin always had a grandiose way of thinking. We weren't talking about cutting off one of his limbs—*we were making history*. We hadn't killed three men to simply open a door—*we had made history*. If I adopted that way of thinking, I could justify any action as well.

Maybe I should.

"On with it," Theasin barked. "If you won't, Essellian will."

I almost had his damn eldrin do the honors, but I didn't want to miss out on hurting the man, so I decided to just allow his dictatorial demeanor to slide.

"Stay as stiff as possible," I said as I grabbed Theasin by the shoulder and shoved him into a better position. "I wouldn't want to miss."

Theasin glowered at me, his gaze so icy, it lowered the temperature of the room. I preferred his arrogance to his anger, but both were still amusing. Hadn't Theasin seen what I had done to a relickeeper? If I wanted, I could kill both him *and* his eldrin.

Despite that, I was impressed by Theasin's unwavering dedication to this process. He didn't flinch when I lifted my weapon, nor did he grimace or look away when I put all of my strength and speed behind the slash.

It'd take a normal man quite a bit of effort to slice a limb clean from the body, but I wasn't a normal man. With my enhanced strength, I lopped Theasin's left arm off with a clean strike—and with surprising accuracy. I hadn't been joking about potentially missing, but his stiff stance and lack of trembling made it easy.

Theasin couldn't maintain his cold exterior forever, though. He groaned in anguish and collapsed to his knees as blood gushed from the new injury, squirting outward and almost splattering me with scarlet. I removed my coat and threw it around him, but Theasin jerked away from my gesture, breathing through his teeth in quick and shallow gasps. Sweat sprouted from every pore on his face.

Despite his protests, I wrapped my damn coat around him anyway. I tied it tight around his shoulders to stifle the flow of blood. Theasin shivered and allowed me to help, but the moment I finished, he reached for his severed arm.

"You want this on the pedestal?" I asked.

If Theasin hadn't been in blinding agony, I was certain he would've popped off with some sort of insult, but luck was on my side today. All he did was reply with a curt nod. His sweat dripped onto the floor.

I picked up his still-warm arm and briefly imagined what Theasin would do if I used it as a plaything for a short while. I decided against it, but I smiled to myself as I set the bloody limb down in the center of the magical fixture.

Theasin continued his labored breathing, but he was surely healing. What a wagon wheel.

And like everything else in this damn lair, the pedestal started glowing, so I assumed we had done *something* right. Theasin's arm sank into the bone of the pedestal, disappearing into the shining structure. I squinted to keep out the radiance, but I kept at least one eye open and on the far door.

The whole place rumbled and shook, threatening to throw me off balance. I refused to be tossed to the ground and instead widened my stance.

"Come at me," I growled under my breath. "I'm ready."

The door opened just as the glowing of the pedestal stopped. It groaned as it split down the middle and slid apart, revealing a massive chamber beyond.

And also a creature. A giant creature. So large that its sides touched both walls.

It was the soul forge—a giant slug, tan in coloration, similar to sand—but unlike a slug, it was semi-translucent and clear enough to see a few feet into its insides. Even from outside of its final chamber, I could see the dark shadows of bodies stuck in the soul forge's interior. The damn beast had hundreds of people, mystical creatures, and animals all stuck in odd positions, as though frozen in a disgusting block of fleshy ice.

It was at least twenty-five feet tall at the "head" and when it moved, its semi-gelatinous body rippled. Hundreds of arms jutted out of its back. When they were still, they looked like spines, but when they moved—or bent at the elbow—they appeared more like corpses attempting to escape their grave.

"What in the name of the Death Lords is that monstrosity?" I muttered as I took several steps back.

Hellion leapt to my side. Markus clung to his mane, his injures and weakness still apparent. He stared into the next room, but Essellian's lights didn't reach the hideous monster. I was the only one who could see the giant slug.

"Where is it?" Theasin hissed. "Where is the soul forge?"

I pointed straight ahead as I took a moment to calm my nerves. Why was it so grotesque? Was there a reason? An explanation? A purpose? When I had imagined the god-creatures, I had assumed they would be elegant and pristine —beauty made flesh.

This was anything but.

"Essellian... take me in." Theasin motioned to the giant chamber, his breathing still pained.

His eldrin positioned himself so that Theasin could climb onto his side. Without two arms, it made the task entertaining, to say the least. To Theasin's credit, he managed to grab hold of his relickeeper and plant a boot into a foothold long enough to be carried into the next room.

"Hellion, stay close," I commanded.

My gut twisted with the feeling of betrayal and dread. I didn't trust the freakish god-creature, and I certainly didn't trust Theasin. Something told me I might have to make my own way out of this pit.

Hellion, Markus, and I entered the chamber after Theasin and his eldrin. The room felt as welcoming as a slaughterhouse. The smell of blood and offal washed over me in waves, as though the slug were exhaling, and its breath were laced with death.

"You have done well to make it here, Children of Balaster," the slug said, its voice booming, deep, masculine, and somehow ancient. Its tone reminded me of someone who was tired—or perhaps just didn't give a shit.

Theasin stepped off his relickeeper and stumbled a few

steps before catching himself. My coat, soaked in Theasin's blood, was still tied tight around his shoulders.

"Soul forge," Theasin said, half-shouting. "I've braved your trial of worth, and I've come for my reward."

I took a step back, wanting to distance myself as much as possible from this exchange. I wanted my reward, yeah, but I wasn't about to address the death slug until it had finally bonded with something.

"Hmm," the soul forge groaned, its foul breath crashing over us. The many arms on its back flailed about. **"Yes. Your essence is suitable to become a god-arcanist—and your thoughts please me greatly. Step forward, Child of Balaster. I will bond with you so that you may become a scholar who transforms all of existence with your knowledge."**

Theasin took a shaky step forward, but he was stopped when his relickeeper placed a single claw on his uninjured shoulder. Essellian didn't attack or prevent Theasin from proceeding, but for a handful of seconds, Theasin didn't move. The two of them stood there, frozen and silent.

Then Theasin jerked his shoulder from his eldrin's grasp and continued his short walk to the soul forge.

Essellian shook its head, and although the beast had no eyes or voice, it seemed as though it were... upset. Perhaps distraught.

But I had never been good at reading people. Everett had always been the one with a knack for empathy.

Theasin stopped in front of the soul forge, allowing only three feet between them. The massive slug groaned a second time, but instead of the beast emitting the stench, something else happened. It felt as though the air had been sucked from the room, and my lungs burned for a few moments when I tried to breathe. Fortunately, it didn't last long. A terrible presence blanketed the area, threatening to steal something from me. I just wasn't sure *what*.

Then Essellian shuddered and shook. It thrashed its head once before the glowing threads of its body began to subside. Essellian turned for the door—perhaps to run away—but he didn't make it far. The magic that held him together broke away and faded, causing his body to slowly fall apart, piece by piece. His glass, metal, and ceramics shattered on the floor as he crumpled. Whatever heart he'd had in his chest had likely disappeared as well...

Theasin barked and fell to one knee. He grabbed at his forehead, once again trembling from overwhelming agony. His arcanist mark bled at the edges.

"Inferior life only taints the rest," the soul forge said, its tone one of apathy. **"Just as it is important to prune plants, it is equally important to cull life. With you as my god-arcanist and scholar, we shall pass judgment on all of life and make it stronger in the process. You have my word as Xarkri the Second Soul Forge."**

I didn't like the sound of any of that.

It reminded me of the Dread Pirate Redbeard. He had said—on multiple occasions—that the weak were things for the strong. He had claimed that anyone killed by pirates deserved it because they hadn't been strong enough to defend themselves.

Which was why I needed to get stronger—to protect myself—but could I ever defend myself from a god-creature that could suck the life out of nearby beings like it were drinking a pint of rum? I doubted it.

And that frightened me, though I was loath to admit it.

Theasin, still kneeling, held out his only hand. The soul forge didn't move forward to make contact. Xarkri shuddered, and the dark shadows of bodies inside its semi-translucent slug body twisted and moved.

Xarkri's many arms waved back and forth. **"There is useless life about—a power source for my growth and strength. Before we bond, I must consume."**

Another exhale. Another crushing force of life-stealing energy. Was the soul forge trying to kill me? I grabbed at my chest, but my heart beat strong. I whipped my attention around to Hellion and Markus. Although they both appeared shaken, neither was dying like Essellian had died.

Was the monster killing us?

"I'm not *useless life*," I shouted. I'd attack this sad sack slug in a heartbeat—all my manticore venom would be his to choke on. "I'll—"

Theasin gestured to me, Hellion, and Markus. "Wait, mighty soul forge. They're serving me. I need them."

The oppressive magic lifted from me, and for a moment, I could breathe normally.

"But you do not need the rest," Xarkri ominously stated.

"No," Theasin replied, his voice low. "I don't need those insects."

The crushing force intensified, and at first, I thought the soul forge was still going to drain our life. Instead, more shadows appeared inside of Xarkri's body—and a few new arms sprouted from his back. Who was it consuming? The Second Ascension thugs we left a few rooms back?

"I am satisfied," the soul forge stated. **"Now the oldest source of light must bear witness to our bonding."**

The oldest source of light?

The entire chamber shook as the ceiling peeled apart. I held my breath, my attention on the smoothed stone circling and moving, opening wide and upward, all the way to the surface. It took several minutes, and the scrape of rock irritated my ears, but I couldn't look away. Was the soul forge altering its lair? Could it do that?

"What's happening?" Markus asked.

Hellion growled. "Keep quiet, boy. We don't want any attention."

The tunnel to the surface opened like the mouth of a fish, wide and oval. A pillar of afternoon light shone down into the chamber, illuminating a circular area that included half of the soul forge and its disgusting body. Slime dripped from its skin, falling to the floor and forming puddles of tannish-transparent ooze.

"This is the moment I have lived my life for," Theasin said, breathless. "I'm ready. Bond with me." He managed to get to both feet and stood. And then he held his hand out, no shaking in his stance.

Xarkri slithered forward a few feet until his slug-like body came into contact with Theasin's hand. The moment they touched, a blinding rose-colored light filled the room. Then, half a second later, it shot up through the new tunnel, piercing into the sky and draining all other color from reality. The pillar of rose-light was all I could see, even with my eyelids shut.

I held up my arm, trying to block out the radiance, but it seemed futile. I clenched my jaw and hardened myself, though an odd noise filled the chamber along with the light. It was... laughing? Manic cackling, to the point it reminded me of plague-ridden mystical creatures.

Was it Theasin?

Sure enough, when I managed to open a single eye, I spotted him with his head thrown back and his laugher pouring out in waves. An arcanist mark shone on his chest —a twelve-pointed star unlike the seven-pointed star other arcanists got for their marks on their forehead. It was the god-arcanist mark, the one that distinguished him from the rest of us.

The pillar of rose-light vanished with a whoosh of wind.

I took a breath, my heart hammering.

Theasin's laughter faded into a pompous chuckle. He was still missing an arm, but it didn't seem to bother him. He ripped off my bloody coat and threw it to the floor. He had a scar—faded and twisted—but it was clear the arm would never return. Was it a punishment from the soul forge? Or payment? I suspected the soul forge could fix Theasin's arm, if it wanted, but perhaps it was a sign?

"Yes!" Theasin ran his gloved hand through his disheveled hair, his megalomania on full display through his crazed smile. "*This is what I've waited for*. This is the power I need! This is what will change the world! More than my plague! More than anything else I've ever created!"

His triumphant shouting got me nervous. I stepped to Hellion's side, confused by Theasin's statements. Was he the creator of the arcane plague? Or was he the creator of some *other* plague? Either way, this dastard was insane—absolutely consumed and touched in the head.

Worse than Redbeard. And I had never thought I'd meet a man more depraved than him.

But humanity, *somehow*, continued to surprise me with its vileness.

"Xarkri, my perfect eldrin," Theasin said, more grandiose than anything he had said before. "Together, we are unstoppable. Together, we will make this world right."

"The world is filled with the weak and useless," the soul forge said, its voice booming up the tunnel to the sky. **"They should be filled with pride to add their flesh, matter, and souls into something greater than themselves.**

But the Children of Balaster are stubborn. They will resist —they always resist. You must be prepared. Seek out the Children of Luvi and the Children of Astros. They are of a greater breed and ilk."

I had no idea what that monster was talking about, and I didn't want to find out.

"We're leaving," I whispered to Hellion. "Right now."

My manticore tilted his head to the side. "But you don't have your magical items."

"To the abyssal hells with my promised items. After what I just saw, this creature'll need to kill one of us to make them anyway. If I'm lucky, the Autarch will have another mission... Something along the lines of what I did for him in the past. Best to stick with *those* tasks."

"As you say."

"Besides," I added. "We have three mystical creatures just waiting for us back in the other room. They'll get us a few shiny coins."

"What a-about me?" Markus whispered.

"What about you?" I growled.

"Take me with you. I'd rather be a pirate of the *Third Abyss* than return to the Second Ascension."

Markus must've put two and two together—he knew his comrades had been killed to feed the soul forge. I wondered if the Autarch had known that would be a price of bonding... Probably.

"Fine," I snapped. "Congratulations. You've hit the bottom of the barrel, and there's nowhere left to fall. Everything from here on out is nothing but improvement." I waved to my eldrin and pointed to the door.

Hellion turned and headed for the door out of the massive chamber. I followed close behind, glancing over my shoulder as I went, keeping my eyes on Theasin the entire time out. He didn't acknowledge my departure. He didn't even seem to notice.

He was too busy running his one hand along the body of the soul forge, coating himself in the slime of the creature.

Humanity truly was messed up.

None of them were to be trusted.

4

THE FABLE OF THE HYDRA'S FIFTH HEAD

HEXA D'TENNI

Before the events of Warlord Arcanist *(Book 6)*

We had certain traditions back in my home city of Regal Heights. As a hydra arcanist, I had an obligation to uphold those traditions, even if I was far from my family. My eldrin, Raisen, understood. He followed me out onto the atlas turtle in the middle of the night. The majority of the guild was asleep, which meant we wouldn't be interrupted.

"It's cold," one of Raisen's heads said.

The other three heads grumbled complaints. They all spoke at once, making it difficult to understand what they were saying.

"Shh," I hissed. "Stay focused. I don't want the islanders to come out and ask questions."

"Okay," the first head said.

The second huffed.

The third chuckled. "Those islanders wouldn't understand."

"Yeah," the fourth head said. "And they're squeamish."

Hydras had a deadly beauty. Raisen's black scales were curved at the tips, creating a prickly surface that could pierce skin if people weren't careful. His four sets of golden eyes glowed in the moonlight. He was fat in the belly, but his necks had the athletic sleekness of snakes. I loved him. He was everything I had ever hoped.

It was a shame so many people were afraid of hydras. The canyon we lived near was filled with giant land shrimp and hydras, and everyone knew their lifecycles. It was a matter of great importance. I had lost my fear long ago.

Most people didn't know this, but hydras lived deep in canyon caves. They didn't move around much—a full-grown hydra was large enough to crush a whole galleon under its weight. Instead, hydras slept for most of the day and then waited for the canyon shrimp to come out at night. Once the shrimp got close, the hydra would strike out with its multiple heads, gobbling up the delicious snack.

I ran a hand through my puffy hair, my fingers getting caught in the unruly curls. I tugged my hand free and then stopped near the pond in the middle of the atlas turtle. Raisen sat next to me, his four heads glancing in every direction.

We were alone. At least I hoped so.

No one else in the Frith Guild was from Regal Heights. Sometimes I felt like an outsider because of that one fact. People like Volke, Atty, Fain, Illia, and Zaxis told stories of their islands. Adelgis was bonded to a creature that came straight from the ocean. I was the only one who had a land-based eldrin, and I hadn't been born anywhere near the water. All my traditions and practices were considered *weird* and *exotic*.

I rubbed at the scars on my arms. In Regal Heights, they had made me popular. Here, they were just a reminder that I was different.

Funny how that worked. So many things in life were a matter of perspective.

"Are you feeling okay, my arcanist?" all four of Raisen's heads asked in unison.

I nodded. "No worries. I'm ready." I pulled a serrated blade from a sheath attached to my belt. It was a bone saw—the type of blade meant to saw through cows, goats, and caribou. "Are you ready?"

Raisen's heads nodded at different rates—one slow, one extremely fast, two with no rhythm whatsoever.

Hydras respected a willingness to embrace pain, especially when it was beneficial. The citizens of Regal Heights understood this as well. It was foolish to fear pain—pain was just the mind's way of warning the body that harm had been done, nothing more. If someone wanted to have control over their life, they had to control their mind as well. They had to fight through the pain to become their best self.

Hydras embodied that philosophy.

"Five is sacred," I whispered.

Raisen extended one of his necks to its fullest extent. Then he lowered the head and closed his eyes.

Five was a magical number. The number appeared everywhere in life. Five fingers on each hand. Five toes on each foot. And it wasn't just with humans. The blossoms on apple trees always had five petals. Sand dollars had five markings. If you flipped a sea urchin over, you would find a five-petalled flower.

And we used five to designate important milestones in

life. At age five, people were no longer babies but kids. At age fifteen, they were considered adults.

People from the islands didn't respect the number five. I had tried to convince a few of them, but they never listened.

"On the fifth day of the fifth month," Raisen whispered. "This is an auspicious sign."

I lifted an eyebrow. "When did you get so wordy?"

"Adelgis has been teaching me things in my dreams," one head replied.

I laughed under my breath. "Yeah. I can see that. Moonbeam has been sleepin' a lot."

"Is there a reason you delay?" another head asked.

"No." I knelt and placed the sharp edge of the blade against Raisen's extended neck. "I'm just... reflecting."

A hydra's fifth head was a sign of age and maturity. It was also a sign of progress and growth—hydra arcanists were considered amateurs until their eldrin had at least five heads. After tonight, I'd ascend to the next level. When I returned to Regal Heights, my family would be proud. I had waited for this day for a long time.

I sawed into Raisen's flesh, cutting through the scales and immediately hitting the spine. The other three heads hissed, but it wasn't loud. They stifled themselves, keeping quiet, even as blood gushed from the new injury. With all my weight, I cut down into Raisen, sawing through the bone and continuing through the throat and muscle. Blood coated my trousers, boots, and gloves.

With a deep breath, I sliced through the last of Raisen's flesh. I half-laughed as the head collapsed to the ground, the golden eyes vacant and staring in opposite directions. The other three heads examined the lost limb, still hissing.

I scooped up the head, surprised by the weight. I held it close. The blood weeping from the arteries didn't unnerve me. Raisen was a part of me, after all. Nothing about him—not the blood, not the viscera—would ever disturb me.

He felt cold. Most reptiles did, I supposed.

Raisen and his remaining three heads quaked and trembled. I hugged the severed head and watched with rapt fascination as the injured neck bubbled and writhed. Hydra magic worked wonders. In a matter of minutes, new muscle, bone, and veins slid out of the injury, forming *two* additional heads.

Now Raisen would have five.

One head looked like the other three. A simple head with scales and eyes and large fangs. The fifth head, however, was different. It had horns and spines under its chin, distinguishing it from the others in majestic ways. Every fifth head of a hydra would have these regal additions —they were the *king heads* or the *queen heads* if female. They would act as the main speaker, and their scales, bones, and muscles would be thicker—they'd be much harder to slice through.

Once the two heads were done forming, the king head lifted up higher than the other four. It stared at me with its slit irises, and I stared back, grinning like an idiot.

"I can't wait to make it back home," I whispered.

"It will be an interesting day," Raisen's king head said, his voice a little deeper and more mature than before. "It will be fascinating to mingle with the other arcanists."

I stood, keeping the dead head tight in my arms. "You know what we should do now?"

"What, my arcanist?"

"Trade this head for something." I stared down at the bloody flesh. "We have a master artificer here—Volke's dad. If I can trade this head for a piece of another mystical creature, I could craft my own trinket. Wouldn't that be somethin'?"

Raisen nodded all five heads.

Before I could head back into the guild manor house, someone gasped. I glanced up and saw an arcanist from the *Sun Chaser* standing in the middle of the grassy field. She held a lantern in one hand, and a scarab-like creature—a khepera—in the other hand. What was her name? Vethica! The one who could cure the arcane plague.

She wore thick wool trousers and a leather jacket, hiding the shape of her body under the heavy cloth. Her short, reddish-blonde hair reminded me of Zaxis. So did her glare. She wasn't like most of the women around here in the Frith Guild.

Her khepera was huge—fist-sized, which was gross for a bug—but the rest of it was rather pretty. Its iridescent exoskeleton glistened in the moonlight, and its black eyes glittered like the stars. The khepera's six legs were thin and delicate... Easily breakable.

"What're you doing out here?" Vethica asked, shifting her gaze from the hydra head in my arms to the blood all over my clothing. "Akhet, fly back to the guild house and—"

"Wait!" I shouted as I took a step forward. "I can explain."

For a long moment, nothing happened. The khepera, Akhet, moved his antenna around, waiting for further instructions.

"Well?" Vethica barked. "Are you gonna explain or not?"

I laughed once, caught off guard by her forceful personality. I liked that. Reminded me of Illia, in a way. I straightened myself and hugged the dead head close. "I'm performing a ritual. It's sacred for us hydra arcanists."

"All by yourself? In the middle of the night? With no one around?"

"No one else would understand."

Vethica held her lantern up a little higher, one eyebrow lifted. "Why wouldn't they understand?"

"No one in the Frith Guild is from Regal Heights," I replied with a shrug. "And none of them are hydra arcanists."

After a long exhale, Vethica slowly made her way over to me. She didn't seem disturbed by the blood or severed head. She barely gave them a second glance as she stood by my side. Up close, I could admire her tall cheekbones and sharp features. Beautiful.

"I lived close to Regal Heights before I joined the crew of the *Sun Chaser*," Vethica said. "I didn't know that was where you were from."

I nodded. "Born and raised." I motioned to Raisen. "My eldrin, too. I can't wait to go back there someday."

"I've never seen a hydra up close."

Raisen lifted his five heads, and Vethica petted the king head, careful not to cut herself on the sharp horns or prickly scales. Her khepera buzzed his wings.

"Everyone has been digging up any and all information on those god-creatures," Vethica muttered.

"Okay?" I asked. "So what?"

"Apparently, hydras are closely related to the *typhon beast*."

I furrowed my brow. "What is the typhon beast?"

"It's a dragon with a hundred heads." Vethica half-smiled and nudged my shoulder. "It could regrow heads that were cut off. And its fire could burn anything."

"And the heads could speak in a language that caused

insanity," Akhet chimed in, his voice *way* too cheery for the information he was providing.

Raisen's king head snorted. "Interesting."

I hefted the corpse head up into my grip and forced a single laugh. "Doesn't scare me. We have the world serpent on our side. And besides, hydras are super difficult to kill. Raisen and I will be here until the end, just you wait and see."

Vethica's smile grew. "I like that kind of mentality."

For whatever reason—perhaps it was because today was the fifth day of the fifth month—I felt bold. I leaned in a little closer to Vethica and tried to flash her my best smirk. "Well, I like the cut of your jib. Perhaps we should spend more time together."

I knew I was covered in blood and probably sweaty from all that bone hacking, but I didn't care. Why wait? Waiting was for cowards, and Hexa d'Tenni was no coward.

Vethica stopped smiling. She gave me the once over and then narrowed her eyes. "What're you trying to say?"

That had me worrying. Had I offended her? What if she didn't like women? What if she didn't like *me*, for whatever reason? But I shook those thoughts away and steeled myself. Maybe I wasn't clear enough.

"I mean, we should have a few drinks together," I said. "Just the two of us. Alone. Candlelight. Everything that implies."

I had never been with anyone, so I worried I was coming on too hard. Would she leave? Be disgusted? Think I was insane for doing this all so suddenly? Within the span of two seconds, a swarm of butterflies appeared in my stomach, and then died, filling me with dread.

But then Vethica's smile returned. Excitement shot through me, reviving the butterflies and lifting my spirits.

"I like the sound of that," Vethica said. "Maybe we can talk more about Regal Heights over a few drinks."

"Or we talk about the typhon beast," Raisen interjected.

It was cute that Raisen thought he would be joining us.

I walked with Vethica back toward the guild manor house, my giddiness preventing me from speaking. I had never known a woman as forceful and beautiful as Vethica. I couldn't believe she didn't have someone in her life.

This was an auspicious day. A wonderful day. A day I wasn't alone in this guild.

"I have to warn you, I'm a little weird," I finally managed to say. I glanced down at the blood smeared across my clothes.

Vethica winked at me. "Don't fret. I like 'em weird."

"Me, too," Akhet said, his wings buzzing.

And for the first time in a long time, my face grew hot and red.

5

THE FABLE OF THE DREAMWEAVER (PART 2)

ADELGIS "MOONBEAM" VENROVER

During the events of World Serpent Arcanist *(Book 5)*

Weaving dreams amused me in intellectual ways.

Dreams were intimate, after all. Individuals didn't typically share their subconscious thoughts. If I were conducting research or writing a lengthy tome on how the minds of individuals worked, their unfiltered and naked thoughts would be a boon.

But that wasn't the case.

No one wanted me to sift through their thoughts—they were afraid of what I would find. Not necessarily because individuals were hiding terrible secrets, but because they feared my judgment. I found that to be the most interesting —and depressing—aspect of all. I hadn't realized how inse-cure some individuals could be. Even the slightest of social faux pas and they would retreat into their own heads, wondering if anyone had seen or judged them for it.

I had food stuck between my teeth for at least an hour. Why didn't my friends say anything? Was that what they were laughing about when I returned to the table? Were they mocking me? Do they all secretly delight in my grossness?

And those thoughts and anxieties manifested themselves in dreams all the time. So many individuals dreamt of losing their teeth—all a deep-seated fear of somehow appearing disgusting and unkempt.

I shook my head. The dying sunlight shone through my bedroom window, and soon a new batch of dreams would begin. The guild house on top of the atlas turtle was home to dozens of arcanists and their eldrin. Their dreams acted like instruments in an orchestra. If I focused, I'd be able to hear individual tunes, but if I just sat in my room, their collective music would bleed into my own dreams and create a chorus of images too bizarre to understand.

But tonight, I had someone to focus on.

Biyu.

The *Sun Chaser* had been destroyed by the Second Ascension when they had attacked the Isle of Ruma, which had left the little cabin girl with terrible anxiety. Most of her thoughts revolved around losing her home and family, and I didn't want her dreams to sour into nightmares.

I would help Biyu if I could.

I rested back on my bed and stared up at the ceiling. My ethereal whelk, Felicity, floated around my head, her iridescent shell shimmering in the lantern light. In most ways, she resembled a giant sea snail, no bigger than a cat, but the six tentacles that hung from her body were a notable exception. She wiggled them around as she twirled through the air, unhindered by gravity.

"Will we be weaving dreams tonight, my arcanist?" Felicity asked.

I nodded.

"Have you given thought to what I asked?"

"Yes," I said. "But I'm uncertain how to improve my dreamweaving. What more is there to do? It feels more like an art to alter someone's dreams—like painting. Do you want me to improve by composing better dreams?"

"Now that you're free of the abyssal leech, I think you can improve your magic substantially. Perhaps you can manipulate multiple dreams at once? Or perhaps you could... um... wake someone up?"

"I find it frustrating that—as an ethereal whelk—you don't know the answer."

I realized the answer to my own question half a second after asking it. Young mystical creatures didn't typically know all of their powers or limitations. Felicity would discover her powers at the same time I did.

"I apologize, my arcanist," Felicity muttered, her tentacles drooping.

"No need. I should be the one offering an apology. I never should have made such a comment."

It was a shame I didn't have any of my father's journals with me. I had read most of them, but I couldn't remember every aspect of every mythical creature he had studied. He probably discussed the limitations of ethereal whelks—he *loved* pointing out the limitations of *weaker* creatures—yet all those notes escaped me. I remembered reading passages about dreamweaving. Perhaps my father had assumed the ability was useless, and thus had stopped any further experimentation in order to focus on grander projects.

That sounded like him.

I closed my eyes and waited. Cool night air wafted into my room. Spots of color filled my mind's eye the moment individuals in the Frith Guild began to dream. Their mental artistry always started as shapes and gradually morphed into pictures—though they were typically incoherent.

"Some of them are sleeping," Felicity said with an airy giggle.

Using my magic, I mentally tugged at the images and colors, pulling them like loose strings hanging off a tapestry. The threads of dreams were connected to memories, fears, anxieties, and creativity. If I manipulated a dream long enough, I could follow the thread all the way back to the source. That was how I could see people's memories, or even know their deepest desires and fears.

It was a useful ability, but one that people found vaguely pointless. Even Captain Devlin had been dismissive of my dreamweaving.

Felicity—always linked into my thoughts and emotions —traveled with me into the realm of dreams. "*Don't fret, my arcanist,*" she said, cheery in all regards, even through her telepathy. "*Your powers will grow. Tonight, you'll have a break-through. You'll see.*"

She said that every night.

Regardless, I appreciated her illogical optimism. If I pushed my ethereal whelk magic to the limit, perhaps I would ascend to a new level of mastery.

A bright flash of color stole my attention.

It was Biyu. Her dreams were vibrant—more than anyone else's in the guild. The moment I sensed it, I focused my attention and magic. Tonight, I'd weave her dreams of castles, princesses, and unicorns. I had done so for dozens of nights, and no matter how often or how long I made the dreams, Biyu insisted on having them again.

It amused me how often children wanted to drown themselves in the same activities—over and over again. I shouldn't have complained. When I had been a child, cooped up in my family's estate with few friends, I had often read the same few books until I had destroyed the spines and ripped some of the pages.

I wove Biyu's dream until a glittering castle of gemstones and ivory filled her thoughts. I created her a white dress made of snowflakes and feathers, and she twirled around the dream-castle, leaving a cold flurry in her wake. When she came to a stop, she found herself surrounded by adoring servants and *princess friends*.

"We must have a royal ball," Biyu announced.

Unlike in other people's dreams, I remained present, clothed in fine scholar robes. I clapped along with the others in the dream, as did Felicity—her little tentacles creating quiet, slapping noises.

Biyu smiled wide. "That's how we'll determine who marries the sovereign dragon arcanist! He's a prince from the Argo Empire. We must be on our best behavior."

The frivolity entertained me, but since I had woven the same dream for Biyu for countless nights in a row, I ironically felt a yawn coming on.

"*Try improving the dream*," Felicity said with her telepathy. "*Improve your magic.*"

I tugged on Biyu's dreams, following the mental tether to her deeper memories.

I hated seeing them. Most of her life before joining the crew of the *Sun Chaser* involved a tiny port town in the middle of nowhere. Her parents, away most of the day, rarely saw or spoke to her. And the last time she had interacted with them had been the day her father had sold her to the Dread Pirate Redbeard.

Apparently, the pirate captain had wanted a little girl so he could harvest her eyes.

From what I could gather in the memory, the eyes of

children were a delicacy to manticores. They craved them above all else, and many hunters used the eyes to draw manticore cubs out into the open so that young hopefuls could potentially bond.

Biyu's memories of losing her eye were so painful that I had avoided them altogether.

Disheartened, I stopped tugging on Biyu's dreams—I didn't want to see anymore.

Someone touched my arm, and I opened my eyes in the dream to see the young Biyu. "Adelgis," she said. "Join me. I need your help."

This hadn't happened before. I tilted my head to the side. "Oh? What for?"

"The prince will be here soon," Biyu said with a smile. She turned to her unicorn eldrin. "I need a glowing rock from the moon, and a piece of ghost coral from the abyssal hells—those will be my gifts for him. Won't they be beautiful?"

Biyu smiled as she stared up at me. Here—in the world I had created for her—she still had both of her eyes. I didn't know if that was a gift or a cruelty, since it was unlikely she would ever have her missing eye back in her lifetime. But having both eyes pleased her beyond reason. I knew because of her many thoughts on the matter, even in the dream.

"Those rocks will be extremely beautiful," I said. In reality, fetching stones from the moon would be impossible, but tonight, we were in a dream. "The perfect gift for your betrothed."

Biyu nodded and took hold of my elbow. "Where is *your* betrothed? Who are you with?"

"I have yet to find someone."

"Oh, no." She placed both hands over her mouth. "Then

we shall find you someone at the ball!" She clapped her hands and her dream-unicorn trotted over. "We must find someone for Adelgis at once!"

The unicorn nodded.

"There's no need to get upset," I said, waving away the comments. "I'm content and happy. We needn't focus on this aspect."

Biyu shook her head. "But... on the *Sun Chaser,* you were always alone in the storage room. And in the Frith Guild, you stay away from the others. You're not happy. You're sad. I can tell." She took hold of my elbow, this time, with a firm grip. "If you're scared, just tell yourself: *Look forward, not behind. Have hope, not regret.*"

Before I could interject, Biyu hastily continued, "When I was stuck on a pirate ship, the baby unicorn in the hold told me to whisper that phrase to myself. It helps me! It'll help you too. Everyone likes you, Adelgis! You should have confidence."

I smiled, but it was bittersweet. I enjoyed her comments, but I knew the reality.

Everyone didn't like me. But her assessment—that I lacked confidence—was accurate.

"I'll try at self-improvement," I said.

Biyu hugged my arm. "Don't worry. I'll help you. I want to repay you for the dreams."

"I appreciate that."

"We'll both help each other, okay? I'm not... I'm not perfect, either." Her voice faded as she spoke, her delight dying into something serious.

To lighten the mood, I wove the dream to the next stage of the story—the prince arrived, along with a parade of trumpeters, arcanists, and cavalrymen. They entered the ballroom with a glorious burst of color, music, and bombastic energy. Biyu's eyes lit up, and she gasped as the handsome prince rode in on a unicorn of his own.

It was then that I made myself invisible in her dream. I didn't want to speak with her on the issue of confidence—or how I could improve. What if I couldn't?

"*If you hesitate, you'll never further your magic,*" Felicity said.

"*There's nothing left to improve,*" I replied via telepathy. "*I can see her memories. I can see her fears. Where else will I go with this?*"

"*Perhaps you can change memories?*"

I mulled over the possibility, wondering what the ramifications would be to altering someone's experiences. Would it change them? Would it harm them? Would they ever know? An interesting concept, but one that would require someone *willing* to have their memories altered, if I were to practice without ethical questions standing in the way.

"*No,*" I said. "*Not that.*"

"*There must be something else you can do, my arcanist. Please, think.*"

I dwelled on my limitations. Currently, I could only alter the dreams of individuals who were nearby. Perhaps I could change that?

"*It's worth a try,*" Felicity said.

Biyu giggled with the other princesses of her dream. Would she be happier with different memories? Erasing the Dread Pirate Redbeard? Or the pain of her missing eye? No. That was a part of her. Just like the chant the unicorn had taught her. What right did I have to change that?

"*Don't focus on Biyu, my arcanist,*" Felicity said. "*Focus on someone far away. Someone you're familiar with.*"

Whom did I know well?

I kept my eyes closed and focused on the bubbles of

colors and shapes that represented nearby dreams. There were so many in the guild house—I recognized Zelfree's and Volke's. Both of them I had helped through tough times, and their colors were ever vibrant in my mind's eye.

Tonight, Zelfree dreamt of a man named Lynus, and Volke dreamt of the world serpent.

I pushed those from my mind and continued grasping outward. The atlas turtle sailed quickly through the ocean waters, taking us to the lair of the world serpent so that Ryker could bond with it. How was I supposed to reach anyone? We were so far away from civilization.

"*Think of someone you're close to,*" Felicity chimed in. "*Like your sister, Cinna.*"

Cinna...

She was hundreds of miles away.

But Felicity had had a great suggestion. Cinna was my closest relative—the only one in my family with whom I had a meaningful connection. And it was night—Cinna hated the darkness. She went to bed as soon as the sun tucked itself away behind the mountains. She would be sleeping now.

With all my concentration, I reached out, beyond the edge of the atlas turtle shell. We were in the middle of nowhere, and the complete lack of colors or images cut at my confidence as my magic stretched out far beyond my physical location. Would this work? Could I actually improve my magic?

"*They say the only way to overcome your weaknesses are to know them, and then to act against them.*"

"*And my weakness is being poor at magic use?*" I quipped.

Felicity's telepathy communicated a sad sigh. "*No, my arcanist. Your weakness is how quickly you become disheartened.*"

I tensed, my physical body on the verge of feverish. Was she right? Did I hesitate too much? Did I give up and just allow life's current to take me? I went along in most situations. I rarely changed anything or altered my course in a drastic way. I didn't enjoy *rocking the boat*, as the islanders said, even in my own life. Had those hesitations hurt me?

With my teeth gritted, I reached even farther beyond the atlas turtle. My magic made me feel as though I were flying —a form of astral projection where my mind floated away from my physical body, wandering the world while I sat in my room in the Frith Guild.

Just as I was about to give up, I saw a flash of color and shapes. At first, they were vague, but the longer I dwelled on them, the clearer they became. The images were... of my family home. Someone was cooking, and there were bear cubs in the garden, all wrestling each other for a chance to come inside and have some of our cook's famous pie.

The type of whimsical stories only a dream could weave. Was this Cinna's dream?

"*It is!*" Felicity cried, her telepathic voice soaked in excitement. "*You did it, my arcanist! You found your sister!*"

Had I?

I took a breath, and the tightness in my chest loosened. That hadn't been difficult. It had been almost too easy. How had I not realized I could find dreams so far away from me?

I knew why—I had never tried. My powers had been within my grasp the entire time, yet I had done nothing to seek them.

That thought almost made me laugh.

Fueled by the desire to test my new limits, I left Cinna's already pleasant dream and reached out into the darkness. Something that intrigued me was that I couldn't seem to see or feel the dreams of others. Cinna lived in the White City of

Ellios—a couple thousand individuals should've been sleeping in the nearby area. Yet I saw nothing of their dreams. Perhaps Felicity had been dead-on with her assumption. If I wanted to see someone's dreams at this distance, I needed to be familiar with them.

Whom else was I familiar with?

My heart seized in my chest as an immediate answer came to mind.

My father. I knew him well. Could I see his dreams?

Did I *want* to see his dreams?

"*You could see his memories, my arcanist,*" Felicity whispered with her telepathy. "*Perhaps we can discover important information we could report to the guildmaster.*"

Once again, Felicity was on to something… but I dreaded seeing my father's thoughts. For the longest time, I had hoped my father hadn't been a party to the treachery happening all around us. To watch his descent to evil through his own memories would haunt me for the rest of my life.

"*You must, my arcanist. Don't look away from the truth. Those who bury their heads in the sand and refuse to deal with reality… They're the weakest people of them all. It's a route of cowards, not heroes.*"

Her words settled into my thoughts, but my chest remained tight.

"*What would Volke do in this situation?*" Felicity asked, though I knew she didn't expect me to answer.

Again, she was right. Heroes never hid from the truth. If I wanted any hope of making things right—of correcting the damage done by my father—I would have to know what actions he had taken.

"You're right," I said aloud, though it was odd to use my

body when my mind felt so far away. "I'll try to reach out to my father."

With all my concentration, I searched farther than I ever had before. The distance daunted me—how far away was my father? Had he left this world and gone to another? Or perhaps he was dead? I didn't know, and I wondered if I'd ever be able to confirm if either of those situations were true.

Then I found something. Another splash of color. Another flash of images. But not my father...

It was the abyssal leech—the mystical creature that had resided in my body for several years while it had grown and matured to the age of bonding. Why had I found the leech's dreams? Why not my father's?

"You and the leech are forever connected," Felicity mused. *"It suckled from your soul and magic, meaning it'll always be similar to you in many ways. More so than your father."*

I hadn't considered that.

But I ignored my own failings and instead focused on the leech's dreams. The images and colors were difficult to nail down, since the abyssal leech was so far, but the harder I concentrated, the clearer they became.

The leech dreamed of me. The realization startled me, but only for a moment.

The dream consisted of me studying. Me in my room. Me speaking with Felicity.

It made logical sense. Of course it would be *me*. I was—metaphorically speaking—the creature's wet nurse. An odd emotional question struck me. Did the leech... miss me?

That wasn't relevant.

Instead, I tugged at the leech's dream and pulled out some of its memories. I needed to see what had happened after my father had taken the leech from my body. Whom had the leech bonded with?

The creature's thoughts weren't difficult to sort through. The leech had few, and what it observed was mostly through its host.

Then I heard my father's voice and focused on that. Fog surrounded me, rendering the images blurry.

"You must master your powers quickly," my father stated, the ice in his voice all too familiar. "The key to our eventual success will be in your ability to manipulate god-arcanist magic. Are you listening?"

"Yes," someone replied, though the image was clouded, and I couldn't make out who it was. "I won't fail you."

"Not me. You mustn't fail *the Autarch*. I promised him you would have these abilities, and I don't intend to be made a liar."

"I understand. I swear."

"Good," my father snapped. "And protect your abyssal leech eldrin with your life. It's the last one. There can be no mistakes."

My magic broke and failed me. In an instant, I was jerked back to my body in the Frith Guild, my head spinning and my chest tight. I sat up on my bed and gasped for air. Sweat dappled my honeyed skin, and I rubbed at my arms to calm the increasing chills.

"My arcanist?" Felicity asked. She floated close to my head and ran two of her tiny tentacles through my long, black hair. "What happened? Are you okay?"

After another deep breath, I nodded. "I heard my father's voice."

"I saw. In the leech's dream."

"My father... He's been helping the Second Ascension for years."

Felicity made a squishing noise—a snail sound for *disappointment* and *sadness*.

I shook my head. "You needn't worry. I... I will handle this. I will think of a way to help the Frith Guild undo everything he has done."

"I will be by your side," Felicity said, her singsong tone uplifting.

"I need to find his dreams again," I said as I lay back down.

"Not now!" Felicity gently tugged on my hair. "You're exhausted. Your dreamweaving has taken its toll. Try tomorrow night. And the next. Use your magic until you find the leech again—and your father. Perhaps we can unravel the plans of the Second Ascension. Together."

Was that why I was shaking? Was it exhaustion?

I stared at my unsteady hands, my mind pulsing with a dull agony. I did feel spent. Perhaps Felicity was correct. I would need to rest before I could continue my investigation.

And if I *could* discover the Second Ascension's plans from afar... it would be a mighty boon for all of humanity and magic-kind.

6

THE FABLE OF THE KIRIN ARCANIST
ORWYN TELLIA

Before the events of Warlord Arcanist *(Book 6)*

The Autarch had decreed that I would become a god-arcanist. He had said I would bond with the fourth god-creature to emerge from the halls of fate—the powerful and awe-inspiring *sky titan*.

I held the sky titan runestone firmly in my small hand, admiring the white marble and vague carvings. The sky titan had a similar shape to a bird, but all the legends claimed it had no real body. It was a creature of air—only incorporeal. The journal I had read claimed the mighty beast couldn't be harmed by weapons, nor could it be touched by anyone other than its arcanist.

Intriguing. What would the god-creature feel like?

I stared out at the ocean waves as our ship headed into port. The last half of our trek would be across land—which I preferred. While the waters of the vast ocean provided soothing sounds and fish aplenty, I couldn't ride horses or other animals while cooped up in the hold of a seafaring vessel.

Our ship had three masts, and two decks below, but I wasn't sure what type of boat we rode on. Well, I couldn't call it *a boat*. A sailor had gotten offended when last I had said that, but I wasn't familiar enough with sailing to know what differentiated a ship from a boat. All seafaring vessels were the same to me—some larger than others—but essentially equal.

"Look!" a sailor called out. "It's movin' around again! The kirin. *The kirin.*"

I smiled, unable to stop myself. My eldrin must have awoken. I turned around, overcome with joy the moment I spotted her majestic silver coloring. Her cloven hooves made soft *clop, clop, clops* as she trotted her way to me.

Kirin were unique mystical creatures, both in appearance and magical ability. They were the shape of a horse, though more slender and delicate, and my eldrin moved with the grace of a master dancer. Unlike horses, who had coats made of hair, kirin had the scales of dragons. When my eldrin moved, she shimmered like a fish which had caught the sun.

And much like unicorns, kirin had horns that jutted from their forehead. A horn of crystal—twisted and antler-like—glittering in even the dimmest of light.

The sailors always took note when she moved across the deck, their mouths agape.

"So pretty," a deckhand mumbled as he swabbed a bit of spilled ale. He kept his eyes on my kirin until she reached me. "Amazin'."

My kirin, Lith, stood at my side and lowered her head until our eyes met. My emerald irises didn't compare to the tiny night skies that Lith had—her eyes twinkled with a hundred tiny stars, though one couldn't see them until up close.

"You're beautiful," I whispered as I ran my fingers through the silver threads of her wild mane. "Did you sleep well?"

"*I did*," Lith replied telepathically, her voice a calming presence.

"Did you have dreams?"

"*Only of the sky titan, Orwyn, my destined.*"

Most people didn't understand that kirin were the mystical creatures of destiny. They were the only creatures born with an innate vision of whom they would bond with. There was no trial of worth required—kirin just *knew* whom their one and only arcanist was. And that person was always someone destined for greatness, be it good or evil.

I liked to imagine my greatness was good, but the Autarch had assured me hundreds of times that both *good* and *evil* were subjective terms. Thieves were "evil," but not when they stole bread to feed their starving families. Knights were "good," but not when they burned down the heartland of enemy territory. Sometimes, great destruction was needed for the new to grow—like wildfire clearing away the undergrowth in old forests.

So it didn't matter whether my kirin suspected I was good or evil. At least, that was what the Autarch thought, and I would never challenge his assessment. He knew best.

Lith pressed her delicate, horse-like nose into my cheek. Her breath smelled of saffron crocus. I closed my eyes and nuzzled against her, content to be close.

"You."

The gruff voice caught me off guard. I snapped my eyes open and found myself face-to-face with my guardian for the trek—Akiva the King Basilisk Arcanist.

He wore gray-scale armor so finely fitted to his body, it might as well have been a suit of second skin. It reminded me of the kirin, so sleek and elegant. But kirin weren't muscled, like Akiva. They were graceful and dainty. Akiva moved with the confidence of a predator, whereas kirin only ate fruits and vegetables, and even then, they did so infrequently. Their stomachs were finicky and easily agitated.

Akiva narrowed his dark eyes. "Tch," he said. "Are you deaf, girl?"

"Orwyn," I said. "My name is Orwyn."

He hardened his gaze. "We've almost arrived at our first destination."

Lith stepped closer to me and ducked her head down until her silver mane covered her twilight-eyes. "*My destined —must this arcanist be so aggressive?*" Her telepathy conveyed her trepidation.

"*What does your future sense tell you?*" I telepathically asked as I stared at Akiva.

He gritted his teeth, his muscled body growing ever more tense as the seconds passed.

I knew people disliked it when I didn't answer them right away. And I knew they found it disturbing when I stared for long periods of time without saying anything. But there were more important things in this world than politeness. Kirin, as well as their arcanists, could use their magic to *sense* when they were close to an individual of significance—someone whose decisions or actions could affect great swaths of land or many people.

It wasn't infallible because fate wasn't written in stone, but my kirin abilities had helped me identify worthwhile individuals my entire life. I wasn't about to second-guess it now.

Before Lith could answer me, Akiva grabbed my upper

arm with a grip that bruised me through my long robes. He jerked me close, and I caught my breath.

"We must disguise your eldrin," he stated, his anger barely caged. "Or we're leaving it on the ship. *Do you understand me?*" Akiva tightened his hold on my arm, the pain intensifying. "Just nod if you're not going to speak, girl. I don't have patience for *games*."

Lith snorted and her twisted horn of crystal flashed a muted red.

I held up a hand—kirin weren't creatures of violence, whereas king basilisks were agents of death. There would be no point to a straight fight. Lith wouldn't stand a chance.

"I have a trinket that will cast an illusion over Lith," I said, my tone calm. I knew how to control my voice, even if Akiva's impatience had startled me.

"Then use it," he commanded as he released my arm. "We're heading into town."

Akiva turned on his heel. The winds of the port rustled his copper hair, but it had been cut short enough that nothing got close to his eyes or ears. As he strode across the deck, the sailors leapt back to their chores, none of them glancing his way.

King basilisks had the ability to turn individuals to stone with just a glance—and their arcanists were no different. Everyone here knew Akiva could murder everyone on this vessel without so much as growing tired. It had made the voyage uncomfortable.

I rubbed at my upper arm. "Did you sense anything?"

Lith shook her head. *"I'm sorry, my destined. His frightful presence disturbed my concentration."*

Akiva the King Basilisk Arcanist...

The Autarch had told me to abandon Akiva if he ever became compromised, or if it even appeared as though he would lose a fight. *He's disposable*, the Autarch had said. *And now that he has nothing to live for, he's merely a tool. Don't worry about his safety—use him for any purpose, even if you must throw him to the wolves to advance across a single river.*

Akiva was my only guardian for the first half of the trek. The Autarch had said it would be best to move in small numbers, especially for the god-creatures no one knew had spawned yet. Unfortunately, because of the Frith Guild, more and more guilds, monarchies, and grandmaster arcanists knew of our plans. We had to remain hidden for as long as possible, and we couldn't yet reveal we knew the location of two other god-creatures.

I removed a bracelet trinket from my slender wrist and hung it around Lith's horn. The moment I secured it place, Lith was shrouded in an illusion made from the magic of a *hulder*. There were no mystical creatures better suited to illusion craft than the hulder, and Lith became indistinguishable from a white unicorn clad in knight's armor.

Illusions couldn't make things invisible, so Lith's horn was covered by an illusion of a helmet that wrapped around the unicorn's horn, obscuring the twisted and jagged quality.

"Are you ready for the city?" I asked as I scratched at her scaled neck.

"*Yes, my destined.*"

"Then we should hurry, before our guard becomes too agitated."

Port Rocklin, positioned between two hills, had enough greenery for a king's garden. Grass, flowers, trees, and vibrant bushes dotted the surrounding landscape. If I had to guess, I would have said the name *Rocklin* had been given ironically, as there weren't many rocks that I could see. The setting sun, casting orange rays across the beautiful land-scape, practically set the world on fire.

I led Lith off the ship and headed down the pier. She stuck close to me, as she wouldn't ever speak to anyone else, not under any circumstance.

Akiva kept my pace. He wore a heavy cloak that fell just past his ankles, covering his magical scale armor. The cloth itself was weighted, preventing it from blowing open. The extra weight didn't bother him—he moved without sacri-ficing agility—but he kept the hood up and pulled so far forward, it covered his arcanist mark and half his sight.

My strawberry blonde hair fluttered about, and I had to secure it back with a tie I had fashioned from strands of Lith's mane. I had an arcanist mark that revealed I was a kirin arcanist, but I wasn't afraid of others seeing. Few people had the education to tell the difference between a unicorn and a kirin. Most would assume my mark was just bizarre, or that my unicorn had a "funny" horn.

"My magic will be weaker the longer we continue this trek," Akiva said under his breath, his gruff voice audible, even when he was trying to keep it low. "We're getting farther away from Nyre the more we head north."

I knew an arcanist's magic didn't work as well when they were away from their eldrin, but I had never seen the effects in-person.

"Will you be okay?" I asked.

Akiva glared at me from under his hood. "Individual arcanists won't cause me any problems, but we should avoid guilds, especially any of them with grandmaster arcanists."

"Like the Crag Knights, Crimson Arrow, and Frith Guilds?"

Akiva replied with a single curt nod.

I had no love for combat, and the white marble rune-stone weighed heavy in my pocket. I didn't want to disappoint the Autarch. We had to find the lair of the sky titan as quickly as possible, though I knew it wouldn't be too long. Ever since Theasin Venrover had become the soul forge god-arcanist, he had been able to sense locations of great magic and life. He had told the Autarch where he suspected the fenris wolf and sky titan were, and I didn't doubt Theasin's godly powers.

Akiva grabbed my upper arm again and jerked me to the side—narrowly saving me from running face-first into a dockworker wheeling cargo away from a local ship.

"Watch it," Akiva hissed.

I nodded, though I knew this would likely happen again. My thoughts—as well as my kirin magic—often had me distracted.

"Can you sense anything, Lith?" I asked telepathically.

"I haven't tried yet."

"Can you now?"

"The bustle of the city disturbs me, my destined."

I bit my lower lip and glanced up at the impressive wooden walls around the docks that separated them from the city proper. Guards patrolled the top, dockhands hurried around the warehouses and gates—the place pulsed with life, and Lith and I weren't accustomed to such crowds. Our tiny home village had been quiet all times of the year.

Akiva kept hold of my arm and led me through a ten-foot-tall gate and onto the cobblestone of the main road. He never let go, even as we traveled for a block and then turned into the first tavern we came across. Lith stopped at the door and waited. With the illusion, she looked too tough to attack, and most people in this small city seemed the honest type, rather than pirates in disguise.

The moment I stepped into the tavern, the smoke and smell of dirty ale caught me off guard. I coughed and half-choked, but Akiva didn't stop his trek. He led me beyond the serving counter and all the way to the back corner of the crowded dining area, beyond one of the wooden pillars that held up the second and third stories. He sat me down on a well-worn oak wood chair and then tapped a single finger on the table.

"Stay here," he commanded. "And I'll arrange accommodations."

His voice and attitude... I sensed a bit of apathy and irritation. Perhaps the Autarch was correct, and even Akiva knew he was just a tool. He certainly acted like one. Was it even worth my time to use my magic to sense his value? To see if he was an individual of destiny?

I held up a hand before he could leave. Akiva stopped and glared down at me, though he said nothing.

"Um," I murmured. "May I hold your hand for a moment?"

I knew it was an odd request, but that didn't matter. Kirin magic worked better when I could touch the individual in question. Along with his destiny, I would be able to sense more about him and his personality.

"Why?" Akiva eventually drawled.

"You know why," I said, turning my hand palm up. "You've seen me assess individuals before."

He said nothing as the sounds of the tavern danced around us. Sailors eating. Soft music from a local bard playing a flute. The tavernkeeper keeping up a loud conversation near the front door. I ignored it all and kept my eyes on Akiva.

Those other people weren't here to change the world. We were.

Akiva didn't move. He met my gaze with a cold one of his own. But then a moment came where I saw the fire die—as though he just didn't care one way or the other what happened this day.

He placed his hand on mine, and I was struck by the harshness of his skin. He had been through many fights, and even though his arcanist magic could heal callouses before they formed, they didn't remove the muscle and tension brought about by hours training with a gun or sword.

My kirin magic came effortlessly to me. Although most suspected I was young—in my twenties, a few had said—I had been bonded for nearly four decades now. Lith and I had waited for the right moment before leaving our village and accomplishing the Autarch's grand goal. During that time, I had mastered my manipulation, augmentation, and evocation. Kirin magic—all by itself—was weak, but that didn't matter. I had the potential to sense Akiva's tether to destiny.

Most people had no tether, sadly. Some had a weak thread of destiny. Some were woven into the tapestry of life, forever destined to alter the world through their actions— great leaders, healers, and innovators. What would Akiva be?

I closed my eyes. The magic whispered in my ear.

He... was tied to... something grand...

Akiva's life was interwoven with destiny, but not... the strongest I had ever felt. The choices he made could alter something major, perhaps crucial to the Autarch's plans. Or maybe against them. Kirin couldn't see the future, after all. The most I could do was determine whether or not Akiva was important to the events of the world—vague feelings of worth.

His personality wasn't as prominent as his destiny. It felt taciturn, but I didn't need my kirin magic to know that. To my surprise, a twinge of sadness and loneliness crept into my senses.

Akiva ripped his hand from mine and growled a curse under his breath.

"You look possessed," Akiva muttered through clenched teeth. He shifted his gaze to the tables around us. Tavern patrons stared in our direction, some with lifted eyebrows or half-smiles.

I had been in a trance-like state, and I suspected the non-magical men had never seen anything like it. Perhaps they found it amusing?

Akiva placed a hand flat on the table and then leaned down until he was a few inches from me. In a gruff whisper, he said, "We mustn't draw attention to ourselves, *girl*. Unicorn arcanists don't start daydreaming to use their powers. Stay focused."

I nodded and offered him a smile. "Your life is mingled with destiny. You have the potential to do great or terrible things."

He narrowed his eyes and grumbled something else I couldn't determine. Then he stood straight. "I won't repeat myself. I can just as easily carry an unconscious body to the god-beast's lair. Keep that in mind."

"You should be proud," I said, ignoring his threats. "Not many people have a strong bond with the fate of the world."

With a look of mild bewilderment, Akiva turned away and headed for the noisy tavernkeeper, not even bothering to answer me. I watched him go, wondering what accommodations he would arrange, but a moment later, I stopped caring. It didn't truly matter. I had greater concerns.

"And my name is Orwyn," I murmured to myself, even though I knew he was long gone. Did he remember it? Surely he did, but a piece of me wondered if he considered my name odd.

I ran my hand into the pocket of my robes and comforted myself with the weight of the white marble rune-stone. The memory of the Autarch ran through my mind. Of all the people I had sensed, *the Autarch* had been the most tied to destiny. His actions and decisions rippled the entire tapestry of the world. Soon it would never be the same, and it all came about from his glorious goals and ambitions.

And I would be a part of it...

Memories of my childhood village played in my thoughts. I never even saw Akiva return to our table. I only knew he was nearby when he finally scoffed to draw my attention.

"What did I say about daydreaming?" he asked as he pushed a bowl of soup and a cup of rum over to me.

Well, I thought it was soup. The thick, brown liquid had the consistency of gravy. Goat chunks and carrots "floated" throughout most of the bowl. *Drowned* might be a more apt description.

I took a spoonful and scrunched my nose.

So much salt.

Then again, I was vaguely aware that Port Rocklin exported salt from mines not far to the west. Perhaps that was why they had named the town *Rocklin*. Because of the *rock* salt.

Akiva held a bowl close and ate his gravy-soup with a wooden spoon. He didn't look at me while he ate—he kept his gaze shifting from one person in the tavern to another.

"Do you think our enemies are nearby?" I asked.

"Our enemies are *always* nearby." Akiva glanced over. "Eat."

I pushed the bowl away. "I don't care for this type of food."

"I don't care about your preferences. You need your strength, and we should blend in as much as possible."

I stared at the gravy-soup. My stomach twisted at the mere thought of consuming it all. Akiva didn't seem to mind the food. He ate it so quickly I doubted he even tasted it. Once finished, he shoved the bowl away and tapped his knuckles on the edge of the table—an anxious tic?—his attention once again on the other patrons.

"Is soup your favorite food?" I asked.

I thought it was a normal and innocuous question, but Akiva slowly turned to face me with equal parts irritation and exasperation. "We needn't discuss food. It isn't relevant."

"But food is what brings people together. It's a part of life that all civilizations share. You can learn subtle things about an individual through their favorite meals, or even influence them with the right dining experience."

"I doubt that," Akiva growled.

"Well, for example, my mother said the way to a man's heart is through his stomach."

"The way to a man's heart is between the fourth and fifth rib." Akiva shoved the bowl of soup closer to me. "Now shut up and eat."

I pursed my lips and stared at the "food" before me. Nothing he had said had influenced my decision to ignore the meal. The grayish goat meat, marbled with gristle, made me wonder if this port town even had fresh ingredients.

"*My destined,*" Lith said telepathically. "*There is a dragon arcanist arriving at port. The denizens are becoming anxious.*"

"A dragon has arrived?" I furrowed my brow. *"Here, of all places? Is it an adult?"*

"Yes. Fully grown. The awestruck children claim it's the eldrin of a master arcanist."

"What kind of dragon?"

"A pyroclastic dragon."

I held my breath for a moment, my chest tight. Dragons had the most difficult trials of worth out of any mystical creature—most of which involved a high risk of death. Pyroclastic dragons dwelled on the sides of volcanos and were said to be some of the most fearsome fighters. My mother had told me stories of old-world berserkers. They had always been bonded to pyroclastic dragons. Always.

Akiva tensed and became unnaturally still. After a strained moment, he whispered, "Something arrived in town. Something powerful."

I lifted both eyebrows, impressed he seemed to sense the pyroclastic dragon arcanist and his eldrin.

"Stay here," Akiva commanded.

He didn't wait for me to respond. He stood and left the tavern, his focus so singular, I suspected he forgot there were others nearby. I waited with bated breath, though excitement coursed through me more than fear. I had lived most of my life in a tiny village, one hidden within a glitter-wood forest that created illusions powerful enough to confuse travelers. We rarely had visitors, and I wanted to see as many mystical creatures in-person as I could.

Akiva returned a minute later, his gait powerful and quick. He almost ran into a man, but the half-drunken patron was smart enough to leap out of the way. The moment Akiva reached our table, he motioned to the door. "There's a master arcanist in town. We're leaving. Now."

I tilted my head. "What if he's an ally? The Autarch knows many powerful arcanists."

"We aren't going to risk anything. There's no need to make contact." Akiva pulled me up from my chair and strode toward the back of the tavern. "We'll travel through the night."

"To a different inn?" I asked as Akiva pushed open a door and led us into the kitchen.

He never answered.

We stormed past a woman tending to a fire in a brick fireplace. A large pot filled with the gravy-soup sat bubbling over the flame. The woman, dappled in sweat, snapped her attention up at us. She held up a hand, on the verge of saying something, but Akiva didn't slow. He yanked me all the way to the opposite side of the kitchen and out the back door.

Akiva maneuvered us around a stack of freshly chopped firewood and then made a harsh turn for an alleyway between buildings. The sun had set, and the darkness impaired my vision.

"*Lith,*" I called out mentally. "*Come to me. We're leaving.*"

"*Of course, my destined.*"

"No one in the Frith Guild is bonded to a pyroclastic dragon," I said.

Akiva stopped at the end of the alley—right before stepping onto the cobblestone road—and then turned to face me. "How do you know it's a dragon?"

"My kirin told me."

He released my arm, his eyes narrowed. "It *could* be the Frith Guild. They have a master mimic arcanist among their ranks. Or they could've recruited someone. Word of the god-arcanist has already spread to multiple port towns."

"Volke Savan," I whispered. "The second person to bond

with a god-creature." My thoughts drifted for a moment. I had met him—I knew I had—near the Autarch's Excavation Site. Absentmindedly, I muttered, "The Autarch said Volke's soul has tainted the world serpent. And he said—"

"*Enough*," Akiva hissed. He glanced around the corner. After a cart and horse trotted by, he grabbed my shoulder and directed me out onto the street. He walked behind me, keeping closer than technically polite.

A roar pierced the early evening sky. I whipped my head around and brushed my reddish-blonde bangs from my eyes to get a better look at the creature making the ruckus.

The pyroclastic dragon was halfway across town, but it was still easy to identify. It stood nearly three stories tall, and when it exhaled, a waft of black smoke spewed outward. Unlike other dragons, who had scales and horns, pyroclastic dragons had skin made of hardened magma. The cracks in their skin glowed with the intensity of lava, and shimmers of heat filled the space around them like mirages in the desert.

The dragon's eyes, as bright as bonfires, shone a fiery red. When the beast opened his mouth, it appeared to be an active furnace of flame. His throat glowed with heat, and his tongue was magma—gooey and malleable, moving and dripping from the dragon's mouth, burning everything it touched with temperatures high enough to melt bone.

"The dragon is beautiful," I murmured.

Akiva ground his teeth but said nothing.

I wasn't sure where we were going. Akiva, fortunately, directed me with the confidence of a man who had lived in Port Rocklin his entire life. We passed several shops and smiths, and I briefly wondered if there were any influential people in town. Could I sense the destiny of everyone here before we left? Definitely not. I didn't have the strength—or the range—to sense much beyond a few feet.

The clear sky and waxing moon gave us enough light to see the shop signs clearly, despite the late hour. The dragon at the docks acted like a lighthouse, warning us away.

Akiva's focus never wavered. I glanced backward several times, but he never met my gaze. He kept his eyes straight ahead.

"Couldn't you kill the pyroclastic dragon?" I asked. "King basilisk venom is the deadliest in the world."

"Nothing will reveal our plans and location faster than news of a dragon arcanist dying due to king basilisk venom," Akiva stated.

"Because you're one of the last king basilisk arcanists in the world?"

He said nothing.

"Or is it because your methods are so well known?" I thought back to my conversation with the Autarch. "You assassinated the queen in Thronehold, didn't you? Would grandmaster arcanists recognize your handiwork, and—"

Akiva tightened his grip on my shoulder enough to hurt. "Quiet, girl," he growled. "We needn't discuss anything. No more talking."

I wanted to protest his arbitrary rules, but I decided against it. The citizens of Port Rocklin gave us odd glances as we stormed by, and I didn't want to draw any more attention to us than we already had. Unfortunately, Lith galloped up the road and joined us. Thankfully, her unicorn illusion was perfect and unbroken, and I hoped no one had taken any real note of her.

"Isn't the pyroclastic dragon wonderful?" I asked telepathically.

Lith nodded her head. *"The light of its body is the source of inspiration, my destined."*

"It's a shame we can't meet him."

"I don't think that would be wise. Several dockhands hurried up the road claiming that the dragon arcanist was here searching for criminals. It could be here for us."

Criminals?

It always worried me when I heard people refer to the Second Ascension as *villains.* Didn't they understand that the Autarch was destined to rule? If they didn't struggle against him, there wouldn't be any need for conflict. If they understood that gold kirin only bonded with the most ambitious and talented individuals, they would realize that it was the *will of magic itself* that he decided the course of history.

All of this death and destruction was the result of weaker individuals fighting against destiny. It was no different than an infant flailing around and then blaming its parents when they had to step in. Children should just behave, and no punishment would be needed.

I had been so wrapped up in my own thoughts that I hadn't noticed how far we had gone. I returned to reality to spot the north gate up ahead. The doors were open—Port Rocklin likely didn't shut the gates often—and the two guards posted by the wall were too busy gawking at the distant pyroclastic dragon to bother checking me or Akiva thoroughly.

Once we stepped outside the city, my feet began to ache.

"Ride with me, my destined."

Lith trotted ahead and then turned so that I could mount her. Akiva released me and waited as I pulled myself up onto my eldrin's back. Although she wore an illusion, I felt her scaled coat beneath me. She was sleek like a snake, and I patted her gently to let her know I was ready to go.

The cobblestone road faded into a dirt path as we traveled away from the city. Akiva never tired, even as we approached the midnight hour. My eyelids drooped several times, but I forced myself to keep them open.

The road turned and wrapped around the outside of a forest, taking us farther and farther away from Port Rocklin. Where was the next town? Would it be exciting? New? Interesting? Nothing compared to my hometown village. The glitterwood and abundance of shardshrooms had provided us with enough magic to power everything from a single forge to a large mill. Magic had been our way of life, and we had been self-sufficient. Every other town I had seen since leaving required trade and mundane methods of development.

It was underwhelming.

I stopped reminiscing and tried to focus on other things.

Some individuals would get bored with long periods of silence, but I drifted into my own thoughts, getting lost in their maze-like quality. The few times I forced myself back to reality, I glanced over at Akiva. He stared straight ahead, his determination apparent. He seemed... livelier than before.

I stared at him, and eventually, Akiva sensed my gaze. He glowered in my direction, his dark eyes pinning me in place.

"What?" he barked.

"Do you miss your hometown?" I asked.

I must have somehow caught him off guard. His expression softened, revealing bewilderment. Finally, he huffed and turned away. "No."

"You have no love for the place of your birth?"

"I don't consider it *the place of my birth*." Akiva shook his head. "It's better described as *the place of my death*."

I pushed back my bangs and tilted my head. "You look alive and healthy to me."

Akiva forced a single laugh. It was bitter enough to taste.

"Girl, I don't mean I literally died, I mean the Akiva of my memories isn't the Akiva you see today. I try not to think of my home island. It's no longer a place that brings me happiness."

"*Ask him why,*" Lith said telepathically. "*I'd like to know.*"

It was a shame she refused to speak to anyone but me.

I patted Lith's silver mane and asked, "What happened on your home island?"

Akiva remained quiet. He mulled over my question, and just as I thought he might never answer, he exhaled and replied, "The Queen of the Argo Empire ordered the death of all king basilisks and their arcanists."

"Oh, my. But why?"

"Apparently, she had dealt with too many king basilisk assassins, and she decreed that the entire race of mystical creatures needed to be wiped from existence."

"She didn't kill you," I said in an overly positive manner, trying to inject optimism where there was none.

"She murdered my whole family," Akiva stated, his voice dead and monotone. "My brother. My sister. And... my daughter. Sometimes I wish she had gotten me, too."

"*Such tragedy,*" Lith said.

I held my breath, my throat tight. "*Perhaps I shouldn't speak to him further. I didn't mean to agitate him.*"

Without me prompting, Akiva continued, "The queen paid for her transgressions against my kin. But that didn't change reality. It didn't change the fact that pieces of me are gone forever."

"The Autarch helped you achieve revenge?" I whispered.

I knew they had made an agreement, but I had never known the details.

Akiva replied with a curt nod.

"The Autarch is amazing," I said, smiling. "He'll set the world right."

He gave me an odd glance. "I take it he helped you achieve revenge as well?" Akiva asked.

I shook my head, the bounciness of my hair a fun sensation. "I've never had a reason to seek revenge. But the Autarch did help my village." I touched a finger to my chin as I debated about whether or not I should tell him any details. Akiva had been open with me—shouldn't I return the gesture?

"I lived in a place that sequestered itself from the world," I murmured. I closed my eyes and pictured the clear river, mystical mushrooms, and houses built in and around the trunks of massive trees. "We didn't trade with anyone. We never mingled with outsiders. We referred to ourselves as *the keepers of kirin*." I opened my eyes and smiled. "Our village is the only place kirin are born in the whole world."

Akiva said nothing as we continued our travel.

"My family, and the overseer of the village, cared for the kirin until they found the individuals who were meant to bond with them. They had cared for a gold kirin for years— it's the rarest of the kirin, and everyone knew whoever it bonded with would be special."

I closed my eyes a second time, trying to remember all the details, even the horrific ones. I continued in a whisper, "But sickness came to our village. I don't know how or why, but one by one, the people and kirin foals began to die. They had boils, and rot, and many couldn't eat. It was... terrible."

I had spent hundreds of sleepless nights trying to care for the ill. No matter what I had done, they had slipped away from me. A sense of helplessness had set in when my own mother had developed the boils. Her insides had bled, and whenever she had coughed or defecated, crimson had poured from her as though she had been stabbed.

"My father left and vowed he would bring back someone who could help," I muttered. "We waited for months, and half the village died, including the overseer, but eventually, my father came back victorious. He returned with an artificer named Theasin Venrover, and an apothecary by the name of Cane Helvetti."

"Theasin?" Akiva asked. Then he shook away the thought. "Continue."

"Theasin said he and Helvetti could cure the illness, but he demanded he be allowed to take some of the dead bodies, including the kirin. It upset a lot of people, but we had little choice. Theasin and his relickeeper gathered the rare materials from our glitterwood, but Helvetti was the one who crafted the cure to our ailment. He administered it to everyone, including the gold kirin. That was when... That was the day they bonded."

Akiva lifted an eyebrow. "Helvetti is... the Autarch?"

I nodded. "That's right. He decided to stay in our village and become the new overseer, and everyone wanted that— no one wanted to see the gold kirin go. Theasin returned from time to time, sometimes bringing visitors to our village, when that had previously been against the rules... But everyone loves him. He's talented beyond his years, and every kirin arcanist could sense it." I smiled wide. "And look at him now! He's a god-arcanist."

"So it seems," Akiva drawled.

I didn't understand why Akiva wasn't as enthusiastic as I was. Wasn't he happy to be friends with Theasin?

"Helvetti only took the name of *the Autarch* when he announced to the village that *now was the age of the second coming.* He gave a speech about the need for god-arcanists, and how he had been chosen to lead humanity into a new age of magic. He told us about the outside world—about dread pirates, murderers, and corruption that ran through the hearts of long-lived rulers."

Akiva gritted his teeth. "I remember speaking with the Autarch about the queen of the Argo Empire. He seemed to know of her transgressions intimately."

"That's right! Helvetti—I mean, *the Autarch*—wanted to make things right. So, he took some of the kirin foals and eventually made agreements with powerful arcanists around the world. The Autarch set into motion the return of god-creatures and referred to his plan as *the Second Ascension.*"

"*I remember those days,*" Lith said. "*Everyone was so excited. We've worked tirelessly for decades for this moment. Why must so many guilds attempt to stop us now?*"

"*I don't know,*" I replied. "*They probably don't understand our reasoning.*"

A harsh wind rushed over us, bringing with it a biting chill. I shivered and pulled my robes close. The white marble runestone remained at the edge of my thoughts—I was always aware of the weight in my pocket, even as I reminisced about my childhood.

"I'm cold and tired," I said.

Akiva stopped walking, and Lith followed suit. Without a word between us, Akiva motioned to a grouping of three trees. Lith carried me over, and I understood why Akiva had led us off the road. The three trees—with thick trunks and canopies—blocked most of the wind. The flat ground and lush grass were suited for a resting spot.

I dismounted from Lith and sat next to one of the trunks. Would I be able to sleep? I suspected so. I had lived most of my life in a vibrant forest—I had slept on countless tree branches, and I enjoyed the smell of dirt and vegetation.

"Here." Akiva pulled off his weighted cloak and unceremoniously threw it over me.

It landed heavily, covering my entire body, including my head and face. With a grumpy frown, I pulled the cloak around my shoulders and snuggled into it. The garment smelled like sweat, iron, and copper. It was an odd scent, but it was one I immediately associated with Akiva.

Lith tucked her legs under her body as she lay down next to me.

With all of the approachable charisma of a corpse, Akiva crossed his arms and turned his back to me, his stance wide. Was he acting as a lookout?

"Don't you need to rest?" I asked.

"No," he said, curt.

"We could take turns."

"I said I don't need rest, girl."

"Everyone needs rest, though." I hugged his cloak. "Won't you get cold? Don't you want this back?"

Akiva glanced over his shoulder and glowered. "Enough talk. You said you needed rest—*so rest*."

I held my tongue and turned my attention to the moonlight streaming between the leaves of the canopy. A handful of fireflies danced around us, and it reminded me of the grove just outside of my home village. Many nocturnal insects called the grove home.

"Do you have a favorite type of bug?" I asked.

After a powerful exhale, Akiva's shoulders slumped. He didn't answer, he just tilted his head back and stared at the stars overhead.

I didn't know what else to say, so I held my breath and stared at my hands as I wrung them together. Perhaps my own charisma wasn't enough to uphold a conversation. It was possible. I wasn't accustomed to the ways of the world outside of my village.

"My daughter's name was Silke," Akiva said, unprompted.

Startled, I tensed and stared at him with wide eyes. I waited, uncertain of what to say.

Akiva chuckled, but it was low and dark—something ironic or sad. "When she was just a lass, she discovered the moths on our island. They were silkworm moths."

I knew of silkworm moths. They were ivory and delicate —beautiful, like kirin.

"She asked me if I had named her after the moths," Akiva said, his voice growing quieter with each word. "I hadn't. But no matter what I told her—or explanations I gave—she never believed me. Silke was convinced she had been named after the moths. And after that... she loved them. She raised the worms in her room, named them all, and even remembered each one after releasing them as moths..."

He was whispering by the end, to the point I almost couldn't make out what he was saying.

After another powerful exhale, Akiva returned to his normal gruff voice and volume. "Silkworm moths are my favorite insect."

"They're gorgeous," I said.

Akiva nodded.

I pulled my legs up to my chest and wrapped my arms around them. Then I rested my head on my knees and closed my eyes. "Maybe I'll dream about them."

He said nothing.

Lith rested her head on the grass by my feet. "*I hope you do, Orwyn, my destined.*"

In the middle of the night, my shivering became a whole-body quake. I couldn't keep warm, no matter what I did. And Lith was no help. Kirin—much like scaled dragons and lizards—didn't exude heat. I leaned against her, but it did little for my warmth.

At some point before the dawn, the cold vanished. Fatigue killed my curiosity, and I didn't care how or why it happened. I was enveloped in a comforting warmth that chased away all dread and nightmares. It was pleasant and allowed me to sleep easy.

I awoke slowly.

My hair had come undone during the night, resulting in a strawberry puff atop my head. I rubbed at my eyes and through a haze of grogginess, realized I was resting against gray scales. Not Lith's scales—but Akiva's armor. It took me another whole second to realize he was still in it. I had been sleeping on his shoulder.

With silent movements—quick and somehow gentle—he leaned me away from him and onto Lith. Then he stood and moved away, returning to his position away from me, his arms crossed. I yawned and stretched, confused by his sudden exit.

"Did you get any sleep?" I asked.

"No," he replied, curt.

"Hopefully, I didn't make much noise throughout the night."

"I wouldn't have noticed."

He said everything with an almost blasé tone, as though

this were all beneath him. Did he think I hadn't seen him next to me? Was he trying to hide it? The thought caused me to giggle. Had Akiva gone out of his way to help me sleep?

He had.

The sun rose over the distant mountain tops, illuminating the world around us. Fatigue wore at me, but excitement provided a second wind as I forced myself to my feet. Perhaps we would enter another town, and I'd have a chance to sense the destiny of those who dwelled within.

Lith stood as well. She stretched and shook out her coat. *"Good morning, my destined."*

"Good morning," I said. "Did you sleep well?"

"Very."

Akiva motioned to the road with a jut of his chin. "Let's go."

After a long yawn, I walked to Akiva and handed him his heavy cloak. "Thank you."

He grunted something as he threw it over his shoulders and secured it into place. He said nothing else.

I pulled myself onto Lith, and she trotted to the dirt path. Akiva matched her pace and then waved his hand to indicate what direction we'd take. Lith started forward, but she stopped a moment later when she realized Akiva wasn't following. She turned around, and I furrowed my brow.

"Are you okay?" I asked.

"He's following us," Akiva stated. He unhooked the cloak over his shoulders and then tossed it to the ground. It landed heavily, sending up a puff of dust. "It seems as though I'll have to deal with this one way or another."

"The pyroclastic dragon?" I asked.

"Him and his arcanist."

I caught my breath. "You think they're here to stop us?"

Akiva didn't answer, but I knew that was his way of saying *yes*.

We didn't have time to plan or strategize or even run. The ground rumbled for a few seconds, and then the pyroclastic dragon came into view a second later. He emerged from the earth like a fish bursting out of the waves. Fire, smoke, and heat gushed outward from his massive body. He was a few hundred feet from us, but that didn't matter. He was so massive—and so hot—that the heat could be felt from where we stood on the road. His white-hot claws burned holes into the ground wherever the beast stepped.

His arcanist, a man clad in full plate silver bone armor—likely made from the skeleton of a fire-immune jinn—rode atop his head. The arcanist's armor covered him from head to toe, and even if I would recognize the man, it was impossible for me to see his face. The man carried a compound longbow—perhaps six feet in length—the type of weapon only dragon riders used, to pierce enemies from the safety of their mount's back. A quiver of arrows, every one made from the same fireproof material as the man's armor, hung on the neck of the dragon.

"Stay back," Akiva commanded as he held up an arm.

Lith trembled beneath me. I held on to her, hugging tightly, trying not to tremble myself. When Akiva leapt forward to confront the pyroclastic dragon and his arcanist, I couldn't bring myself to say or do anything.

"*Lith,*" I said telepathically. "*We must hide.*"

"*The dragon can sense tremors made by even the faintest footsteps.*"

She was right—what was the point of hiding? Perhaps I could talk the man and his eldrin out of fighting. What if he knew of how powerful the Autarch was? Would he cease his pursuit of us?

Akiva didn't make it far. The pyroclastic dragon vomited molten magma like a diseased volcano. The melted rock hit the ground and caught grass, shrubs, and nearby trees ablaze. Akiva shielded his eyes from the heat and leapt away, his reflexes impressive.

"Surrender," the arcanist shouted from atop his dragon as he notched a silver bone arrow. "I am Quinton Quake, master arcanist of the Evening Seekers Guild. If you come peacefully, you'll be brought before the proper authorities to answer for your crimes. If you fight, it'll be your corpses they bring before the justicars."

"You're a damn fool if you think you can stand against a king basilisk arcanist in a one-on-one fight," Akiva said, both confident and slightly apathetic.

"My sources say you're far from your eldrin." Quinton laughed. "Who's the fool now?"

"The one who relies on an unproven advantage."

Quinton pulled back on the drawstring of his longbow. "Enough. You and the kirin arcanist have bounties on your heads. You're coming with me—dead or alive."

He knew I was a kirin arcanist? And he had known where to find us? I wanted to ask him *how*, but my curiosity didn't beat out my dread.

Without his eldrin nearby, Akiva would have to fight in a weakened state. Would all of his magic work? And if he were injured, he wouldn't be able to heal as well. He could easily die. But what else was there to do?

Akiva evoked venom into the palm of his hand. The blackish substance dripped from his fingertips, hitting the grass and killing the plants instantly. With all of the strength he could muster, Akiva splattered the venom toward the dragon—the beast was huge, and even a single drop could be lethal—but the extreme heat wafting off the pyroclastic dragon evaporated the venom before it even had a chance to connect. In a blackish vapor, the venom dissipated.

"Is that all you've got?" Quinton yelled, a chortle on his breath. "Pathetic."

He fired an arrow. It whistled through the air, but Akiva managed to duck away. The arrow slammed into the ground, burying itself halfway in the dirt. Steam sizzled off the arrow, and I suspected it was superheated just from being in close contact with the dragon.

Then the pyroclastic dragon slashed the air with his claws. Hot wind rushed over Akiva—and even reached me. The heat stung my eyes, and for a moment, I had to close them and look away. When I returned my attention to the fight, I realized Akiva must have had the same problem because he was almost hit by another terrible vomit of molten magma.

Akiva tumbled to the side, his forearm over his face. His gray-scale armor glittered in the morning daylight, and I could see a patch on his legs that had been burned through. Was he hurting? Would he be okay? My chest twisted at the mere thought.

Despite the injury, Akiva took a fighting stance and rushed for the dragon a second time.

Could he survive the heat? The dragon arcanist was likely personally immune to the extreme temperatures, but king basilisks weren't.

Akiva's eyes shone a bright gold, and I glanced away, my heart beating twice as fast. "*Lith! Don't look!*"

"Close your eyes," Quinton yelled to his eldrin.

I couldn't see anything, and the next clash left me dreading every second. I opened one eye—that wouldn't save me from turning to stone if Akiva caught my gaze—but I needed to know what was happening.

Akiva headed for the body of the beast by leaping over molten puddles of burning rock. The flames singed his body, but he moved with the determination and confidence of a seasoned warrior. The dragon arcanist shot another arrow, but Akiva tumbled to the side, narrowly avoiding the attack.

"Don't let him touch you!" Quinton roared, smacking the dragon's neck.

The pyroclastic dragon—blind but able to sense tremors—spun around and vomited more magma in Akiva's direction. The beast's quick movements, combined with his substantial weight, caused the ground to quake and rumble. The nearby trees lost branches' worth of leaves, and a crack formed across the road.

The dragon slashed the air again, superheating it with his white-hot claws. Akiva closed his eyes, ending his stone gaze, but managed to leap away from any harm with noteworthy agility. He couldn't keep this up forever, though. Was I just going to sit and watch while he slowly died?

"Just destroy everything," Quinton shouted.

His eldrin stepped forward, and his whole body lit up with an inner blaze. Akiva hesitated and then moved away, but he wasn't fast enough to clear out of the area. The dragon lunged forward, glowing like molten lava, and thrashed his entire body around the woods, *melting* trees on contact and devastating the landscape in a matter of seconds. Bubbles of flames spewed from his dragon body as he moved. He swung his tail, leveling another cluster of trees without a second thought.

Akiva rolled and ducked, but the inferno of heat took its toll. Singed and burned in multiple places, he struggled to avoid the steam and fire. With the grace of a master fighter, he managed to escape the devastation, but I suspect it was because the dragon was creating so much smoke and ash. It became difficult to see, and Akiva used that smokescreen to his advantage.

However, the dragon leapt from the pyre he had created and smashed back onto the main road. His body had returned to its normal state—no longer bright-hot lava. The beast swished his tail, and he turned his head in Akiva's direction without ever opening his eyes.

Akiva's luck would run out at some point. And he was already tired.

"Stop," I yelled out. "He's bound to me and follows my commands! It's me you're after!"

I had said everything without much thought—I had just wanted to help. I didn't want to see Akiva injured.

Quinton whipped his head around in my direction, and with a tap of his free hand, his eldrin turned to face me. The mighty dragon swirled his lava tongue, and the arcanist pointed.

"Kill her," Quinton commanded.

"Run, Lith," I said, my voice unsteady. "We can... we can distract them."

But my eldrin continued to tremble beneath me. She didn't even reply telepathically. She remained stunned by dread.

The pyroclastic dragon lunged down the road, shaking the earth with each step. Akiva managed to open his eyes, and his look of panic was honestly surprising. With reckless disregard for his own safety, he ran forward, jumped over some of the magma strewn across the ground, and raced toward the dragon's tail.

The dragon—sensing Akiva's movements—couldn't be snuck up on. He whipped his tail at Akiva, attempting to burn the man in half with his lava-like body. Akiva rolled under, avoiding the lethal blow to his body.

But that didn't stop the arcanist from attacking me. The moment he was close enough, he fired his arrow, aiming for my chest. It took all of my willpower and courage to lean to one side, but even then, I hadn't been fast enough. The arrowhead cut through my robes and effortlessly sliced the flesh over my ribs. The burning sensation hit me so hard, I was momentarily blinded by sheer agony.

Lith sprang backward several seconds too late. She half-stumbled and tripped as she retreated without turning to face away from the dragon himself. I figured we would die here—we couldn't outrun this beast, nor could we hide—but the dragon let out a soul-shattering screech and threw his head back in terror.

I remained confused until I spotted Akiva. He had touched the dragon's back leg with his hand, and in the process, burned his entire palm and most of his forearm. He stumbled away, cradling his severely charred limb. The dragon spasmed, which resulted in magma gushing out of his body at random points.

Lith jumped back again, her body so tense from anxiety, she was practically a spring.

No one had time to catch their breath, however. Although Quinton's eldrin was caught up in his death throes, the man slid off the side of the dragon and then evoked his own magma. Akiva attempted to dodge, but the splatter of the superheated rock caught him on the hip. He groaned and collapsed down on a single knee.

Although Quinton's longbow was impractical for non-mounted combat, he still notched the last arrow he had and fired it anyway. The arrowhead caught Akiva in his already injured hip, but just barely.

But Quinton must have momentarily forgotten whom he was dealing with. Akiva's eyes shone a bright gold, and the *instant* Quinton's gaze met Akiva's, he locked up. And then I watched with fascination as Quinton's body hardened and drained of color. He had succumbed to the basilisk curse—turning to grayish stone and ultimately dying.

The dragon collapsed a moment later, the magma in his body cooling at a rapid rate. It only took a few minutes before the pyroclastic dragon became black and inert.

My injury healed quickly, but I hated the bloodstains on my torn robes.

"Lith," I said. "Lith, don't fret. They're dead."

"*Yes, my destined.*"

"Let's go to Akiva. He looks like he needs our help."

"*Surely, we can wait here.*"

"Please, Lith. We must. Do it for me."

My kirin hesitated, stomping her feet and shifting her weight back and forth. I urged her with a gentle kick to the sides. Finally, she trotted forward, avoiding the dragon by giving it a wide berth. We maneuvered past the statue of the dragon arcanist and only came to a stop once Lith was beside Akiva.

Blood wept from the injury on his hip, but the hole in his leg had been cauterized by the magma. He remained kneeling, and his breathing came out in rasps.

"Are you okay?" I whispered.

Akiva slowly lifted his head. Blood poured from his hairline, streaking down his face like a scarlet waterfall. It ran over one eye, which he kept closed, and then over his lips and finally dripped off his chin and splattered against his armor.

I hated fighting. I couldn't stand it. Couldn't deal with it. The blood disturbed me. It always had. It reminded me of everyone who had died in my village... everyone who hadn't been able to stop the bleeding or the boils or the pain...

Akiva took a deep breath. "Go," he finally barked. "Follow the road. Quickly. Some of the Autarch's lackeys are waiting there for us."

"Aren't you coming?"

He smirked as he pressed a hand on his injured hip. "No."

"Well, I can't *leave* you."

Akiva darkly chuckled. "Get out of here, girl. The mission was an easy one. Take you from one location to the next. We're almost there. It's a straight shot."

"I need you to protect me."

"I've dealt with the threat. Anyone who arrives in town now will be too late." He shook his head, his blood dropping onto the ground around him. "Besides... they'll be looking for me. I'm the assassin. I'm the one who has killed several dragon arcanists."

"But—"

"*Go*," he commanded, glaring up at me.

"You're tied to destiny," I said, more forcefully than I had ever spoken to him before. "You must come. You have to."

"*Perhaps his destiny was keeping you alive,*" Lith said telepathically. "*He's done that. And the Autarch did say to leave him if ever he became a burden.*"

I hesitated, my body stiff. The Autarch had predicted this. He knew I'd have to leave Akiva behind in order to fulfill my grand path in life. But how? What magics did the Autarch have that allowed him such knowledge?

Lith turned for the road. "*We should head out.*"

"No," I said aloud. "No."

"*My destined?*"

The Autarch said that "good" and "bad" were subjective

and arbitrary. Perhaps it was "good" to save a life, but not the life of a murdering assassin. If they were subjective—if it were all pointless anyway—I didn't want to leave Akiva.

I slid off Lith's back and landed next to Akiva.

"Leave me," he growled. Then he tensed and his body convulsed once, as though he were holding back vomit or swallowing blood that had bubbled into his digestive system from odd angles.

I knelt next to him and held his arm, my hand shaking the moment I felt the hot blood.

"Please," I said. "I'll help you. There will be other arcanists in the next town. There has to be."

"They'll turn us in for the bounty," Akiva said through clenched teeth. "Stop being a damn fool. *Go*."

"When you see Silke next, do you really want to tell her you died on the side of some unnamed road? Bleeding to death? All alone?"

He shot me a dark glare, and for half a second, I thought he might activate his stone gaze and kill me.

But I persisted. "Wouldn't you rather tell her you helped to change the world? So that people weren't killed by foolish monarchs ever again? Wouldn't you want your story to have ended in glory?"

Akiva swallowed hard but said nothing. Then he tightened his hand on his injury. "I can't walk. Not until I heal. And without Nyre nearby... I might not be able to."

"Ride Lith," I said.

Lith snorted, and I knew she didn't want to get anyone's blood on her beautiful scales. But we all had to make sacrifices.

"I'll help you," I said as I attempted to wrap my thin arm around his bulky torso. "I might not be strong, but I've enough strength to help you mount. Please."

"I'm not worth it," Akiva whispered, his tone laced with venom and anger. He turned away from me, his eyes closed. "You can make it on your own."

"I don't care about your preferences," I said, mocking his tone and voice. "I want you to accompany me, *boy*. Get on the kirin. Now."

I wasn't sure if now was the time for playfulness, but something about my "speech" had gotten Akiva to half-smile. Even in the face of death, he seemed to think my impersonation of him was amusing. More blood gushed from his injuries, but he relaxed enough to lean some of his weight onto me.

"I might not... be able to stay conscious," he muttered.

"I'll take care of everything."

"Orwyn," he said—the first time he had ever said my name. "If you must, just turn me in for the bounty."

"That isn't going to happen." I squeezed my arm around him. "Come now. Few ever experience riding a kirin. Fewer still have ever laid eyes on a god-creature. You will do both. Let's go. Together."

7

THE FABLE OF DEATH LORD CALISTO

EVERETT "THE FACELESS" ZELFREE

Before the events of Knightmare Arcanist *(Book 1)*

I t wasn't difficult pretending to be a pirate. Well, so long as we were in port. All it took was copious amounts of drinking and card games, both of which I had mastered in my teenage years.

Our current pub, nestled in Port Crown, housed all sorts of questionable individuals. Dancers entertained on a stage, but a few times I spotted knives on their belts and vials of poison by their shoes. Everyone here knew a fight was always possible.

Four of us sat at the same table—the four arcanists aboard the *Dark Flag*. Technically, it had been Captain Redbeard's second ship in his growing pirate fleet. He had secured the *Dark Flag* while he had still been masquerading around as a mystic seeker. The moment the ship was finished, Redbeard had skipped port and never paid the shipwrights—ironic, because Lynus and I ended up stealing it from him.

Captain Redbeard currently sailed on *The King's Revenge*, a vessel named after his reaper's vindictive power.

Sitting at the table, we had *me*—Everett Zelfree—but I often took the name *Simon* to confuse people. Few knew my real name outside the Frith Guild. I was obviously the most handsome and talented at the table, and the others could barely contain their jealousy. The more drunk they became, the more their anger rose to the surface. Or perhaps it was because I was winning and taking all their money. Either or.

Lynus sat next to me. He knew me and my real name. We had known each other since we were children living near Red Falls. Lynus had the physique of a man who crushed rocks in his bare hands and ate two dozen eggs for breakfast. Manticore magic would do that. Not that I was complaining. His copper hair, rough stubble, and intense gaze made him the second-best-looking man at the table.

Drake sat across from me. His gut put pregnant women to shame. Too much booze, not enough walking. Plus, he was a wyvern arcanist, so his winged half-dragon flew him wherever he wanted to go. His teeth jutted so far out of his mouth it was like they were lonely and wanted to participate in the card games. *Someone* had to be the worst-looking man at the table, and Drake was a good sport for taking the title.

Ivy sat on the other side of me. Her whitish-blonde hair put ice to shame. It went well with her black unicorn eldrin—a rare variant of the unicorn that few ever bonded with. Most crew members on the *Dark Flag* spoke at length about her curves, thick lips, and how her thighs could choke a man to death, but I wasn't as smitten with those details. She was the best-looking —and worst-looking, technically—woman at the table.

I took a swig of my rum as I examined the cards in my hand. I would win this round. Not because of luck, but because of the king of kirins I had hidden in my sleeve. As long as no one else revealed that card at the end, I would win, and the pot was currently three gold leafs. A hefty sum. More money than an entire mortal family usually saw in a year.

"So," Drake said as he scratched at his gut. "Lynus... When you takin' a new name?"

Lynus ground his teeth. He glared at his cards like he intended to set them all on fire. "I'll do it soon enough."

"*Lynus* sounds like the name you give to a sick kid, ya know what I'm sayin'? Weak. Nothin' to it. Old fashioned. If you want help in takin' the territory from Redbeard, you'll need to sound fierce."

"I said, *I'll take a new name soon enough, fool.*"

"What about your manticore? It gonna take a new name?"

"No," Lynus stated. "*Hellion* is good enough." He threw half his cards into the discard and drew new ones to replenish his hand. "Besides, manticores are just big cats. And cats do whatever they please. I couldn't force him to take a new name, even if I wanted."

Pirate names amused me. I understood why they were taken—most families disowned their thieving relatives, and most pirates wanted the tough façade of having an intimidating name. Some pirates wanted to keep their real names hidden, just in case someone figured out something important about their past.

But why rename an eldrin? I could come up with reasons, sure. Perhaps the eldrin's name wasn't suitable for a pirate ship. No pirate wanted a moon rabbit named *Floof.*

But still. There were fewer reasons to rename an eldrin. Hellion was a fine name. Why change it?

My eldrin, on the other hand, tended to get mixed responses. *Traces* wasn't an imposing name, but it was enigmatic enough.

Ivy fanned her cards out and moved them around. She smiled as she said, "Lynus, have you considered a name like Redbeard's? You have that ginger look." Ivy pointed to his hair. "Metallic, almost. Maybe you could be... *Matchstick*. Or *Carrot Top*. Or *Flamer*."

Drake sputtered and laughed, which only got Ivy chortling alongside him. I restrained myself, even though I thought some of the names were amusing. But Lynus hated Redbeard. He would never take a name similar to Redbeard's, that I already knew.

"Why did you pick the name *Ivy*?" Lynus asked, never acknowledging her comical suggestions. He looked over his cards with renewed interest in the game.

"I grew up near a place called the *Garden of Poison*," she said, still mirthful. Ivy smirked as she set her cards facedown on the table. "It's a bizarre little place that grows only poisonous plants—everything from nightshade to hemlock. The gates on the inside were covered in frostbite ivy." She fluffed her icy blonde hair, allowing some strands to catch the lantern light. Several tavern patrons glanced over to get a better look at her. "I loved the frostbite ivy, but my mother never allowed me to touch it."

"Just like you don't let anyone touch you?" Drake said, his voice too filled with bitter resentment to just be a joke.

"Exactly," Ivy said with a laugh. "Poisonous *and* beautiful. Ivy is the perfect name." Her icy-blue eyes shifted back over to Lynus. "Maybe you should name yourself after an animal that frightened you as a child. Maybe you could be *Hawk* or *Wolf*."

"Animals don't frighten me," Lynus muttered, his attention fully on his cards.

Drake sat forward in his chair. "I bet you wanna know why I picked my name."

"No one cares," Ivy said, rolling her eyes. "It's so boring and predictable, anyway. You're bonded with a wyvern, which is a type of lesser dragon, hence the name *Drake*. Get it? *Get it*?" She laughed and dismissively waved her hand. "No creativity whatsoever."

Drake frowned so deep his whole face twisted in anger. He seethed loud enough I could practically hear the anger bubbling inside of him. Or maybe that was his lunch. It was hard to tell.

"I feel like the name *Simon* is ironic." Ivy smiled in my direction, but her eyes drifted down to my cards. I held them close—I wasn't distracted by her fluttering lashes.

"It is," I said. "My mother would get my brother and me confused, so she just called us both *Simon*."

Drake's anger quickly shifted to confusion. "Really? Your mum did that? You musta been unloved as a kid."

"Oh, she hated me. We never got along. Sometimes she'd say I was worthless."

It was Lynus's turn to laugh. He threw down his hand, forfeiting the game. "You're such a liar," he muttered. "Look how easy those words roll off your tongue. I'm surprised it's not forked."

I flashed a toothy smile. "Well, Ivy had a story with her mother. I didn't wanna be left out."

Ivy smirked and then tapped the table, calling for everyone to be in or out. Drake showed his hand—he had a few sets, including one with the king of sea serpents, but nothing groundbreaking. Ivy revealed after, and I couldn't help but smile.

I revealed my hand, including the king of kirins I produced from my sleeve, resulting in the highest set among the group. I grabbed the coins in the center of the table and slid them over.

"You win an awful lot," Drake said as he slammed a fist on the arm of his chair. It was powerful enough that the table shook. "Too often."

"You've always been a terrible loser." But then Ivy shot me a cold glare. "But Drake has a point. You do win too often."

I shrugged. "This is a game of strategy. It requires skill and the ability to understand probable chance. You know me. I'm good with numbers. I'm quick on my feet. I'm surprised any of you play cards with me, to be frank. This is my arena."

"You *are* good with numbers," Drake said, stroking his large chin. Then he frowned again, diving straight back into anger. "But I don't buy it. I make this oath right now—on the abyssal hells—I'm never gonna play another card game with you, *Simon*."

"Fair enough."

"You sure you aren't lyin' to us?" Ivy asked, her eyes narrowed.

I shook my head. "I know you'd both shoot me if I cheated. I'm not foolish."

"Heh. Perhaps..."

Again, Lynus laughed. He didn't look my way or even call me out for my lying, but he knew. He was the only one who always knew.

After a few more drinks, I retreated to my room.

Port Crown had two types of inns: the luxury inns meant for pirate captains who suddenly found themselves swimming in wealth, and rundown inns meant for idiots who couldn't wait to spend their coins on booze and companions. The rundown inns always smelled of sweat, smoke, and rotting jerky. I had stayed in *way* too many of the dilapidated inns to ever want to return.

Which was why I opted for the fancy inn, even if I'd have to fork over all my card winnings to pay for it.

Lynus stuck close to me as we headed up to the room. The luxury inns didn't smell too bad, and they provided you a bottle of wine for the evening. The beds had down feather comforters, and each had its own wash basin with fresh water. The height of extravagance for a pirate.

Our eldrin waited back on the *Dark Flag*—along with everyone else who couldn't afford to sleep in an inn for the night.

As Lynus and I climbed the stairs to the third story, I half-stumbled and grabbed onto the railing. The booze had gotten to me. Lynus offered his shoulder, and I held fast. I swear he got stronger every time I saw him.

We continued up the steps, and Lynus glanced over at me with a frown. "Redbeard is still out there," he muttered.

"You need to learn how to relax," I said, leaning most of my weight on him. "We've been fighting him for years. We'll get him eventually."

"Heh. Right about that time you help me build a ship, huh?"

I laughed and shrugged. "I said I would, but you know I've been busy. The cost of a proper ship... I'll need to do a lot more work, or take a lot more loans, before we can make it happen."

Lynus grew tense and quiet.

When we reached the top of the stair landing, he turned for the narrow hallway. The owners had incense burning on multiple trays, masking the bodily odors that filled every room.

Once we reached the door to my room, I used the inn key and threw it open. We both walked in, and I braced myself for the impending conversation. Lynus wanted Redbeard dead, and it hadn't happened yet. Unfortunately, Redbeard was a reaper arcanist. Whoever killed his eldrin would end up dead in return, thanks to the *king's revenge*. Unless we tricked a fool to kill Redbeard's reaper for us, we weren't going to make much progress on this front.

And fighting at sea had taken its toll on my desire to go sailing. Wars between pirates involved all sorts of under-handed strategies, and avoiding our enemies was becoming a difficult challenge.

Lynus shut the door once we were both inside. I stumbled away from him and then grabbed the bottle of wine sitting on the dresser. Using my dagger, I yanked the cork out. Then I plopped myself down on the edge of the bed and took a long swig. Lynus sat at the table, his bulky frame almost too much for the small wooden chair.

He turned to face me, and I held my breath. I really didn't want to have a conversation about Redbeard. I wanted to relax.

"You got a name for me?" Lynus asked.

Name? It took me a long moment of silence to remember what he was referring to.

"Bruiser," I quipped.

"I'm bein' serious."

"Shouldn't you have taken a pirate name ages ago?" I asked. Then I took a longer swig of the wine. It wasn't good, but it *was* alcoholic. "You've been running on red waters for a while now."

"I should've," Lynus said as he leaned one arm onto the table. "But I never think of myself as a real pirate. As long as I'm working with you… It's different. It's *us* against *them*."

I chortled to myself. The only reason Lynus was even running with these thugs was because I asked him to help me infiltrate the ranks. He wouldn't be here if it weren't for me. But he never seemed to resent me for it. It was *us* against *them*, or so he said.

Lynus sighed. "Besides, I'm not very creative."

"I understand." I glanced over and offered him a half-smile. "Nothing ever comes to me, either."

"You'll think of somethin'. You're clever."

"Perhaps." I gulped down another mouthful and then shuddered. My thoughts blurred at the edges, and my body felt more limber than ever before. I rested back on the bed. "I should have taken a proper pirate name. Just to avoid suspicion."

"We still have time. We're not famous yet. But once we oust Redbeard from these waters, people will talk. We'll need names then. Real ones."

Lynus wanted desperately to take this territory from Redbeard. It was probably for the best. If I helped Lynus take the waters around Port Crown, it'd be easy for me to masquerade as a pirate and gather information for Guild-master Eventide.

"We'll get him eventually," I said.

"I know." Lynus slammed his hand on the table. "But I hate that he runs free. I want him dead, Everett."

"Quiet with *that* name," I hissed.

"Feh. We could think of a few names right now, if you want."

I searched my mind for a name I thought was intimidating and dastardly. I drew a blank—names weren't inherently intimidating, after all. It was the deeds associated with them. The *people* associated with them.

So, who was the most intimidating person I knew?

"Have you ever heard stories of the Death Lords?" I whispered, staring up at the canopy that surrounded the bed. Why hadn't I noticed the canopy before? I blamed my drunkenness. The thought got me chuckling again.

"Who are the Death Lords?" Lynus asked.

"Do you know much about the abyssal hells?"

"Not too much."

I waved a hand in the air. "There are five levels to the abyssal hells."

"I know that." Lynus ground his teeth. "Get to the interesting parts."

"Okay, okay." I glanced over and frowned. "You have an anger problem still, you know that, right?"

"It's served me well."

"Whatever. Listen. The Death Lords rule over the lost souls on the third level—*the third abyss*."

Lynus sat a little straighter in his chair, his attention focused on me and *only* me. "Go on."

"According to legend, each of the Death Lords is bonded to an abyssal dragon. That's how they got their title. The abyssal dragons led them to the gates of the abyssal hells, and then granted them powers over all who dwelled within."

I had heard hundreds of stories when I was younger. The abyssal dragons supposedly sought murderous individuals of the darkest ilk. Each Death Lord was worse than the last—something about their souls helped grow the ghost coral, which in turn, allowed the dragons to produce offspring, thus creating more future Death Lords.

"There is one Death Lord that always frightened me," I said as I closed my eyes. "Death Lord Calisto occasionally rides his dragon out of the abyssal hells to consume entire villages of people. They say he's the smartest of the Death Lords—cunning and always willing to use a ploy. His eldrin is the oldest living dragon, and he wears artifact armor made from ghost coral—some of the strongest and most beautiful material found in the entire world. But that's not the best part."

"What is?" Lynus asked, his eyebrows knitted.

"Ghost coral absorbs magic from abyssal creatures. Death Lord Calisto made himself the armor so that none of the other Death Lords could kill him."

"This man sounds like you," Lynus muttered with a laugh.

I smiled. "Maybe."

"Are the abyssal hells an actual place?"

"Oh, yeah," I said as I nodded. "Well, that's what I've heard, at least. You can't find the entrance unless you're bonded to an abyssal creature, though."

"What else do you know about Calisto?"

"He's a fiend."

"I got that," Lynus growled. "What else?"

While lying on the bed, I brought the half-empty bottle of wine to my lips. With the wisdom of a drunken teenager, I attempted to drink from the bottle, but I ended up spilling it on myself and the blankets. I smiled and once again chortled to myself.

Soaking in terrible wine, I attempted to remember some of the stories about Death Lord Calisto. Most stories involving the abyssal hells weren't pleasant. They ended or started in tragedy, and one too many individuals were killed or maimed.

But there were a few stories that bucked the trend…

"Death Lord Calisto had a lover," I said, opening my eyes to once again stare at the canopy.

Lynus huffed. "And?"

"It was a man. Some warrior. I think."

For whatever reason, that got Lynus's attention more than anything else. "And what happened?"

"They met out at sea." I held up a hand in dramatic fashion as I recalled the tale. "Calisto wanted to slaughter the man and drag his soul down into the abyssal hells, but the warrior put up a valiant fight. So valiant, in fact, that their duel ended in a draw. Both men were so determined to *kill the other* that they sought each other out the following winter."

"Who won then?"

"Neither of them," I said with a laugh. "The legend says their fights were so catastrophic that they caused storms to rage across the seas. That's why winter storms are worse than others—again, according to the stories. It's an echo of their battles." I sighed and then shrugged. "But they grew to have a deep respect for one another."

Lynus laughed. "Is that what the kids call it these days?"

"Heh," I said with a smirk. "Calisto crafted the warrior a suit of armor made from ghost coral, and the man later crafted an arrow made from a king basilisk—*Death's Arrow*—and presented it to Calisto as a gift. You know things are serious then."

"Why do I have the feeling this doesn't end well?"

"Because love is a lie and nothing good lasts forever," I quipped. "The warrior was later killed. I forget how. It wasn't by Calisto's hand, but it happened."

Lynus said nothing.

I shrugged. "Death Lord Calisto supposedly sought out a true form phoenix arcanist and struck a deal to bring the warrior back to life. As part of the deal, the Death Lords would forever leave the phoenix arcanist's family alone. Or something. A lot of details are fuzzy."

"Yeah, I got it. Go on."

"All these stories have a twist ending. Calisto and the warrior never met ever again. After he was resurrected, the warrior ended up disappearing. Not sure why. After that, Death Lord Calisto became more ruthless and brutal—killed two other Death Lords and dragged thousands into the depths. Hate will do that to a man."

I yawned. There were other stories with Death Lord Calisto, but I couldn't remember them all. Not now. Perhaps in the morning. Still drenched in alcohol, I pulled myself up onto the pillows and stretched.

"Why not take the name *Calisto*?" Lynus asked, keeping me from sleep.

"Eh. He reminds me too much of myself. And I'd like to imagine that *one day* I'll find someone who doesn't up and die on me, ya know?"

Silence settled between us. I wanted to sleep, but my thoughts kept returning to potential names. Who else did I fear or admire?

"I thought of a name for you," Lynus said.

"What's that?"

"You're a mimic arcanist, always changing your identity. You're faceless, Everett. Whoever you want to be, whenever you want to be."

"Faceless?"

"That's right."

I chuckled. "You know, a successful mimic arcanist

wouldn't have an identity, right? They would blend in so well that people would never know they existed."

Lynus stood from the chair and rotated his arms. "I'd rather dastards knew *someone* wasn't who they said they were. It creates paranoia. And nothing kills a man faster than fear, dread, and mistrust."

I hadn't thought of it like that, but I agreed with Lynus. "Then I suppose *the Faceless* is a perfect name."

"Once we've chased Redbeard out... We'll take control of these waters and do whatever we please."

I had meant it when I said it—nothing good lasted forever. I supposed I would just have to enjoy the time with Lynus until the next battle.

8

THE FABLE OF THE IMPOSSIBLE TRIAL OF WORTH

EZRIL RIVERS & THE KEEPER OF CORPSES

Before the events of Warlord Arcanist *(Book 6)*

Fifty-seven.

That was how many fools from the nearby fishing village had come into my woods, looking to bond.

Six.

That was how many had turned back and fled to their homes.

Eleven.

That was how many had been injured by my ghouls and then decided it was too difficult to brave the timberland.

Forty.

That was how many I had consumed the moment they had reached me.

Why should I bond with any of these imbeciles? They didn't display any noteworthy traits. They were *born*. They learned to *fish*. They settled down to pump out *children*. And then they died. No ambition. No goals. No imagination beyond the mundane and simple and traditional. They would accomplish nothing, and then their names would be lost to history. They existed for a blip of time simply to pass their genes on to someone else.

And some couldn't even manage that.

They were cowards. They allowed their fear to shackle them to mediocracy. They didn't deserve to become arcanists. They especially didn't deserve *my* magic. I wasn't a typical mystical creature—there would never be another one of me.

At least... that was what I had thought.

Now that the god-creatures were returning to the world, there was a chance I would finally have more siblings. For centuries, it had just been me and the Mother of Shapeshifters. Me—the Keeper of Corpses—and my deformed, blob of a sister.

Once upon a time, people knew and feared us, but humans have short attention spans. During the Age of Monsters, our heyday, we fought off lone warriors and knights, and were worshiped as *elder gods*. But then humanity moved on to the Age of Travel and Conquest. Then all they cared about was reaching the land's end, and who gave birth to whom, and which of them built the most impressive hovels.

Pathetic.

Now I sat in a woodland cave—a small hole in a large moss-covered boulder. The surrounding oak trees, raspberry bushes, rivers, and groves were my domain. This was my home—the final one. I was done with aimlessly wandering the world, and this tranquil location would serve as my final domain.

So long as the idiotic fishermen would leave me alone.

The wind shifted, and from deep within my boulder

cave, I caught the scent of a human who had entered my woods.

Ah. Lucky number *fifty-eight*. How would his journey end? Would he be wise and turn back? Would he be clumsy and injure himself? Or would I get another fine meal before I began renovations?

I wanted to relax and wait for this lump to reach me—so I could devour him like the rest—but the winds shifted again, and I caught the scent of *three others* who had entered my woods. Why were so many determined to bother me today?

Insufferable nuisances.

EZRIL RIVERS

I limped through Winfelt Woods, my heart beating out of rhythm. I wheezed as though my lungs had a hole in them, and my whole chest burned like the sun were lodged in my ribcage. My weak body struggled with even the most basic of tasks. I gritted my teeth, pushing forward despite the ever-mounting pain.

What use was there in complaining? I would hurt whether or not I voiced any displeasures, so I tried to focus on the things that *didn't* hurt, like my good leg. And... well, that was it.

At least I had my good leg. I patted it like a faithful dog that had served me for decades.

"Oh, there he is," a man called out, his voice laced with relief and exasperation.

"Finally," a woman replied with a sigh. "I did *not* want to spend another moment in these woods."

They emerged from a cluster of trees, both dressed in Mableville's finest attire—sturdy overalls and baggy linen shirts. Their tall boots were caked in mud, and I suspected they had just come straight from Gale River.

Everyone fished at Gale River this time of the year, after all. It was the only one with a dam. Harper River and Tangle River were viable options, but the denizens of Mableville waited until autumn to fish along those riverbanks. They were all so predictable.

The man approached me with a deep frown. What was his name again? I think it was Gann, but I couldn't place it. I rarely had the energy to leave the medicine house, and it wasn't like any neighbors ever came to visit me.

"C'mon," Gann said. "I don't know what you're thinkin', but Caregiver Lana is worried sick. Let's be gettin' back home."

I said nothing as he approached. I was too busy catching my breath.

The woman—Holly?—motioned to the south. "Let's cut through the bushes here. We'll be back in the village before noon."

"I'm not going back yet," I stated through ragged breaths.

The pair exchanged worried glances before returning their attention to me. Gann stepped over a root protruding from the dirt and finally closed the gap between us. He placed a hand on my narrow shoulder and squeezed.

"Winfelt Woods is no place for a boy with your condition," he said.

I slowly pushed his hand off my shoulder and tried not to give him a sarcastic glower. I wasn't *a boy*. I was twenty-five years old—long past the coming-of-age ceremonies and well into adulthood—but that didn't matter much. I was forever "the sick kid" who lived in the rundown building at the edge of our fishing village. See? It had the word *kid* in it, so clearly, I wasn't a man. Airtight logic.

"I already told you—I'm not going back yet," I said.

"Don't make this difficult, Ezril. You'll thank us later for catching you before anything bad happened."

"How did you even know I had left?" I asked. No one in town was a master detective—or even a normal detective, for that matter—and there was still fishing to do.

Both Gann and Holly glanced at the clump of trees they had emerged from. Standing between two trunks, and looking rather put-off by the whole ordeal, was none other than Trent.

With his thick, curly hair and squared jaw, Trent would have probably passed for a "handsome young man." Well, if it weren't for the fact that he was missing his right arm from the elbow down. It ended in a thin nub, no joint at all.

And he also had scars on the right side of his face. Not the dashing kind of scars that girls swooned over. The jagged kind of scars caused by infected injuries.

Unlike me, who had been born a *tad* misshapen and weak—a shriveled leg and sunken chest, nothing major, right?—Trent had come across his deformities the old-fashioned way. Pirates.

Years ago, Trent had been caught up in an attack, and ever since then, we had lived together in the same medicine house. Caregiver Lana took in all the unfortunate souls, no matter how broken they were.

"I figured you'd come this way, Ezril," Trent said. "Lana sent me looking for you as soon as she realized you were gone. Did you really think your presence would go unnoticed? You're such a hassle."

Trent and I—and the others from the medicine house—didn't get the privilege of dressing like fishermen. We both wore long, white tunics and loose cotton pants. The type of *one size fits all* clothing they handed to all the inhabitants under Caregiver Lana's protection. Or perhaps they were *avant-garde* clothes, and Trent and I were the most fashionable bachelors in town. All a matter of perspective, I supposed.

Again, Gann placed a hand on my shoulder, this time with the forceful direction of someone who was going to *make me* comply with his demands. It happened all the time. I was weak, so people thought they could push me around. And they could—I didn't have much strength to fight back—but that didn't make it much better.

"Do I need to carry you?" Gann asked, not because he was concerned. It was a threat.

"I'll walk," I said, keeping my tone neutral.

Gann, Holly, and Trent turned toward Mableville, and my insides twisted as I followed them. If only I had made it out of the medicine house without no one noticing...

I limped behind them, my left leg slightly shriveled, and my ankle twisted. Sometimes, when I saw my whole body in a mirror, I thought I looked like a half-dehydrated grape. I tried not to think about it. I straightened my posture and attempted to walk as "normal" as possible. If anyone asked, I'd say this was my *saunter stride*.

"There are ghouls in these woods," Trent said as we made our way to the one road through Winfelt Woods. "I doubt you would've been able to outrun them, Ezril."

I didn't answer. He just wanted to mess with me, and I couldn't think of a witty comeback to the statement. I probably *couldn't* outrun them.

"There are more than ghouls out here," Holly whispered as she glanced around. She wrung her hands in front of her. "Haven't you seen the bodies? For the last six months... All those deaths..."

"We don't need to discuss any of that," Gann said.

"They're just bones. Picked clean. Ghouls don't do that. Ghouls go for the organs and leave rotting skin behind…"

"What did I just say, Holly?" Gann shot her a glare. "Enough of that. We're almost out of the woods."

The oak trees thinned as we neared the edge. My legs ached and my lungs burned, but I controlled my breathing and forced myself to stand tall. I shook from time to time, and I hoped no one would notice, but it couldn't be helped.

THE KEEPER OF CORPSES

I dug my claws into the dirt, irritated when the scents died away. The village denizens had gotten my hopes up, but now I would remain hungry. In theory, I could consume my progeny—the ghouls that wandered the trees would come if I summoned them—but I never enjoyed devouring my kin.

Then again, I could always wander into their disgusting trash pile they called a town and simply eat my fill.

Perhaps, if they made me wait too long, I would.

EZRIL RIVERS

I sat on my bed, staring out one of the many windows in the medicine house. The large common room housed our beds, our eating tables, and the lone bookshelf sadly stocked with five meager books. One was a recipe book. Two were educational material on architecture, which included how to construct dams, mills, and different types of bridges. The last two books were journals written by cowardly adventurers who barely explored the nearby area before returning home.

I had read them all several times. I could season goat

meat and describe the detail of a nearby lake with shocking ability, but it hardly seemed worthwhile.

To be fair, I had to admit that *five books* were better than *no books*. And the structural integrity of dams wasn't too dull.

The orange rays of sunset shone through the uneven glass of the windows. Any moment, Caregiver Lana would light the lanterns. Then we'd have an hour or two more before we had to rest. Party time. Woo.

Three children rushed by, each screaming something about the rules of touch-n-go. When they dashed by my bed, I pulled my legs up to allow them more room. They laughed and giggled, and I should've told them to stop, but I wasn't in the mood to interrupt their games. They each had their own aliment that kept them tethered here, and they'd hurt later, but for right now, why not have fun?

Trent entered the common room from the medicine house's entrance hall. He strode forward with his head held high, but I knew where he had been. The injuries he sustained from the pirates messed with his insides, specifically his bladder. He remained at the medicine house, despite his overall health, because he sometimes needed *assistance* in matters people deemed personal.

Sure enough, Caregiver Lana entered shortly afterward. If I had to guess her age by looking at her, I'd have said she had lived three lifetimes. She walked with a pronounced hunch, the skin on her face hung so much her slumped forehead made it difficult for her to fully open her eyes, and her white hair would fall out if someone blew on it.

Despite that, she walked with spring in her step—as though nothing would hold her back from completing her life's mission to help the unfortunate.

"Everyone, listen up," Caregiver Lana announced, her voice warbled by age. "Arcanists have arrived in the village."

The three kids—Brack, Sasha, and Ethan—stopped dead in their tracks.

Trent and I glanced over.

And that was it. Us five. No one else.

"They're mystic seekers," Lana continued. "No need to be frightened if a few arcanists visit. Answer any questions they have about Winfelt Woods and everything will be fine."

Mystic seekers? Winfelt Woods?

I bit my tongue and returned my gaze to the window, trying to feign disinterest. The appearance of mystic seekers troubled me, however. They sought rare and dangerous mystical creatures, either to gather for kings or queens, or to kill them.

There was something interesting hiding in the Winfelt Woods. Something powerful. There had to be! Forty people had disappeared since entering the woods, after all. Most creatures didn't have that high a mortality rate for their trials of worth. Well, some dragons did, but there was no way there was a dragon in our woods. So, it had to be something else.

A mystic creature unlike anything anyone here had ever seen.

I wanted to seek it out and take its trial of worth, but I couldn't get five feet from this damn medicine house before someone dragged me back "for my own good."

"Are the mystic seekers hunting for ghouls?" Trent asked.

Caregiver Lana shrugged. "Perhaps. They've grown in number lately. They may need to be culled."

Ghouls were terrible mystical creatures. They used their magic to remain invisible until life wandered by. Then they would attack without warning, slashing at their victims with diseased bone claws.

If someone wanted to bond, the ghoul's trials of worth involved eating human flesh—typically from someone the hopeful arcanist had freshly murdered.

I wanted to become an arcanist. Desperately wanted it.

But I couldn't stomach the thought of eating human flesh. I just couldn't. Even though I had tried to convince myself it wouldn't be terrible—I could live through the experience, right? I still just couldn't bring myself to accept that reality.

And murder wasn't really *my thing.*

The three kids ran to the entrance door, probably excited to meet arcanists in person. Mableville didn't have a resident arcanist, after all. Why would it? We were out in the middle of nowhere. And we fished. If I ever became an arcanist, I'd leave our redneck village behind in a heartbeat.

For some reason, Trent sauntered over to my bed, his half-arm tucked close to his body, as though he were trying to make it less noticeable.

"What're you up to?" Trent asked in a suspicious tone.

I stared at him with my best neutral expression. "Whatever do you mean?" I batted my eyes in comical confusion. "I'm too sick to do anything other than lie here on my bed."

"Cut the act," Trent growled, keeping his voice low. He leaned in close. The twisted scars on his face reminded me of a crude child's drawing. "Why do you keep leaving the house?"

"So that you can practice your snitching skills," I quipped.

"You think you're funny?"

"The funniest one here."

Trent grabbed me by the collar of my tunic, his one arm

plenty strong—I sometimes wondered if all his physical activity was his way of compensating for the loss. He jerked me forward, enough to have the fabric of my clothing dig into my skin.

"You were going to search for the killer mystical creature in the woods, weren't you?" Trent asked. "*Admit it.*" He shook me again, this time twisting his grip on my collar so that it tightened around my throat.

I held his wrist and forced a tight smile. "You got me," I said. "Nothing gets by you, master sleuth."

"What's in the woods?"

"I don't know."

Trent loosened his grip, and the collar of my tunic no longer hurt me. "So, what was your plan? Wander out there and just *hope* you don't die like the rest of them? What's wrong with you?"

I sardonically nodded with the last of his words. "What else am I going do, *Trent*? I can't leave the medicine house." I motioned to the window. "The woods are at least a ten-minute walk. And it's not like anyone in the village will tell me what's going on."

"You'll die," Trent said, his scarred face contorting in confusion. He released my clothes and stepped back. "You realize that, right?"

"Better than sitting here and doing nothing," I said with a shrug. I wanted to sound tough, but that wasn't the case.

Trent stared at me for a long moment, his eyes—a light shade of amber—searching mine as though he might find a different answer.

I shrugged and turned away. "What does it matter? The mystic seekers are here to search the woods. I'm sure they'll use their arcanist magic to capture the beast, which means I'll never get my chance. My only options now are either *find a ghoul before it eats me* or *hope life gets a lot more interesting living with three children and an elder lady.*"

"Don't be so dramatic," Trent said with a scoff.

Caregiver Lana herded the three kids away from the entrance door. Then she lit the lanterns around the common room, smiling the entire time. The last of the sun died just as she lit the final lantern.

Trent shifted his gaze from the kids to Lana and then back to me. "You're a fool, you know that, right?"

I lifted an eyebrow. "Better than being a blowhard."

He grabbed me by the collar again, this time almost on reflex. "*Listen,*" he said through gritted teeth. "The village takes care of us out of the goodness of their *little hearts.* They give us food and blankets, and Caregiver Lana dedicates her whole life to make our lives better. Maybe you should be a bit more thankful for what you have and not throw it away."

"Just because they're willing to care for me doesn't mean I'm bound to them for all eternity." I pushed his hand away with as much strength as I could muster. Thankfully, Trent just let go. I rubbed at my throat. "Besides, wouldn't it be better if I became an arcanist? Then they wouldn't have to provide for me."

"You're going to die," Trent stated.

"Well, they wouldn't have to provide for me then, either."

I had meant the last part to be a dark joke, but Trent gritted his teeth and glared. "You think that mentality is good for the kids to see? Stop being selfish. They look up to you."

The little ones had problems like mine—things they were born with. Brack's joints became swollen, to the point he couldn't move. Sasha would bruise and bleed at the slightest bump and was often bedridden. Ethan, for whatever reason, had lungs that filled with mucus that Caregiver Lana had to help him cough up on a daily basis, lest he half-suffocate at night.

I stared at the three as they prepared for bed, each folding down their blankets and carefully untying their only boots. Then I stared up at Trent. "Maybe I just want to feel like I'm in control of my own life."

He caught his breath, on the verge of saying something, but opting for silence.

"Maybe," I continued, my voice a whisper, "I'd rather try for greatness and *for once* not have someone hold me back and say, *you aren't capable of greatness.*"

Something in my words struck a chord with Trent. His grip loosened, and when he took his breath, he hesitated a second time, unable to speak. Then he released me and mulled over my statement.

"Those mystic seekers will find whatever is in the woods," Trent said. "No doubt in my mind."

I nodded.

Trent lifted his stump arm and rotated it about. "But they're currently gathering information around town, which means they likely won't leave until morning."

"Probably."

"So, what would be your plan if you went out into the woods right now?"

I scratched at the black stubble on my chin. "Well, my plan would probably be... *limp around in the dark until a ghoul found me.*" With a sarcastic look, my eye half-lidded, I added, "I could always fall into a ditch and die. That'll be my backup plan."

Traversing Winfelt Woods at night was difficult, even for people in full health. What made Trent think I could wander out there and not have problems?

"Do you enjoy testing the limitations of my patience?" Trent snapped.

I shrugged.

He sighed and then motioned over to Caregiver Lana. She hobbled around the front door, clearly waiting for the mystic seekers to visit.

"Once we're questioned, you know Lana will insist on snuffing all the lights," Trent whispered. "We can explore the woods then."

"We?" I asked, one eyebrow to my hairline.

Trent smirked. "You have two functioning arms. I have two functioning legs. We can explore a decent amount of the woodland if we work together."

"Uh-huh. And let me guess. Once we find the creature, I'll be stuck with my backup plan while you bond with the beast."

"I'm not going to kill you," Trent said, his anger flaring again. He took a breath and ended it quickly, but I could tell I was killing his desire to remain calm. "Listen, creatures have a trial of worth, don't they? Whatever happens, the mystical creature will decide which of us to bond with."

I cogitated on his proposal, and while it was risky, I appreciated the plan for what it was. Trent thought he could best me, but he wasn't being condescending. He was treating me as an equal—saying we could help each other get there, but then we'd compete like any normal fellows.

"Why take me?" I asked. "You could probably run off and do this on your own."

Trent shrugged with his good shoulder. "It was your idea. I'm trying to be fair."

I chuckled. "Fine. It's a deal. Once the lights are out, we'll borrow a lantern and head out into Winfelt Woods.

THE KEEPER OF CORPSES

The undead never slept. There was no need. Our bodies didn't require rest, and it was easier to sneak up on unsuspecting victims in the middle of the night, while lesser beings chose voluntary unconsciousness.

Despite my hunger, I remained in my lowly boulder cave. The wind rustled the oak leaves and carried with it an aroma of vegetation and people. At least ten individuals—two groups—had entered my woods, most of which wore cured leather and carried gunpowder.

I hated gunpowder. It had a distinct smell that agitated my nose.

What were these fools hoping to accomplish?

I hoped they had come to kill me. Not because I wanted a final death, but because nothing eliminated boredom faster than combat. Some of the intruders were arcanists—orthrus arcanists, to be specific. Those two-headed dogs could track over long distances, which only increased the likelihood I'd see combat this evening.

Excellent.

EZRIL RIVERS

"I thought you said the mystic seekers would wait until morning?" I asked as we traversed the uneven surfaces of the woodland. The roots, along with the catkins dropped by the oak trees, made every surface a lumpy mess.

Trent scoffed. "I thought they'd wait until they had more light, but apparently, the undead are more active once the sun sets."

"How do you not know that by now?"

"Some of us don't make plans to wander into the *death woods*," Trent said, glancing over his shoulder.

"Still."

I carried a lantern in one hand and a shovel in the other. We didn't really have weapons, so I had to settle for the only large tool the medicine house had in its shed. Trent kept watch ahead, clearing the path a bit by kicking rocks and branches out of my path. I appreciated his efforts, though I couldn't seem to find the courage to say it to him.

The shovel fascinated me for a moment. The head—clearly crafted by a talented smith—had been shaped to resemble a dragon's head. The wood handle, though worn, still had the etchings of scales. I wondered why the medicine house had such a unique tool.

"Are you paying attention?" Trent asked.

"I'm always paying attention." I limped a little faster until the distance between us was only a foot or so. "But just in case I wasn't—what're you bellowing about?"

"This is the farthest I've ever gone into Winfelt Woods."

I glanced around, unable to see much beyond the soft glow of the lantern. Could Trent recognize certain areas of the woods? By the abyssal hells, they all looked the same.

With a shaky hand, I half-closed the shutters on the lantern, dimming our light. If there were ghouls nearby, they would surely spot us, but maybe this would make it harder for them. I hoped.

Trent stopped dead in his tracks. I stumbled and collided with him, surprised by his balance and steady stance. He held up his one arm. "Listen," he whispered.

I held my breath.

"I don't hear anything," I muttered.

"Yeah... There were the sounds of insects and owls before."

"There were?"

Trent offered me a glare. "Yes. And now there's nothing. Which means something is nearby. Something the animals want to avoid."

I mulled over his observations. "Interesting. Ghouls?"

"I suspect so."

"Then we should head in another direction." I gestured to an opening between trees. "Ghouls don't wander around. They stay still—like crocodiles—waiting for a victim and then striking when the moment is right."

Before we could discuss the matter further, a new sound echoed throughout the trees. It was the heavy footfalls of men, along with the crunching of twigs and undergrowth. People were making their way toward us, some of whom grunted out curses and irritations.

"The mystic seekers," I said.

Trent nodded.

I snuffed the lantern. The thick oak tree canopy blocked most of the moonlight, giving us only a few slivers to work with. Then I poked Trent and pointed to a larger tree for us to move behind. He half lifted my weight and helped me rush behind the trunk.

The mystic seekers tore through the woodland, chopping down any shrub in their path and pushing forward at a decent clip. Their lanterns shone bright, giving away their position, even if the sound of their destruction didn't.

Five two-headed dogs—a few hundred pounds each—sniffed at the ground. One head would occasionally bark, and the other head would turn back to the mystic seekers to yell out when they had found something.

"What are those?" Trent whispered.

"Orthrus," I replied. "They have a powerful bite, and

their arcanists have magically enhanced strength and endurance."

"Will they find us?"

"If they wanted to. But I doubt they care about us. They're here for mystical creatures, and we're far from that."

The mystic seekers drew closer and closer, their parade of destruction loud enough that everyone along all three rivers could hear what was going on.

"We're close," one orthrus shouted, his gruff voice laced with excitement. "The scent is strong in this area."

The group of arcanists and their retinue hurried their pace. They rushed past our location, never even bothering to slow or speak to us. A few of the orthrus turned their multiple heads in our direction, but they clearly considered us of no importance.

There were five orthrus, five arcanists, and five mortal men. The men carried the lanterns, along with rope and nets. The arcanists all wore silver badges that flashed in the lantern light—a sign they were all mystic seekers from the same company.

Trent cursed under his breath.

"We should follow them," I muttered.

"What's the point?" Trent asked. "They're gonna beat us to the punch."

"It's not over until it's over," I said. Then I motioned for him to hurry. "Maybe we'll still have a chance to bond. *C'mon*. Let's go."

Trent offered me his good shoulder. I hesitated for a moment—he hadn't done that before, and I usually disliked accepting help from others. In this instance, however, I was thankful he had. I wasn't about to run anywhere.

Together we hustled after the mystic seekers. Even without

a lantern, it was easy to follow their trail. They practically left a road in their wake, and Trent was strong enough to carry most of my weight. I helped by running along with my strong leg, and it didn't take us long until we caught up with the group.

The smell of the woods shifted dramatically the farther we traveled. I wasn't familiar with battlefields or graveyards, but I imagined they smelled like this portion of the woods. Just as Trent had pointed out, there were no animal sounds here, and the ground was muddier than usual. My mind played tricks on me—were there bones protruding from the ground? But it was too dark to confirm my suspicions.

Trent stopped before we entered a large, circular grove. On the opposite end of the clearing was a boulder—the massive and tall kind that had slid down on a mudslide from the nearby mountain during a terrible storm. It had to be twenty feet in height and several tons in weight. The boulder had been in these woods for a while now—moss covered the north side, and the stone had sunk into the dirt.

The boulder had a crack through it, creating a small cave. It was too dark to see inside, and even as the lanterns were brought closer, I just couldn't make out the interior of the boulder. The orthrus gathered around the entrance, their hackles raised and each head growling. The five orthrus arcanists pulled out pistols, and the five men readied their nets.

One arcanist stepped forward. He wore thick leather armor, and packed his flintlock pistol full of powder. "Oh, mystical creature," he called out. "You have nothing to fear. We're arcanists come to help you."

Help?

I held back a sarcastic laugh. Mystic seekers were often hired by royalty or wealthy merchants to gather up rare creatures, either for trinket creation or to allow certain individuals—such as their children—to bond with mystical creatures they were too lazy to find on their own. Was that really helping the creature? It was debatable.

A low and guttural growl emanated from the darkness of the boulder cave, and a cold shiver ran down my spine. The arcanists and their orthrus took one hesitant step back.

Whatever dwelled in the boulder cave wasn't a ghoul, of that much I was certain.

THE KEEPER OF CORPSES

What fools.

With no urgency, I uncurled myself and stood, my boulder cave barely enough to contain my body. The stink of gunpowder filled my grove, but at least I would finally eat.

"I'm Karric Daan," the orthrus arcanist shouted. "What shall we call you?"

His two-headed dog stepped forward as though to protect his arcanist. What a joke. Weak beasts should know their place.

I stepped out of my boulder cave and stared down at the intruders in my woods. The humans ranged in height, from five feet to roughly six and a half. At the shoulder, I stood eight feet tall, my body wolf-shaped, and my entire being made from the corpses of other creatures. Dogs, cats, humans, unicorns, drakes—their rotting bodies were fitted together like a poorly constructed jigsaw puzzle, pieces jutting out of me at random.

The sharp horns of a minotaur protruded from my shoulders, the talons of hurricane hawks formed my back claws, and the broken iron bones of drake skulls—sharpened to a deadly point—constituted my fangs.

I was an amalgamation of whatever corpse I had come

across, and the skulls of the deceased were located at random spots around my torso. My wolf-like shape, quadruped and without human hands, was because I was born of the progenitor behemoth, a god-creature who was also a quadruped.

These pathetic arcanists didn't understand what they stood in front of.

"What in the name of the death lords is that?" one of the other arcanists whispered.

Karric Daan, his eyes wide and his pistol hand shaky, stared up at me with his mouth agape. He swallowed hard, buried his hesitation, and held up his weapon. "Who are you, beast? Identify yourself!"

"I have gone by many names," I drawled, both angry and hungry after a short slumber. "Your kind has called me the *Charnel Hound*, and the *Cadaver Collector*, but the name I now answer to is the *Keeper of Corpses*."

The ten men and five mystical creatures glanced between each other, looking for leadership. None had heard of me. A pity. I wanted them to know the danger they had unearthed. Ignorance was their shield, and they held it proudly as only fools could do.

"We're here to take you on a journey," Karric Daan said. "We have a ship, and, uh, quarters for a mighty beast your size."

"I will go nowhere," I said.

The orthrus growled. Smaller dogs always had more bark than bite.

Karric Dann straightened the belt around his pants. "Are you bonded with someone?"

"I am not."

"Well, look here, that's a problem. You're a mighty beast, Keeper of Corpses. Don't you wanna be bonded with someone as powerful as yourself? Maybe a prince, perhaps? A prince of a whole darn kingdom?"

I snorted and bit back a laugh. "Titles do not make one important."

"Well, you aren't gonna find anyone worthwhile in this back-alley dump. Come now. Let's get you somewhere proper."

I flashed my jagged and sharp fangs. The orthrus tensed, each set of eyes locked on my every move.

"Here's how this will go," I said. "Either you'll leave my woods, board your pathetic sailing vessel, and live to tell this tale, or I'll be forced to add your bodies to my collection. The choice is yours."

The men in the grove grew silent and tenser than before. Would they be wise and accept my mercy? Of course not. Mankind never did anything *wise*. They bashed their head on a wall until they fashioned themselves a tunnel—no cleverness to their tactics or schemes.

Karric Dann lifted his pistol.

It seemed he had made his decision.

The imbecile shot at me, and the round bullet found a home in my chest, but it didn't matter. I didn't have blood. Or weak points, like vital organs. I didn't even feel pain. His puny bullet shattered a skull in my torso—but I would soon replace it with his.

I lunged forward, mouth opened wide, and crunched down on his body, enjoying the sensation of his hot blood bursting from his body. With enough force to crack stone, I shattered the man's body in my maw, the crackling noises enough to get me laughing.

His orthrus was the first to respond. Both heads bit me on the leg, but the beast immediately yipped and jumped away. Pestilence wafted from my rotting skin. Anything that bit or licked me would not soon forget it—they'd be diseased, and likely die within the month.

I thrashed my head from side to side, splattering the grove with crimson. The five mortal men took off between the trees, yelling and screaming as they went. The other four arcanists and their dogs attacked. Two shot with pistols, two stabbed with swords, and all five of the orthrus bit at my diseased flesh, regardless of the damage they would do to themselves.

Dogs were loyal to the point of self-harming stupidity.

I chomped down on Karric Dann a second time, ending his life. One of the arcanists—strength empowered by his magic—cleaved my leg with his steel sword. My limb hit the ground and writhed on its own, the undead bodies groaning of their own accord.

It didn't hurt. It didn't even matter.

I turned and crunched down hard on the man's head. If he wanted to take a body part, I could do the same.

My fangs severed his neck when I applied my full force.

Both the unbonded orthrus attacked me with untold fury. They ripped at my flesh and tossed it aside, determined to defeat me one piece at a time.

A handful of my ghouls burst into the grove, some with blood already on their claws. Had they defeated the five mortals who ran? It saved me the trouble of chasing them down.

The ghouls lunged for the orthrus—they were good children, my little undead offspring.

When another arcanist slashed me with a sword, I crunched my fangs down on him as well. The moment I touched something—anything—it grew weaker and weaker from my magic of decay. I manipulated the entropy and time of an object, wasting it away until it expired. Creatures and objects alike atrophied.

Three arcanists dead to my fangs.

The last two, both with pistols, had reloaded. They fired at my face, likely aiming for my "eyes." They didn't know my eyes were nothing more than glowing patches of crystalized blood. I had no organs, just magic enough to sense the world around me.

Although I was missing a leg, I shifted my weight and then slashed with my front claw. I clipped one arcanist, slashing open his leather armor—and his stomach. His guts spilled out like spaghetti, and while he tried to shove them back into his mutilated body, I caught him a second time with my claws, ending him once and for all.

The last arcanist, shaken by the rampant death all around him, couldn't seem to bring himself to act. He shook, his body moving in jerky motions. I had no idea what he was *trying* to do. All I saw were his convulsions.

I leapt and clamped my fangs around his body. He was stronger than the others and attempted to force my mouth back open. For a brief second, I was impressed—his magic was strong. Too bad he couldn't withstand my entropy.

I killed him too. His blood tasted sweeter than the rest.

Once I finished slurping down his body and adding his bones to my collection, I glanced back to find my ghouls still engaged in combat. They fought the orthrus with all they had, but the dogs were powerful. Each orthrus destroyed two of my ghouls before dying. When I returned to the fray, my children had ceased to exist, but only two orthrus remained.

I leaned down next to my severed leg and the rotting flesh knitted itself to my body. The bones of the other corpses helped in the process—the hands of men clasped hands and held my leg together while I healed.

The orthrus attacked, even before I was finished.

I slashed at one and bit the other. No matter how hard they fought, or what they bit, they were no match. I savored their blood and organs, delighting in their death wails.

So delicious.

I sat in the grove, consuming my meal. I started with the fingers, and then devoured any arms I could find. Each piece of a body added to my own... until I was complete.

Once upon a time, the more I ate, the larger I became. But then it stopped. The Mother of Shapeshifters had said I needed to bond to grow any further. Perhaps she was right, but I had never met anyone worthy of my magic or my little undead children.

The ghouls in the grove had died their final death. I could make more—I gobbled up the orthrus until all five were in my rotting intestines. My magic would seep into their bodies over the coming days, and once they were done baking, I'd birth out ghouls. They'd steal the magic from the corpses of the dogs, and I'd use the bones of men I had slain in order to make a new kind of mystic creature. Ones that were undead.

We'd be a new happy family.

I chortled at my own joke.

The rustle of leaves disturbed my thoughts. I turned my attention to one of the oak trees that lined the grove. All I could smell was the carnage of the recent battle—blood had a powerful odor that masked most others. I didn't realize there were still people nearby.

Two individuals descended from the branches of the oak tree. One had a deformed leg. He crumpled to the ground, shaky. The other was injured and missing an arm. He jumped down and helped the first to his feet.

What a duo.

Had they arrived with the others? No. They stank of fish. Simple villagers. Simple—*deformed*—villagers.

I growled as I got to my feet, my belly full of dead mystical animals.

"Had you been smart, you wouldn't have revealed your presence," I said. "Now, I'll have to kill you both as well."

EZRIL RIVERS

I had never seen a creature so large or powerful. He had defeated *five* arcanists with little effort, and now he was feasting on the gore as though their bodies were his reward.

The giant corpse wolf turned to face us, his glowing red eyes wild with some emotion I couldn't describe. My mouth went dry, and my weak legs nearly buckled, but Trent grabbed my upper arm and kept me standing.

The Keeper of Corpses strode toward us, but I knew we couldn't run.

His gigantic body, made up of other corpses, moved oddly as though each undead body had to work together. The Keeper of Corpses' belly was enlarged and sloshed with thick blood when he walked.

"W-wait," I said, my voice cracking. I took a deep breath and started again. "*Wait.* Oh, mighty mystical creature. We've come seeking your trial of worth." I would've knelt, but I couldn't bring myself to move. And let's face it—I probably would've fallen over.

The charnel hound laughed, his voice deep and taunting. "Then you have made a grave mistake. I have no trial of worth."

Trent placed a hand on my shoulder, his fingers digging into my flesh. He trembled, and I wondered what kind of storm of emotions raged beneath his frozen expression.

"All mystical creatures have a trial of worth," Trent said, forcing the words out. "That's... that's the rule!" He barked the last part as if using anger to bolster his confidence.

"Rules?" The Keeper of Corpses snorted. He strode up to us and stopped only a few feet away. "What makes you think, a pathetic mortal—half of one at best—has any right to tell me what the *rules* are to my existence? I was once worshipped as a god. *I'll do as I please.*"

Up close, it became apparent that the head of the wolf was bodies laced together and locked in place with bones and sinew. The "fur" was corpse hair, some different colors than the rest.

I held up an unsteady hand. "P-please. Wait. Mystical creatures grow in power when bonded. They... they take from their arcanist's soul. It... it's a mutual agreement. Everyone benefits."

"Lies."

"What? No. That's how bonding works. Everyone knows it."

The beast chuckled as he leaned forward, flashing his blood-soaked fangs in front of Trent and me. "*Silence,*" he growled. "Or I'll rip your tongue from your throat."

"At least *then* you'll have the truth in hand," Trent spat. "Ezril is right! It would benefit you to let us compete for your bonding."

"No human is worthy of me," the Keeper of Corpses stated in disgust.

"I'm worthy," I said, no hesitation.

The beast laughed, dark and low. "You're so weak your mother's womb almost killed you."

"I..." My throat knotted, and I struggled to find any clever rebuttal. Still, I stood firm. "I'm worthy."

The beast shoved his rotting snout into my chest, knocking me to the ground. His nose was dry and flaking skin, and his breath had a sickening chill. "From what delusional wellspring do you pull such confidence? *No one is worthy of me.* No one."

Trent took a slow step back, his attention shifting from me to the giant wolf. "If that's true, then test us! Give us your trial of worth. If we fail, then you can just kill us anyway."

"I might as well cut out the extra step."

"Are you afraid you'll be proven wrong?" I asked as I pushed myself into a standing position. "Is that what this is?"

The Keeper of Corpses growled, his threat echoing throughout the grove. Then he turned away from us, his patchwork fur on edge. With his tail angrily swishing from side to side, he walked back to the entrance of his boulder cave and stood next to it.

For a long moment, I thought he had simply ended the conversation and would let us go, but then the Keeper of Corpses turned back around, his red eyes flashing with amusement. He smiled a wicked canine smile, his tongue nothing more than shriveled muscle twisted together. It reminded me of my deformed leg.

"This is what you asked for," the Keeper of Corpses said. "Whoever can move my boulder—at least a few feet in any direction—is worthy of bonding with me."

I caught my breath. The beast had intentionally picked a physical challenge to stump us! Why would he be so cruel?

"That's impossible," Trent said, throwing up his good arm. "Even a healthy man would fail at that trial!"

The corpse monster roared, his threat somehow laced

with the wails of the dead. Trent and I staggered back, shaken by the outburst. It had been so loud, I swear I felt the reverberation ripple through my body.

"You wanted a trial of worth," the Keeper of Corpses growled. "*Now you have one.*" He extended his warped claws and bared his fangs. "Move the boulder, and I will bond with you. Fail, and I'll wreck the rest of your pathetic bodies."

Trent and I turned to each other. His wide eyes and trembling shoulders told me he was at a loss. There was no way either of us could move that boulder. Trent glanced over at the shovel by the tree, but I almost laughed at his silent proposition. Maybe digging away at one side could cause it to roll—but that would take weeks of effort by a single person. Maybe a month. Winfelt Woods was practically all flatlands.

Silence dominated the grove. What could I say to convince the creature to give us a real chance? What hope would we have if it offered yet another preposterous trial?

The Keeper of Corpses leapt forward. I tensed, my blood running with ice as I braced for death.

But the monster dug his claws into the dirt and stopped before us, his voice somehow more haunting as he growled, "When you die, your skull will be as empty as a hollowed acorn forgotten on the forest floor. You're meaningless and frail—a single hole through that head of yours and everything that makes you *you* will drain out into the dirt. *You're nothing.*"

"Give us time," Trent said, once again angry, despite the situation. The injustice of it all killed his fear, apparently. "We can move the boulder if you give us time! *We can.*"

"How much time?" the Keeper of Corpses asked with a chortle.

"A month," I blurted out. "Please. One month. That's all we need."

"A whole month?" The beast huffed, washing me with his foul breath. "Then I'll require you move the boulder a whole *ten feet*. If you cannot accomplish that, your lives are forfeit. I'll drag you back to these woods—no matter where you run—and I'll delight in dismembering you further."

Trent gritted his teeth. "That's not enough time," he muttered under his breath. "It's impossible."

"I accept your trial of worth," I said, trying to stand as tall as possible with only one good leg. "I'll show you. I'll prove that I'm worthy."

Trent stepped closer to me and weakly nodded. "I'll accept. It's better than dying, at least."

"Then so be it," the Keeper of Corpses stated. "Let me see if you're worthy."

Before we left the clearing, I stooped low to pick up a silver badge that had fallen from the corpse of a mystic seeker. Although stained with blood and no longer full of luster, I wanted it anyway, just in case.

Trent grabbed our ornate shovel, though I still thought it foolish to dig our way out of this problem.

Then we fled Winfelt Woods without another word.

THE KEEPER OF CORPSES

Sixty-seven.

That was how many fools had come into my woods.

Fifty.

That was how many I had consumed.

Two.

That was how many I had ever offered a trial of worth to.

What had I been thinking? It was because I had been

full. Had I been hungry, I would've gobbled those two up, but instead, I listened to their pleading and allowed them a chance. It had been a mistake, but one I would delight in. There was no way they could move my boulder. Nature herself had put it in these woods, and mankind had yet to master nature.

I rested back in my den, eager to see their laughable attempts.

EZRIL RIVERS

One day into our challenge—Trent and I had yet to come up with a plan.

We sat on our beds, huddled close and whispering. No one knew of our predicament, and no one cared that we were off by ourselves, either. Everyone in Mableville was too concerned with the disappearance of the mystic seekers.

The silver badge weighed heavy in my pocket. People around the village speculated, but no one was willing to investigate. Fear spread from house to house, and even bathing in the rivers had become a mandatory group activity. I thought it all foolish—if five arcanists went missing, why would a group of four men in the river do any better?

But I was too distracted to question their bizarre logic.

"We need to think of something," Trent said, scratching at his chin. His half-arm stayed stuck to his side, unmoving —a sign he was agitated.

Weren't we all?

I shook my head. "I think we need to consider outlandish possibilities."

"What?" Trent glared. "No. We need to start shoveling the dirt around the boulder as quickly as possible."

"That won't work. The beast said we had to move it *ten feet*. You think we can do that in a month?"

"Maybe we can get people in town to help us," Trent said.

My heart seized in my chest for a moment, and a new idea formed at the edge of my thoughts. "People in town? That's clever... But they'll never work at the boulder. Not with the Keeper of Corpses nearby. And there's no guarantee that monster won't eat them."

But using the townsfolk to do something... It really was a clever idea. But how? How could they help if they wouldn't enter the woods?

Trent huffed. "Okay. Then we'll have to dig around the boulder."

"I thought you said we were competing against each other?"

"Well, I did—but this is different. I thought it'd be a normal trial of worth. Not *this*."

I leaned back on my bed, posting my weight with my arms. "If we both dig, who will the creature bond with?" When Trent didn't answer, I continued with, "Exactly. We need to do something different."

"Then I'm digging," Trent stated. "That's my idea."

"You can have it. Because it's terrible."

He gritted his teeth and narrowed his eyes further. "It's the best we've got."

"I don't think so. Strength alone won't solve this problem. We need something better."

"The creature clearly wants someone strong," Trent said. "That's why he gave us this trial."

"No—the Keeper of Corpses wants someone as great as he is. He made that clear. No one is worthy. If he wanted someone physically strong, he could've had an arcanist ages ago."

"Pfft." Trent stood from his bed and threw his good arm in the air. "What do you know? You're just afraid because you're weak." He strode for the front door. "I don't have time to waste here. I have a job to do—and if you're going to do something else, so be it." He stopped and glanced over his shoulder. "From this point on, we're doing our own thing. We'll see who bonds with the Keeper of Corpses at the end of the month."

I nodded. "I guess we will."

THE KEEPER OF CORPSES

There were *visitors* in my domain, moving around with impunity. The two half-men, and their ridiculous demands —I never should've agreed to give them a trial of worth. However, I was intrigued by their fierceness. Men with more body parts had crumpled faster than those two. Perhaps I underestimated the worth of moxie and grit.

What interested me the most, however, was the difference between the two. The man with one arm would come into my woods twice a day. He brought an odd shovel and dug a slope around my boulder—slow and steady, no matter the weather. One arm made the whole ordeal amusing. He struggled—oh, how he struggled.

But he never missed a day.

The man with the shriveled leg had entered the woods once a week for the last three weeks.

And done nothing.

He didn't dig or alter terrain or even push the boulder— he just examined, searched, and measured points in the woods. The two men didn't speak to each other, and I suspected they weren't aiding each other in this *impossible trial of worth*. Why would they? I couldn't bond with both. One *had* to win. And since the one with a limp wasn't doing much of anything, it seemed the one-armed man would come the closest.

But he wouldn't succeed. He was too weak and the boulder too heavy. A month wasn't enough time. They were both doomed to fail.

EZRIL RIVERS

What was weakness? Was it physical? I refused to believe that. Mankind hadn't invented numbers, letters, communication, and grand stories because they had rippling abs. Sure, some problems in life required muscle—arithmetic alone couldn't carry firewood into the house—but not always.

So what if I lacked physical strength? That didn't speak ill of my moral center. The bulge of my biceps wouldn't determine my greatness, even if it could make life easier.

I passionately believed only three virtues determined true greatness—creativity, courage, and willpower.

Creativity was needed to see things beyond the normal and mundane—to have the initial idea. A creative person developed thoughts, concepts, and solutions to problems that others deemed impossible. A person who lacked creativity would never think of anything beyond their limited world, and problems that crossed their path became walls they could *never* overcome.

Courage was needed to take the risk of a new idea—*to bet on oneself*, even if success was unlikely. A courageous person pushed forward with beliefs and ideals worth fighting for and never shied away from handling problems along the way. A person who lacked courage was a burden. They never tried new ideas. They fell into a simple routine —boring monotony—allowing their life to waste away as they repeated the same tasks *again and again* with no growth or variation.

Willpower was needed to see the new idea through to the end. A willful person *endured* through long processes, never losing sight of a future goal or plan, and strived for greater and better routes at every corner. A person who lacked willpower couldn't follow through with long-term projects. Even if they had an idea and risked it all, they would fail to reach their destination every time.

I didn't need *physical strength* to move the boulder, even though Trent was convinced that was the only solution. What I needed was creativity, courage, and willpower. I had to embody the virtues I held dear.

And on the second-to-last day of the month, during the rain, I would finally see if my plan had worked. Everyone in town had helped, even the three kids in the medicine house.

I prayed to the stars—hell, I even prayed to the death lords, so long as they would listen—that everything would work as I envisioned.

THE KEEPER OF CORPSES

It was the second-to-last day of the month.

Those two fools didn't have much time left, and I was eager for their blood. The man with the one arm hadn't finished his digging. He had dug a decent slope—more than I had suspected—but it wouldn't move my boulder. And two days wasn't enough to make it much better.

He had failed.

I chuckled as I enjoyed the heavy beat of rain

throughout the woods. The scents the water unearthed allowed me to smell the history of the trees. Wolves had once resided here, but I suspected the nearby fishermen had chased them away. Wolf blood stained the deepest soil, and only the rain could uncover the last of its presence.

But there was something else in the woods today...

Tension.

Collective anxiety and uncertainty.

I couldn't fully detect it in the rain, but it was there, worsening with time.

Curious, and somewhat perplexed, I stood and exited my boulder cave. The sounds of distant crashing drew my attention toward the rivers. My ears went erect as I strained to listen. What was making the thunderous destruction? Had some giant creature come to the woods?

Birds shot into the sky by the dozens. Rodents and weasels dashed through the bushes, running as fast as their tiny legs would take them.

If I had a heartbeat, it probably would've elevated, but this was yet another advantage of being undead. The rumble of the ground, the shake of the trees, and the downpour of the rain didn't break my calm. Whatever was coming didn't stand a chance against the Keeper of Corpses.

Then I saw it. The source of the disturbance.

Water. A wall of water.

It rushed through the woods like a wave, picking up dirt, shrubs, and trees and transforming into an opaque brown as it sped toward me. For a moment, all I could do was stare. Where had such a vast amount of water come from? It wasn't purely from the rain. The storms didn't create a land-based tsunami.

It was too late to run. By the time I regained my senses, the water had washed over me with the destructive force of a typhoon. Thankfully, the undead didn't need to breathe, either. The mud, sticks, and rocks battered my rotting flesh as I was swept into the rumbling current. My magic of decay didn't help me swim through the torrent, but I bit onto the branch of an elder oak tree and steadied myself. Although the tree devastation rocked the tree, the roots ran deep enough to keep it upright.

I leapt onto a large branch and then ascended higher until my entire body was free of the waters. I lifted my head beyond the canopy of the woods and stared in the direction the flood had come from. Smoke rose in pillars beyond the tree line, and I recognized the area the fishermen liked to conduct their business.

It was a dam.

Someone had broken the dam.

The man-made lake that had been by the lake was draining into the woods, altering the landscape with its sheer power. At first, I couldn't understand why, but then I shifted my gaze to where my boulder ought to be. It was so massive, the tip of the stone could be spotted above the canopy... but not today.

The flood had moved it.

Shock overcame my thoughts.

It couldn't have... It couldn't have been the work of the half-men.

I just... It couldn't have been them.

EZRIL RIVERS

It had taken some time, but I had convinced the village leaders that my plan was the only way to clear the woods of threats. The bloody silver badge had been my key to success. Nothing motivated the people of Mableville quite like *fear*. When I explained that a dangerous mystical creature would soon grow bored of the woods and come for us, everyone banded together to eliminate the threat.

That was when I had to convince everyone my plan was the one to follow. I used books from the medicine house—the old ones about architecture. Although it would hurt Mableville in the short run, flooding the woods and building a better dam at a new location would help everyone in the long term.

In order to mitigate damage to the village, barriers were built to keep the water from rushing over the houses. While that happened, material was gathered for the replacement dam, so Mableville wouldn't go long without. Additionally, stoppers and walls had been positioned to make sure the majority of the water went to the center of the woods—the location of the boulder.

Obviously, I didn't have the strength to dismantle the dam myself, but the villagers took care of the difficult parts —avoiding the woods—while I did all the measurements, calculations, and planning. It was hard work for everyone involved, and the moment the skies grew dark, I gave the command to execute.

And it went better than I had imagined. Probably too well, to be frank. I hadn't counted on as many trees being uprooted, but that wasn't too much of a problem. The denizens of Mableveille had the materials for a new dam, and they relied on the rivers for their livelihood, rather than the woodland.

It would be difficult for a year or two, but perhaps—if I actually bonded with a powerful creature like the Keeper of Corpses—I could take some of that burden away.

Now I had only to wait for the water to subside. Then I'd

venture out to the beast and claim victory over his trial of worth.

THE KEEPER OF CORPSES

I couldn't believe it.

Damn.

They had done it. They had completed my impossible trial of worth. Well, not the one-armed man, but the other... the one I had counted out immediately. How could someone with such disadvantages in life possibly be the one to rise to the challenge of my bonding?

As the rain stopped and the flooding waned, I stayed in the mighty oak tree, my rotting body soggy and hanging from the massive limbs like a corpse on the gallows.

Somewhere in my core, I felt a spark of excitement. I assumed every mystical creature had this feeling when they met someone they considered *worthy* of their magic. It wasn't just excitement—it was a connection, *a thrill*—a new horizon that hadn't been present before.

The man's soul would help me grow stronger. I would once again take a seat alongside gods.

Days after the flood, when the ground was nothing but mud and muck, I leapt down from the oak tree and shambled my way back to my boulder. It had slid across the ground a good fifty feet and smashed into several trees along the way. The boulder had also toppled over, ruining my cave.

But it didn't matter anymore. I took a seat in the mud and waited for my future arcanist.

EZRIL RIVERS

At dawn, I hobbled out into Winfelt Woods—alone.

Trent hadn't wanted to speak too much after the event. He had been so absorbed in his attempts at bonding that he hadn't figured out what I was doing. Sure, the villagers had been busy with the dam, but Trent had apparently assumed it was plans to make another and hadn't questioned anything further.

I felt for him. He had wanted to bond with a mystical creature as much as I had. But only one of us could win, and my creativity, courage, and willpower had been greater.

The woods seemed more like a mire. Ankle-deep water covered the area, trees were on their sides—some on top of one another—and insects danced in the air as if to celebrate the devastation. I swatted a few away as I sloshed my way forward, my legs already burning ten minutes in.

I flinched the moment I spotted a pack of ghouls standing by the shattered stump of an old oak tree. They stood around it, similar to a group of friends grabbing a drink at a tavern. They spoke, but too quietly for me to hear anything specific.

The ghouls stopped their chatter and turned to face me. Their human-like appearance, with pale skin, red eyes, and shredded clothing, was unsettling, to say the least. I thought the ghouls might attack, but after a few seconds of staring, they returned to their own business. I brushed off my shoulders, muttered a few reassurances to myself, and continued forward, hoping the undead wouldn't follow me.

I wore fishermen's boots—the tall kind that went up past my knees—keeping my feet dry even as I trudged toward my destination. My feet sunk into the mud, and I had to yank them out, which hurt, but I didn't care. Excitement drove away the agony, and the moment I spotted the Keeper of Corpses, my thoughts escaped me.

The wolf-shaped undead sat waiting near the displaced boulder, his silhouette from the early morning light shining in the distance. The canopy had been ruined by the flood, giving us plenty of light. The beast was just as frightening in the day as it was in the night.

One careful step after the next, and I finally made it to the creature's side. I stared up at the Keeper of Corpses, our eyes meeting for a quiet moment.

I motioned to the boulder, now tossed on its side. "Looks like you'll need a new home," I quipped.

The beast's mouth pulled back in an eerie smile. "What makes you think I won't eat you for your impudence?"

Icy dread mixed with my excitement, but something about the Keeper of Corpses' voice put me at ease. I slipped my hands into the pockets of my loose trousers. "That wouldn't happen. I'm too impressive."

The creature chuckled, and I swear the skulls that made up his torso chattered along with him.

"There is a dark truth to life," the Keeper of Corpses said. "A sheep will spend his entire life afraid of wolves, only to die at the hands of the hungry shepherd. Cowardice, ignorance, narrow-mindedness, the inability to escape routine—they will always rob a man of greatness. But you've already learned that, haven't you?"

I waited, unsure if he wanted me to speak.

"Tell me your name."

"Ezril Rivers."

"Bond with me, Ezril. Out of the thousands of humans I've encountered, you're the only one I've found worthy."

With my breath held, I reached out a hand. "I accept."

Something gripped at my chest, twisting inside me and

filling my mind with thoughts I had never had before. The feeling was brief—gone a second later—but when I took a breath again, I was filled with a sense of *power* and *might*. Although still physically weak, it no longer seemed that way.

"I..." I shook my head.

My forehead burned, and I doubled over. With an unsteady hand, I rubbed at the skin above my eyebrows, startled by the etching in my body. I had a nine-pointed star and the image of a patchwork wolf woven between the points. It marked me as an arcanist, and although droplets of blood ran down my face, I couldn't help but smile.

I straightened my posture, my body shaking. "Thank you..."

"You've earned this," the Keeper of Corpses stated. "Remember that."

He stood, his undead body somehow more majestic than before.

"We have one last order of business," I said.

The undead creature stared with red, inquisitive eyes.

"You can't eat Trent."

The Keeper of Corpses offered me a canine smile. "Very well."

Satisfied that I had done everything I needed to, I motioned the creature closer. The Keeper of Corpses walked to my side, lowered his head, and offered his shoulder. The rotting bodies that made up his frame moved and shifted— bone arms formed makeshift stairs. I stepped up, and the undead hands helped me get onto the Keeper of Corpses' back.

"First things first," I said. "I'm just going to call you *Keeper*."

My eldrin snorted. "Lazy."

"It's more efficient." I settled on his back and then continued, "Secondly, we're going to help Mableville rebuild."

"A waste."

"It's needed. And after that..." I patted his skin-and-bones head. "We'll leave this place. Do you know of anywhere we should go first?"

"My sister will be waiting for me," Keeper growled.

"Oh? Well, we can seek her out."

"Perhaps."

"Well, there are greater things for us out there."

Keeper darkly chuckled as he took off through the oak trees. "That we can both agree on... my arcanist."

9

THE FABLE OF CARD NIGHT
FAIN THE RENEGADE PIRATE

During the events of Plague Arcanist *(Book 4)*

It was going to be a weird night, I could tell. Perhaps it had something to do with our new location.

The *Sun Chaser* was as different as night and day when compared to the *Third Abyss.*

Yeah, I understood—one was an airship, the other was a dread pirate ship—but it still surprised me. First off, the *Sun Chaser* crew was mostly women. They seemed ambivalent about their captain, too. Captain Calisto had his first mate, Spider, sure, but there were only a handful of other women that ever dared to run on his vessel.

Calisto was a callous dastard, but his ambition made him a favorite of the crew. He also handled most of the major problems himself, saving the mortal deckhands from facing the worst the seas had to offer.

Captain Devlin wasn't so bad, I supposed. I liked his giant bird—the roc—and he didn't mind I was on his airship, which was surprising. Most people hated my guts. I didn't blame them. Sometimes I hated my own guts.

Wraith nudged my leg, bringing me back to reality. The skull over his wolf face often intimidated people, but I loved seeing his eyes shine from inside the eye sockets. It was cute. I petted the top of his skull, and Wraith wagged his tail.

I sat at a small circular table playing cards with two others—Moonbeam and Karna. I liked them. They were good people. Moonbeam said odd things from time to time, I couldn't deny that, and people got suspicious around Karna, but that was on them, not her.

Overall, trustworthy people.

And I knew Moonbeam had a real name—Adelgis, I was pretty sure—but I didn't much care for it. Moonbeam suited him better. It was his honorary pirate name, after all.

Wraith was under the table, by my leg, his panting creating a fine puff of mist with each breath. Wendigo evoked powerful ice, mostly to chill their victims and sap them of heat and strength, but Wraith wasn't trying to kill anyone here. It was just his nature.

Moonbeam's ethereal whelk was nearby, albeit hidden in the light, and I never knew where Karna's doppelgänger eldrin hid. He could be anywhere. By the abyssal hells —*Moonbeam* could secretly be the doppelgänger, and I'd never know. Their disguises were thorough.

"So, what kind of game are we playing tonight, boys?" Karna asked as she shuffled the cards.

It was a standard seven-suit deck found on most islands and ships. The suits always fascinated me—there were ships, anchors, griffons, kirins, crystals, sea serpents, and stars. The best card in most games was the king of kirins, while the worst card was often the two of anchors. As kids, my brother had often teased me by calling me *a two of anchors.* Now that he was dead, I associated the card with him, and the suit had become my favorite.

Moonbeam stared at me, his gaze intense.

"What?" I asked.

"Maybe the twos will be wild in this game," Moonbeam said. "Then it won't be the worst card."

Believe it or not, I constantly forgot that Moonbeam could hear thoughts. I regretted half the things I thought about.

Moonbeam shrugged. "You don't need to worry. Your secrets are safe with me."

Karna tapped a slender finger on the table. "What game are we playing? If you're not going to pick, I will."

She tossed her golden hair over her shoulder. The lantern light caught some of the strands, causing them to glitter. I enjoyed the beauty, but from my experience, the pretty ones always cost more. And not just the harlots.

Tonight, Karna wore plain clothes. She normally wore outfits that fit her body or showed more flesh than most, but that wasn't the case this evening. Her tunic and trousers had been sewn for a man, leaving her swimming in cloth. Her blue eyes and ivory skin remained flawless, as usual, but everything else seemed... casual. Relaxed.

Moonbeam was an entirely different story. When I glanced over at him, he straightened his posture and lifted an eyebrow. The way he sat—you could tell he grew up wealthy. And he went to great lengths to tend to his long, black hair. His silky locks almost beat out Karna's.

"I do take good care of my hair," Moonbeam murmured as he combed through it with his fingers.

"Stop that," I whispered in a harsh tone. "We're playing card games tonight, remember? You wanted to do something normal."

He nodded once.

The airship creaked as our course turned a bit to the east. The portholes gave us a great view of the night sky, and sometimes I would stand by them and stare out at the stars. Our little storeroom had plenty to see, just not inside of it. Well, unless barrels of rum were someone's favorite thing to admire.

"Okay," Karna said with a sigh. "I'm picking the game. We're going to play *desert rivers*." She dealt out the cards, six to each of us. "Fain will start."

"Why me?" I asked.

"Because you're cute." Karna winked and then giggled.

I frowned as I snatched up my cards. "I'm not in the mood."

She dropped the act—returning to her casual speech and posture—and then sighed. "It's much more fun to play cards with people who like to flirt." Karna placed a hand on my knee. "You're a bit cold, you know."

With a simple graze of my blackened fingers, I evoked ice across the top of her hand. Karna jerked away, likely from being startled—I hadn't evoked enough to hurt her.

"I don't mind flirting," I said as I fanned out my cards and examined my hand. "I just want it to go somewhere. Flirting for flirting's sake seems... childish."

"I'd like to flirt for flirting's sake," Moonbeam interjected, his tone serious.

I laughed once. "Of course, you would."

"I've never been involved with anyone before. I'd like to see a master in action."

Karna glanced over at Moonbeam and gave him the once over. She seemed to contemplate something for a long moment before finally exhaling. "You look like you'd be a lot of work," she said as she walked her fingers over his shoulder. "It's a shame because you're rather pretty."

Karna brushed her knuckles across Moonbeam's honeyed cheeks. He didn't even flinch. He just allowed her to stroke his skin. And he stared at her with the intensity of a corpse. *What was wrong with him?* I thought that all too often.

It must have disturbed Karna, too, because she pulled away and frowned. "Flirting requires both people to participate."

"I'd love any pointers you have," Moonbeam said.

"First off—don't act like a dead fish. Nobody likes that."

He nodded. "Your thoughts indicated you wished I had been more excited by your proximity. Should I act that way?"

"Are we gonna play cards or not?" I asked.

Every pirate aboard the *Third Abyss* would have laughed me all the way to the abyssal hells if they heard any part of this conversation. And where was Volke when we needed him? Probably on the main deck with his knightmare, but still. If he were here, we wouldn't be having these absurd conversations.

Wraith wagged his tail, his skull face poking up around the edge of the table as he attempted to get a better look at what was happening.

We each held up our six cards. Karna flipped over the top card from the deck and placed it in the middle of the table. It was a three of sea serpents—a good start. The whole point of *desert rivers* was to slowly increase the sequential number without going backward. The river was complete if it ended in a king. More rivers could be created if there were enough cards. The person with the least number of cards in their hand at the end was the winner. It was typically a drinking game—you took shots for each card you still had in your hand once it was over.

We had some rum, but it wasn't the good kind.

I'd still drink it, though.

I placed a four of ships on the table and then glanced over at Karna.

She smiled as she examined her cards. "The key to flirting is to be interested, but not *too* interested." She placed a six of sea serpents down. Then she narrowed her eyes at Moonbeam, still mirthful and now giggly. "You should listen to the woman when she speaks, but also add a few tales from your own life. Laugh at jokes—but not too long. If a woman touches you, that's a sign she's flirting."

Moonbeam placed down a ten of kirins. "Should I touch her as well?"

"No," I quickly said as I slapped down a duke of anchors. "Never do that."

Karna shot me a glare. "Don't listen to him, Adelgis. You can touch her in the same manner that she touches you. It lets her know her affections are wanted."

I shook my head. "Nope. It doesn't work. I tried. Women hate that. They'll get weird, end the conversation, and leave in a hurry. I guarantee."

"That's because you're half a corpse and half a cutthroat," Karna said, motioning to my frostbitten fingers and then to the pistol on my hip and the ascot hiding my pirate tattoo. "Adelgis looks like a gentleman. Women *like* attention from gentlemen. He'll get different results."

"No, he won't," I muttered under my breath. Then I pointed to the table. "Are you gonna play or not?"

Karna threw down the king of stars. "Round over. Play the second river, Adelgis." She touched his shoulder and smiled.

Without even waiting for a second, Moonbeam placed a hand on her shoulder and nodded. "Okay." Then he played the two of ships to start the second river.

I couldn't hear Karna's thoughts, but I already knew what she was thinking. And Moonbeam must've actually heard them because he removed his hand and sighed.

"I apologize," he muttered. "I'll wait longer next time before reciprocating."

"Flirting with a woman is a dance," Karna said. She scooted her chair closer to Moonbeam's. "You have to do all the steps correctly—to show the woman you're competent in social situations. They like that."

The airship swayed as it turned south. I glanced at the porthole and admired the stars once again before returning my attention to the game. I set down the five of sea serpents and then tucked my hand into my coat pocket. I always kept a memento of my brother on me—a bracelet of woven winter silver. Kalroux always won at card games.

Moonbeam turned to me as though my thoughts were intriguing. They definitely weren't, but sometimes the oddest things fascinated that man. I never knew with him.

"Fain," he said. "You seem to have strong opinions on socializing in general. What's your advice in regards to flirting?"

"Just pay a harlot," I quipped. "Then you don't have to flirt at all."

"Interesting solution." Moonbeam stroked his chin as if giving my comment serious consideration.

Karna placed her hand of cards down on the table. She rubbed at her eyes, her frustration so apparent even the stars outside could see it. Her beauty never waned, even as she placed her forehead down on the table, dramatically giving up on ever helping either of us master the *dance of women.*

"You know what else is easier than flirting with a woman?" I asked Moonbeam. I pointed at him with a frost-bitten finger. "Remaining chaste."

"That's a defeatist attitude," he replied. "And I never said I only wanted to flirt with women. Several men fit my category of acceptable partners."

I tapped Karna's shoulder. When she glanced up, I motioned to the cards on the table. "Men are a totally different story," I said. "Way easier. No games. Just walk up and tell them you're interested. It'll either go somewhere fast or not at all."

Karna straightened her posture. "Are you suggesting that women just play games with their potential partners?"

The silence that followed the question was thick enough to choke on. I leaned back in my chair and offered a nervous chuckle, though I wasn't sure how to pull myself out of this hole. I didn't want to get us kicked off the *Sun Chaser* because I angered their quartermaster.

"Maybe," I said with a shrug. "All I know is—women are odd. They're thinkin' of a million things. Like how socially competent the person they're flirting with is."

She fluffed her blonde hair and stared at me for a long moment. "Surely you don't think I'm like that, do you? I'm helping you two out."

"You're not straightforward," I said.

"How am I not *straightforward*?"

"You're wearing a disguise. All the time." I sat back up in my chair and ran a hand through my dark hair. "I don't even know what you really look like. If that isn't the biggest game of all time, I don't know what is."

Another pause in the conversation. Another bout of

awkward silence. Moonbeam glanced between us, but he said nothing, and his expression betrayed nothing. Was Karna upset? Would she show us her true appearance?

Finally, she pushed away from the table and stood. "My appearance isn't a game." She took a deep breath and then exhaled, her shoulders relaxing. "When I'm like this—I feel like *me*. Do you understand? I'm comfortable. I'm confident. When I'm not like this—when I look like something or somebody else—it isn't *me*."

Moonbeam replied with a curt nod. "I understand."

She shot him a glare. "I know *you know*. We had a long conversation about it." She clenched her jaw and spoke through gritted teeth as she said, "And you better not tell anyone what you saw in my memories, do you understand me? No one."

"I won't. I never have."

Although I didn't know what they were arguing about specifically, I just shrugged again. "Okay. If that's how you feel, then forget I said anything."

Karna returned her attention to me, her eyes narrowed in suspicion.

"I don't really care what you look like without your doppelgänger magic," I said. "I just thought... you were wearing this appearance as a way of tricking us or something. But if this is what makes you comfortable..." I tossed my own cards onto the table. "Stick with it."

I had felt helpless and worthless too often in my life— what I wouldn't give to find something that just gave me *confidence*. I'd never let it go either.

"Fain understands, too," Moonbeam said, turning to face Karna. "His thoughts mirror yours in many ways."

She turned away and crossed her arms. "Well, you say girls play games, but you two have never been a woman.

People judge your appearance all the time. *Not sometimes.* All the time. And it eats at your confidence..." Once again, she exhaled, more of her frustration escaping her. "But I'm glad you won't insist on seeing the *real me.*"

I shook my head. "Well, as far as I'm concerned, this is the real you."

Karna snapped her attention to me, her expression softer than I had ever seen it before.

"See?" Moonbeam said, smiling. "I told you he understood. You don't have to be so defensive around him."

A moment passed. Then Karna gave *me* the once over, as though seeing me for the first time. She took her seat back at the card table and picked up her hand.

"I still think this game would be more amusing if the two of you learned to flirt," she said as she examined each card individually. "There's no harm in it, after all."

I sighed as I snatched up my cards as well. "Except all the frustration," I mumbled.

"I want to learn more," Moonbeam stated without hesitation. "Please, give me another couple of lessons."

"Maybe the next time we play cards." Karna snuck a glance in my direction and then lightly touched my knee. "I think Fain would rather focus on the game for the time being." She pulled away and quickly threw down a queen of kirins. "Maybe then I'll show you something that will surprise the both of you."

Although I wasn't usually affected by her sultry tone, this time was different. My face heated, and Wraith even poked his head out from under the table again, giving me a strange glance. Karna had never touched me so... gently... before. But she wasn't serious.

Or was she?

I gritted my teeth, my face red.

I just stared at the cards, unsure of what to do with my thoughts.

"*She's interested in you,*" Moonbeam said with his telepathy. "*You should say you're interested as well.*"

Why didn't Moonbeam understand that Karna was a woman who could have whoever she wanted? And she obviously had a *thing* for Volke. I didn't compare to him. I didn't have a chance with Karna. Not now. Not ever.

"*You're wrong.*"

I gritted my teeth as I glared at my cards. I wasn't angry at them—I was just angry at myself.

How should I go about flirting with Karna?

"*Just tell her,*" Moonbeam telepathically said, the communication filled with frustration.

I shot him a glower. *Easier said than done.*

"*I can help you.*"

Then help me.

Karna glanced between us. "Are you boys okay?"

Now wasn't the time for flirting. Volke needed a cure for illness, and this airship wasn't meant for matchmaking. The crew members here were wary of us. What if my attempts to be with the woman backfired, and I got us kicked off the ship?

"*You could try later,*" Moonbeam said. "*But don't give up. Karna appreciates the fact that you left a hard life to pursue something noble.*"

Oh, really?

"*And she likes that you're both marked—her harlot tattoo and your pirate tattoo. She sees it as a sign of similarity.*"

I had never thought of that before. It made me think that maybe we did have similarities that I hadn't considered. But it had to wait. I had to build up my courage, and it would be best to wait until Volke's crisis was over.

"*Just don't give up,*" Moonbeam repeated.

"I won't," I muttered aloud. "Just don't go around talkin' about it.

"Back to the game," Karna said, tapping her finger on the table.

10

THE FABLE OF MOS
RYKER BLACKWATER

Before the events of Warlord Arcanist *(Book 6)*

Being bonded with the Mother of Shapeshifters was a unique experience.

Volke had bonded with the world serpent two days ago, and as Gentel the atlas turtle swam back to the city of Millatin, I waited in my room, wondering what I'd do with myself now that I had bonded to such a bizarre creature. No book or guide or mystic seeker could possibly give me advice. No one had ever bonded with the Mother of Shapeshifters before.

The Frith Guild had been too kind. My soft bed was nicer than what I had back on my home island. I rolled onto my back and stared up at the ceiling, unable to sleep despite the warm blankets and comfortable mattress.

My room looked like a layer of the abyssal hells made real.

Dozens of bats hung from the ceiling, their glowing red

eyes watching me with a single-minded intensity. An equal number of rats scurried around the floor, their claws scratching against the wood, creating an incessant chorus of skittering. Occasionally a bat would flutter around the room, adding its wingbeats to the disturbing music.

I swallowed hard.

A large rat leapt onto my bed, its red eyes wide and glowing. It bounded over my blankets until it stopped on my chest. The rat sat up on its back legs, holding its rodent head high.

"You're not sleeping, Ryker," the rat whispered. "You haven't slept the last few nights."

I shifted my attention around the room, to the many tiny creatures plaguing my space. Then I met the rat's gaze. "Must you... look like this? The noise is... bothering me."

"I can revert to my original form."

Before I could say anything, the bats flew from the ceiling, and the rats rushed to the middle of the room. They piled on top of each other and melted, their flesh sticking together like globs of half-melted butter. I sat up in my bed, my skin crawling as they fused into a single, massive layer of skin, muscle, and eyes.

Did she have bones? I doubted it. She jiggled like a jellyfish as she grew to occupy the majority of my room. Organs —or something like organs—jutted out of her gelatinous body, some writhing, some glistening.

The eyes seemed to come and go. Some would emerge, look at me, and then dip back inside her skin. I held my blanket close, uncertain of what to do or say.

This wouldn't help me sleep.

"Is this better?" the Mother of Shapeshifters asked.

I forced half a smile and choked out a chuckle. "Er, yeah. Better. I suppose."

"I can shapeshift into a great many things. Is there a form you would prefer?"

What would I find comforting? My mind drew a blank. It was difficult to think after everything we had been through. The Second Ascension, the world serpent, the long journey —now my weird eldrin wanted to shift into something less disturbing. What was I supposed to say? *Transform into a pile of babies?*

"R-rabbits," I eventually muttered. "How about rabbits?"

The Mother of Shapeshifters exploded.

It happened so suddenly and without warning, that I yelped in shock and jumped backward on my bed, standing on the corner of my mattress, my back against the wall.

She had exploded into dozens of black-furred rabbits, each with the same red eyes as the bats and rats. They had long ears and fluffy tails, and if they hadn't just *appeared,* I might have said they were cute. Instead, it was unnerving to see all the rabbits roll out of the pile, each leaping away and running throughout my room. Some ran to the bookshelf and knocked over a few empty journals. Others jumped onto the windowsill and clumped together, blotting out most of the moonlight.

A single, fat rabbit hopped onto my bed and stared up at me. "You remain tense," it whispered. "Do the rabbits not please you?"

"I just..." I swallowed again, trying to bury my fear and anxiety. "I'm not accustomed to such things."

"What else can I do to put you at ease?"

"I'm not sure..."

"That is unacceptable," the rabbit whispered, its nose twitching. It hopped closer and then placed its front paws on my leg. "We have been bonded for several days, and you have yet to develop or train your magic. This cannot be tolerated."

It was a rabbit—a cute, cuddly rabbit—yet the last sentence had been spoken in such a slow and icy tone that it was the scariest threat I had heard in my life.

I tightened the drawstring on my trousers, my hands unsteady. I had slept in a tunic and pair of trousers every night I had stayed in the Frith Guild, and I was glad I had. For whatever reason, it disturbed me to think the rabbit would touch my bare skin. Could the Mother of Shapeshifters melt into me like she had melted into herself? My imagination played terrible tricks on me.

"O-once I'm rested, I'm sure I'll have the strength to learn your magics," I muttered. "But I do need to sleep."

The rabbit leaned against my leg, its furry cheek resting on my trousers. "I need to remind you that you never passed my trial of worth."

"I... I know that."

"I bonded with you because I owed your brother a life debt. *He* passed my trial of worth. But you must prove yourself. I won't tolerate an unambitious arcanist."

She wouldn't *tolerate* me? What did that even mean?

And I was already painfully aware that I did nothing to earn a mystical creature of my own. Even before I joined the Frith Guild, I had always been skeptical of my prowess and skill. Guildmaster Eventide had approached me, claiming I would become the first god-arcanist, and even then—deep in my bones—I knew there had to be some mistake. I wasn't special in any regard. I was just... Ryker. A man from an island in the middle of nowhere.

In the end, I was proven right. My older brother, Volke, had been the true world serpent arcanist. Not me. The world serpent had refused to even consider me.

"Maybe you should leave my room," I said as I moved my leg away from the rabbit. "I think I'll be able to sleep if I'm alone. It'll be quieter."

The rabbits swarmed around the room, hopping and scratching and knocking over more books. The fat rabbit on my bed jumped into the herd and disappeared as though diving into water. Then, to my fascination, the rabbits piled on top of one another near my door. Once they reached the door handle, they opened it up and fell into the hallway. A few seconds later, the rabbits stormed out into the guild manor house, leaving me alone in my room.

⁂

I slept, but not well.

After the sun had risen in the morning, I dressed in my formal clothing—a vest, a button-up shirt, fine trousers, and black leather boots. I wandered into the hallway, both my eyelids and my feet as heavy as rocks. Where had the rabbits gone? I didn't see any as I made my way to the staircase and down to the first story.

The new apprentices and journeymen of the Frith Guild gave me quick glances as I passed. I kept my gaze down on my feet, trying not to notice. Most arcanists had a seven-pointed star as part of their mark, but mine had nine points. And the "creature" on my arcanist mark wasn't something distinguishable. It was a blob with tiny eyes, nebulous and disturbing.

I had always wanted to be an arcanist, but I figured the best I would ever bond with would be a will-o-wisp or a sprite—something weak, with an easy trial of worth. Now I didn't know what to do... I didn't even know what to say to the others.

Even my eldrin knew I wasn't worthy of this power.

A part of me wanted to speak to my newfound brother on this issue, but we didn't know each other, not really. He had demonstrated his courage, valor, and resourcefulness in overcoming the world serpent's trial, but that didn't mean he had time to help me with my dilemmas. Who else could I turn to? The guildmaster? But how could she help? No one here knew anything about the Mother of Shapeshifters.

I stepped off the last of the staircase, my gaze unfocused.

"Hey," a gruff voice called out.

"Hm?" I glanced up, surprised to see Master Zelfree only a few feet away.

He wore a heavy black coat, and his mimic, a gray cat, sat perched on his shoulder. Her feline features and bright, two-colored eyes gave her an occult appearance. I stared for a moment, surprised a shapeshifter could be so small and adorable.

"We need to talk," Zelfree said. Then he motioned to the front door of the guild house. "Let's go outside."

He turned on his heel and headed for the door, long before I answered. There was purpose in his step—he didn't slow to greet anyone else or even glance in an unusual direction. I quickened my step to keep his pace.

Zelfree threw open the front door and stepped out into the glorious light of a cloudless afternoon. I squinted as I joined him, my curiosity piqued. Why had he led me outside? Was it because he, too, had a shapeshifting eldrin? Did he want to speak with me on the matter?

We took the path through the Frith Guild gardens, and out to the field and small pond. The sole tree cast a long line of shade, but it wouldn't cover so much ground once the sun was above us. I took the opportunity to shield myself from the rays of the sun by hiding in the shadow.

A black rabbit leapt through the grass and hurried to my side. Its intelligent red eyes betrayed its true nature. My eldrin came to a stop at my feet, her rabbit form charming, even if a bit sinister.

Zelfree fidgeted with his coat, patting at all the pockets.

"You put the flask in the dresser drawer, remember?" Traces asked. "You already had too much, and you didn't want to revert to your old ways."

"*I'll* say when I've had too much," he replied.

"But you did say it." Traces wrapped her tail around his neck like a scarf. "You said *I've had too much* and then tossed it into the drawer and fell asleep. That was you."

"That was *drunk me*," Zelfree quipped. "The two of us don't always see eye-to-eye."

"This time, you did."

"Feh."

The ocean winds whipped across the shell of the gigantic turtle. The smell of salt and fish lifted my spirits. It was a new day. Perhaps it wouldn't be so bad.

Master Zelfree glanced over, his eyebrows knitted together in a look of irritation—or perhaps exasperation, I wasn't sure. "Show me your magic," he said. He looked me up and down. "Something small is fine."

"I, uh, haven't manifested any abilities," I muttered.

Zelfree met the rabbit's gaze. Then he glanced back up at me. "You haven't tried using your magic *at all*? Not even for a few seconds? In private?"

I shook my head. "Before this adventure, I'd never heard of the Mother of Shapeshifters, and I can't imagine what any of my abilities would be. Except maybe transforming or something similar." I shivered. "And that sounds unpleasant, to be honest."

"Curse the abyssal hells," Zelfree muttered. He sighed

and then waved his hand around. "Listen, you're probably gonna have to become comfortable with transformations. It's in the name of your eldrin."

"Well, I figured the Mother of Shapeshifters would transform, yes, but that doesn't mean *I* have to. Mimic arcanists don't change their shape."

Zelfree held up a hand. "*Mother of Shapeshifters* is a mouthful. We're not gonna say that every time. From this moment on, you're a MOS arcanist, got it? Simple. Easy. One syllable."

"MOS?" I asked. With a nervous glance, I met the red-eyed gaze of the rabbit. "She isn't a small, green plant that grows on the side of boulders."

"I don't care. It's easier, and she doesn't care either."

"How do you know that?"

Zelfree knelt and patted the rabbit on its soft head. My eldrin leaned into his hand as he scratched behind its ear. "Because if MOS disliked the name, she would've said so." He stood and slapped his hands together to rid himself of any black rabbit fur. "So, do you know the basics of magic? Evocation, manipulation, augmentation? Those are what most new arcanists start off studying."

"I've heard the words," I muttered. Then I rubbed at the back of my neck as I tried to recall everything I had read. "The guildmaster gave me books to study while we were heading to the world serpent's lair. Evocation creates things, manipulation controls things, and augmentation alters things."

Zelfree slowly nodded along with my words. Once I had finished, he shrugged. "For most shapeshifters, augmentation is the most important. Obviously, altering oneself is the essence of shifting your shape."

"Please," I muttered. "Anything but that. Let's start with something else first."

The thought of *melting* and coalescing back together afterward... I shuddered, unable to fight the goosebumps forming over my skin. What would it feel like? Would I be the same after? What would happen to my organs? To my brain? I knew the magic involved wouldn't kill me... but what if it was as painful as death?

Zelfree sighed.

His mimic tilted her head. "Mother, are you sure this man was the right one to be your arcanist?"

MOS tilted her little rabbit head. "No. But I'm willing to give him a chance."

"And if he messes up that chance?"

"I'll do what I always do with people who fail my trial of worth."

Another bluster of wind whistled over the shell of the turtle. The chill didn't put me at ease. What did MOS do with people who failed her trial of worth? I didn't even want to ask. It no doubt involved a terrible death.

Master Zelfree must have sensed my apprehension. He grabbed my upper arm and pulled me closer. "Listen. Stop getting in your own head. You're deep in this situation. There's no escaping now."

"Was that meant to be comforting?" I sarcastically asked.

"Sort of," he quipped. Then he smiled. "What I'm trying to say is—no use worrying about it now. You're in the situation, and the only way out is to do something about it. So, are you going to do something or not?"

"I'll do something," I muttered.

"Good. Then if you don't want to transform yourself, let's start with evocation." Zelfree released my arm. "Doppelgängers have the ability to evoke misdirection and muddled thoughts. Confusion, basically. Why don't you try that?"

"Why would I be able to evoke the same thing doppelgängers do?"

"Because MOS uses her magic to create new doppelgängers. I suspect your magics will share a lot in common with mimics, for the same damn reason."

I glanced down at my hands, examining the lines of my palms. Evoking confusion didn't seem disturbing. Perhaps MOS's magic wouldn't bother me as much as I feared.

"Will I evoke confusion?" I asked the black rabbit.

It stared up at me, its nose twitching. It said nothing.

Was this the first of many tests? I feared that was the case.

"How do I evoke things?" I asked.

Zelfree held up both hands and glanced between them. "Most people evoke from their palms—it's a way to focus your magic into a location and project it out of your body. It doesn't need to be your hands, but you have a lot of control if you evoke from the center of your palm."

"I focus on my magic and project it outward?"

"Like forcing it out. It requires concentration—and if you lose focus, you'll end the manifestation of your magic, understand? Pay attention when you're using your abilities."

My throat went dry. What if I failed to evoke confusion, and MOS decided I was unworthy? What if I could only manifest weak amounts of magic because my soul wasn't as bountiful as others?

Zelfree patted his coat again, unsuccessfully searching for a drink. Then he exhaled and shot me a glare. "Stop. Thinking. Just do it."

"Can't your mimic transform into a version of MOS?" I asked. "Couldn't you show me how it's done then?"

"Traces can't duplicate MOS's form. We've already tried. MOS's magic isn't normal. It isn't even similar to a dragon's. It's too *abstract*, for lack of a better word."

Abstract?

I dwelled on the word for a long while. When I took stock of our surroundings, a tight knot formed in my lower gut. A group of guild arcanists stood at the edge of the grassy field, each staring in our direction. They had come to watch me practice my magic. I didn't blame them. I wanted to see what I could do, too—I just wished I could've done it away from the audience.

"I am a child of the first progenitor behemoth," the rabbit whispered. "His magic is definitely abstract."

Did MOS have to whisper? It seemed her preferred method of communication.

The rabbit continued in a soft voice, "My father is a creature of pure chaos. He had powers of both creation and destruction, but chaos cannot be tamed. He rarely had control."

"The progenitor behemoth is one of the god-creatures?" I asked.

Zelfree nodded. "It's the tenth beast to spawn once a new age of magic has begun."

The rabbit stood on its large back feet and then stared down at its front paws. "Everything my father touched became warped with his *claws of havoc*, and when I was born, he insisted on holding me, if just for a moment."

I caught my breath. "Wait, you didn't always look like this?"

The rabbit shook its head. "In that moment, I was altered by his chaotic magics. I've never been the same."

Traces swished her tail from one side to the other. "I've heard of the beast's claws. I read about it from Illia's new book. It said when the progenitor behemoth fought the apoch dragon, he died, and his body was cast into a nearby mountainside. A great artificer found the corpse and harvested the *claws of havoc* and then crafted three weapons that altered anything they touched. For better or worse."

She added a spooky *oooohh* at the end of her statement and then giggled. I didn't see what was so funny. There were three *weapons* out in the world made from the claws of a god-creature who was so powerful and chaotic that he altered his own children *by accident*? Sounded terrifying.

"What book?" Master Zelfree asked, one eyebrow raised.

His mimic purred. "A book she found on one of her many adventures. She wouldn't tell me where it came from, but it had all sorts of tales about the deaths of the previous god-creatures. Grim reading, but interesting nonetheless."

"And it took you this long to say something?"

"You've been busy." Traces licked her front paw and then rubbed it across her cat-like face. "It's not my fault we don't talk as often as we once did."

The crowd of arcanists outside the guild house continued to grow. I recognized a few now. Zaxis Ren, the phoenix arcanist, and Adelgis Venrover, the ethereal whelk arcanist. I didn't want to practice my nonexistent skills in front of them. I knew it would disrupt my concentration. I'd never maintain my focus, which would lead to embarrassing myself, leading me to fail even more of my training.

Master Zelfree hit me on the shoulder, jerking me from my whirlpool of depression.

"You think too much," he said. "The thing about using your sorcery is this—you have to do it. You can think about it from now and until the sun sets, but you'll never get better unless you try. Success is grown in the garden of failure."

Intellectually, I knew Zelfree was right. But that didn't

stop me from fretting. Ultimately, I didn't care about what most of the arcanists in the guild thought of me, but there was one person whose judgment I feared.

Volke.

We were apparently flesh and blood, and he had done the impossible while also dragging my bleeding body to the finish line. What if he saw me struggling with basic magic? Would he regret saving me? Regret we were related?

It bothered me more than the simple embarrassment of failure.

"Can we do this tomorrow?" I asked in a quiet tone. "Perhaps indoors? Where no one will see?"

Master Zelfree sighed. "Fine. We'll meet in the library tomorrow."

"Thank you."

"*At dawn.*"

"Y-yes, of course."

I paced my room, unable to escape my thoughts.

"I can do this," I muttered to myself. "Get ahold of yourself, Ryker."

Dark clouds blotted out the setting sun, creating an early night. The gloom haunted my surroundings, and I refused to light the lanterns. I wanted no one to know I had been in my room the entire day, so I remained quiet as I did laps from the far wall to the door. Thankfully, I was alone. MOS had spoken with Zelfree and Karna—the only shapeshifters in the nearby area.

Just me and my inescapable thoughts.

A soft knock at my door saved me from another dive into dread. I straightened my vest and walked over, fearful everyone secretly knew I had been hiding. I held my breath, hoping whoever had come calling would leave.

Another set of knocks, this time louder than before.

I sighed as I opened the door. The man in the hallway startled me.

Jozé Blackwater.

Volke's father.

And... my father as well.

I fidgeted with the handle of the door, tempted to close it again without saying a word. Jozé wasn't what I thought he'd be. He stood with most his weight on one leg, dressed in clothing I associated with pirates—a loose tunic, a sloth belt, a tricorn cap on his head, a bandana around his neck, and heavy leather boots. The stubble on his chin, and his black, unkempt hair, didn't help, either.

Apparently, my father had been aboard the *Sun Chaser* for many years—an airship of mercenaries who didn't associate themselves with any guilds. Until now. Captain Devlin had agreed that his arcanists would help the Frith Guild deal with the Second Ascension, but from what I had gathered, most arcanists on the *Sun Chaser* were once criminals, including my father.

That made sense. My mother had been a thief in her younger years.

"Evenin', Ryker," Jozé said. He tipped the front of his cap and half-smiled.

I bowed my head slightly. "Good evening."

"Do you mind if I speak with you?"

I stepped out of the way to allow him into my dark room. Jozé limped inside, though he did so with a slow and steady stride. When he passed a lantern, he waved his hand and lit the inner wick with his magic. The light chased away the gloom, illuminating everything clearly.

Still a simple room, filled with simple things. A book-shelf. A bed. A dresser. The guildmaster had even been kind enough to provide me with a chest of clothing and valuables.

"You know who I am, right?" Jozé asked as he slowly turned around to face me. He stroked at his chin—he used to have a goatee, but it was overgrown now. "Volke told me… all about his discovery in the world serpent's lair."

"I'm aware you're my father," I said.

"Ah. Good."

I said nothing.

He said nothing.

We both just stood still and quiet, and the longer it went on, the tighter my chest became. My mother hadn't spoken much about my father, and I had always assumed that meant he was a lowlife. But Jozé was an arcanist—the mark on his forehead had a phoenix wrapped around the seven-pointed star. I had seen his rare blue phoenix flying the skies on occasion, and I had known him as a blacksmith long before I discovered he was my father.

It all seemed respectable.

"Zelfree said you were struggling with your magic," Jozé finally said, breaking the uncomfortable silence. "It must be hard to have such an *odd* eldrin."

I let out a sigh of relief. "You have no idea. I'm more afraid of my own magic than anything else." I stared at my hands, noting how badly they still shook.

Jozé leaned against the nearest wall and lifted his bad foot. He took a moment to relax a bit, but he offered me a genuine smile once he did. "So, look—I want to say I'm sorry. But also, I'm glad you're here."

"What do you mean?" I asked.

"I'm sorry I wasn't there for you as a child, I mean." Jozé

crossed his arms, his whole stance rigid. "I didn't know. I swear. Aarona must've been carryin' you when she left the Isle of Ruma."

"I understand. My mother rarely spoke of you, so I don't have much of an opinion of you one way or another."

"Ah. Well." He darkly chuckled. "Apparently, speaking with Volke was just Lady Destiny's way of giving me a test run before I had to speak to another son."

I half-laughed at the joke. What else was I supposed to say, though? I wasn't sure what the man wanted from me.

"Listen," Jozé said, "I came to see you to... break this awkwardness between us, but to also offer my services." He pushed away from the wall and forced himself to stand tall. "I want to do right by you. I'm not an expert mentor, but I do know a thing or two about imbuing magical items. If you ever want to make Mother of Shapeshifter trinkets or artifacts, I'll teach you everything I know."

"We call her MOS now," I said.

"Huh?"

"The Mother of Shapeshifters. We call her MOS."

Jozé slowly nodded, his eyes narrowed in confusion. "Okay. I guess that's a tad easier."

I nodded.

My overworked mind couldn't help but cast doubt on the situation. What if Jozé was disappointed in me? And why wouldn't he be? Comparing me to Volke—I was nothing.

I didn't know if he could sense my sudden shift in mood, but Jozé stepped closer and returned to genuinely smiling. "Well, now that we have all *that* out of the way, I wanted to offer you some advice."

"Really?"

He clasped my shoulder and squeezed. "That's right.

Look, as a new arcanist, you're going to have to go through a lot of steps to master your magic. Don't get discouraged by the small things, hear me?" He tightened the grip on my shoulder. "It's okay to take things one step at a time. Just keep taking steps. You've only failed when you stop."

"That's rather generic," I said as I ran a hand through my hair. "You wouldn't happen to know anything about MOS, would you? Or the progenitor behemoth?"

Jozé gave me a long and silent stare. Then he exhaled. "I don't know a damn thing about the god-creatures. Well, besides that their parts would make for great trinkets and artifacts."

"Hm. Probably."

He released my shoulder and then stepped back. After a quick glance to the window, he said, "Well, Zelfree will help you learn your magic. I'm certain. Just do as the man says. To the letter." Then he moved toward the door of my room. "In the meantime, I'm helping Volke with his funeral."

"*Volke's funeral*?" I asked, half gasping.

Jozé chuckled. "He didn't die. I meant for Luthair. Volke is torn up about losing his first eldrin. Says he wants to honor him before anything else happens."

"Ah. Right."

"But if you need anythin', just come callin', all right?"

I nodded.

Then Jozé headed for the door of my room. I allowed him to go, thankful he had come to speak with me, even if just briefly. Clearly, it was still awkward for both of us. One step at a time.

But he hadn't helped me with my MOS problem. I didn't want to disappoint her, which meant I would have to develop my magic, even if it meant warping my body into unspeakable shapes.

The Frith Guild library wasn't the largest I had been in, but it still impressed me.

They had an entire room dedicated to books on the back of the atlas turtle. How was that not impressive?

Master Zelfree and his eldrin, Traces, sat on a nearby table, watching me with half-lidded eyes. They both looked as though they'd had a rough night. Probably not as rough as mine, however. I hadn't slept at all. Whenever I closed my eyes, I imagined my bones twisting and rearranging themselves—my skull collapsing, my organs bursting out of my skin—all the gruesome aspects of shapeshifting.

My eldrin sat on the floor next to me, a portion of her still in the shape of a black rabbit. It glanced up at me, its red eyes almost twinkling with anticipation. I wasn't as enthusiastic.

"What're you thinking about?" Master Zelfree asked, his tone curt. "You fretting about your magic again?"

"N-no, of course not."

"Then what?"

"Uh..." I searched for a quick topic and finally asked, "How do knightmares come into existence?"

"The ruler of a nation is assassinated or murdered," Zelfree said as he rubbed at his temple. He scrunched his eyes closed and groaned. "Is that it?"

"Well, why didn't King Rishan's death result in a knightmare? Shouldn't there be one in the world serpent's lair?"

Zelfree shrugged. "Well, I wasn't there to see what happened, but from what Volke told me, Rishan and his sister, Evianna, had a duel. Fighting honorably, and then dying honorably, doesn't result in knightmares. Only treachery that results in death. Like assassination."

"So Rishan's corpse *won't* spawn a knightmare?"

Zelfree stopped rubbing and then opened his eyes. He glared at me, his jaw clenched. "You're just stalling for time, aren't you?" He cursed under his breath. "Damn kids these days." Then he slid off the table and walked over to me. His slow gait betrayed his fatigue.

"Look," he said. "I don't know why you're so hesitant. You've been nervous like this since Eventide brought you into the guild. At least with the god-creature, I could understand. It's a big responsibility. But that's not the case anymore. You're already bonded. *This is the fun part.*"

I shook my head and shrugged. "I don't know what to tell you. I've lived on a tiny island my whole life. I've never thought of adventure, or fighting seadogs, or dastards out to control whole nations." I threw my hands in the air. "I never asked to be a MOS arcanist. I'm just…"

"Overwhelmed?" Zelfree asked.

I nodded.

"Well, prepare to be just the right amount of *whelmed*," he quipped. "You don't need to fight seadogs or dastards. That's not in any contract you signed or agreement you made."

"But…"

"All you have to do today is evoke something." Zelfree snapped his fingers. "It'll be over in a flash. C'mon. I need some more sleep, anyway. Just do a little evocation for me, and everyone can go back to their room and dwell. I'll dwell on napping, and you'll do whatever you do that causes you to pace all damn day."

I straightened my posture and narrowed my eyes. "How did you know about that?"

"I have my ways." Then Zelfree motioned to the library. "Go on. Evoke something."

The rabbit at my feet nodded its head.

I let out a short sigh and swallowed the last of the doubt I had been holding on to. Then I held up a hand, my heart practically slamming into my throat. Why was I so afraid? A part of me disliked the change, but that wasn't the main reason. I had been nervous when I entered the world serpent's lair, but it hadn't been until we fought the Second Ascension that I truly understood what was happening.

Everyone, including myself, almost died. Volke lost his eldrin. We were halfway to the abyssal hells, and we barely made it out with our lives. Yet here I was, preparing to go back in. Master Zelfree said I wouldn't have to fight, but I knew I would. I couldn't sit back and do nothing—and MOS was a powerful mystical creature. I had to use my new magic to help others. That was what Volke would do.

I had to as well.

Which meant there was a good chance I would die. A high chance if I were being honest.

Did I want that? No. But Zelfree was right about my situation—I was already deep in it. No turning back now.

I closed my eyes and attempted to force my magic out through my palm. Would anything happen? I hoped so. If I mastered my magic, there was at least a small chance I lived. If I *didn't* master my magic, I was sure to fail. The Second Ascension would come for MOS, and then they'd get rid of me.

Which meant—even though I was loath to admit it—I would have to master shapeshifting as well. I could disguise myself then.

I shook the thoughts from my head and focused. A power rushed through my body, and the sensation gave me hope. I concentrated on my palm, and something happening. An odd feeling swirled throughout my body, tingling as though I had lost blood flow to a limb.

"Whoa," Zelfree said. "You did it."

I opened my eyes and stumbled a step backward, my head spinning. *I* felt confused. Was that supposed to happen?

Zelfree had to grab the nearby table. "Wow. That's way more powerful than anything I've felt from a doppelgänger. Interesting…"

The rabbit hopped onto the nearby table. It gave me the once over as I steadied myself on a nearby chair. "Excellent," it whispered. "But there is more you can do. Evocation can be intensified, and you must learn more."

"Okay," I muttered, the whole library spinning as though caught in a storm.

Traces—seemingly unaffected—just licked at her paw and rubbed her face with it. "Well, that wasn't difficult, was it? So much drama and fuss over nothing."

"We should try it a few more times," Zelfree said as he pulled himself back onto a table. He settled himself and stretched. "Just to make sure you got it."

"You said I just had to evoke something once," I said.

"Well, you need the practice, kid. Besides, it won't kill you to do it a couple more times. Take a seat in a chair and get to it. I want to go as much as you do."

I exhaled as I sat down. Once the spinning stopped, I held up my hand again. Perhaps I should speak with Karna? I had never seen her evoke confusion, but perhaps she would have a few pointers for me.

With all my concentration, I focused again.

And then I wondered what Volke would think if he saw me now…

11

THE FABLE OF THE DREAMWEAVER
(PART 3)
ADELGIS "MOONBEAM" VENROVER

Before the events of Warlord Arcanist *(Book 6)*

Night after night, I searched for the dreams of others.

I traveled the world while sleeping, though I couldn't make out the details of each territory or location. It was more a feeling. The slope of the mountains, the grass of the valleys, the chill of the rivers—I felt them as I passed over during my astral projection. I imagined this was the same feeling an incorporeal ghost might have. Feeling the environment, but never touching it.

And it made sense. My magic came from an ethereal whelk, and ethereal whelks were born from the bodies of drowned children. Their magic stemmed—at some level— from death. It made me wonder if the realm of dreams was somehow tethered to some sort of afterlife. While sleeping, people didn't breathe as much, and their heart rate slowed. Were they closer to death then? It seemed so.

But I shook the thoughts away to focus on my task.

I could reach the dreams of the abyssal leech without much trouble, but it was still difficult to get a clear picture of everything happening around it. Was it because of our vast distance or because I lacked in magical ability?

Tonight, when I entered the dream, I heard something interesting.

"The soul forge's magic is unique," a man said—the abyssal leech arcanist.

The abyssal leech lived inside the man's body, and it was difficult to separate them. When the leech spoke, it did so with the man's mouth. I could only tell the difference from their word choice or context clues.

"The magic that creates the god-creatures is purer than other mystical creatures," the man said again, but this time, it was the leech speaking. "Once we've master this, it'll be easier to manipulate the magic of our enemies. God-arcanists who oppose the Autarch will succumb to our powers."

All the leech did was work on his magic. His arcanist tirelessly focused—even dreamed about—his training. But this information wasn't as helpful as I thought it would be. What did it matter if I knew they were training? I needed to do something more. Something *useful.*

If I had more control over my magic, I'd be able to slip into deeper memories, and view everything, but the distance—once again—hindered me. I had to improve.

Felicity, ever a faithful companion, floated with me in the dreamscape. *"Don't give up, my arcanist,"* she telepathically said. *"We'll find more information. We're bound to!"*

Although my mind was hundreds of miles from my body, I felt the forceful shake of someone jostling my shoulder. It jarred me enough that I lost concentration and I slipped out of my astral projection.

I jerked upright, my heart slamming against my ribs. I

was basically helpless while I searched the world for dreams —my physical body just lying there, on my bed, unable to move until my mind returned.

"There you are," Master Zelfree said. "Get up, Adelgis."

... Finally awake after all that shaking... I could've killed him three times over...

After blinking my eyes for several moments, I glanced up at him. He stood with a casual posture—typical for him —his hands in his trouser pockets, his shirt untucked, and his short, black hair clumped to one side. Had he just woken up? The bags under his eyes told a story of a sleepless night, and he had no boots, just bare feet.

His inner thoughts rattled around my skull. It was difficult to keep his voice separated.

I turned my groggy attention to the window. Night. The glow of the moon didn't compare to the lantern next to my bed, but it still shone through the glass, offering illumination.

"Did you need me to weave your dreams?" I asked as I turned back to face Master Zelfree. "I apologize. I thought they were no longer an issue."

His thoughts turned sour.

... All I need is uninterrupted sleep, dammit... Why must everyone do their oddities after nightfall? ...

"It's not that," Zelfree said, a hint of irritation in his voice. "I want to know what you're doing in here."

"Pardon?"

"I'm a mimic arcanist. I can sense magic—and magic use. You've been doing something in here every night for longer than the stars can remember." He narrowed his dark eyes into something discerning. "Most men your age go out and find real partners. You don't have to create yourself a fantasy world to get your jollies."

... I swear kids get weirder every decade...

"E-excuse me?" It took most of my sleep-addled mind to even process what he was implying. With my face red, and my heart still pounding, I pulled at the collar of my shirt to get some cool air across my body. I used my powers fully clothed, which often left me soaking in sweat, but I hated the idea of awaking naked in front of someone. "I'm not weaving myself fantasy worlds, Master Zelfree. I'm searching for people."

Silence.

Even Master Zelfree's thoughts seemed to come to halt for a moment. Then he regained his composure and said, "Searching how? And for whom?"

"Well," I said, brushing back my long hair. "I'm searching for my father. I thought I might be able to see his dreams, and his memories, and provide the guildmaster with the next few steps of his plans."

Zelfree rotated a hand, motioning for me to continue.

... Is he intentionally obtuse? Sometimes I wonder...

"I don't mean to be vague," I said with a nervous chuckle. "I apologize—I've been improving my ability to, well, *project* my consciousness over long distances to enter the dreams of others."

"You've never told me about this."

"Yes, I know. But we've been busy, and the priorities are—"

"Next time inform me you have these powers," Zelfree snapped, cutting me off. "I don't care how frantic things get. It's important to know."

I nodded once and then sighed. "I wasn't sure it was relevant until I had discovered important information."

"I know you're not an apprentice anymore," Zelfree said, pinching the bridge of his nose. "And I know you're older than a lot of the journeymen here, but you still have a lot of growth. You hurt yourself with that leech stunt, and you shouldn't try to strong-arm your way out of the situation. I can help you."

... Everyone always tries to handle hardships alone... Ha! Even me. But the kid doesn't need to know that...

Zelfree stopped rubbing his nose and then stared down at me with an inquisitive expression.

... Damn. You can hear everything anyway, can't you? ... Even if you can, you know I'm still right...

"Again, *I'm a mimic arcanist*," Zelfree said aloud, almost indignant. "I can have my eldrin transform, and then I can use your magic alongside you. I can help. C'mon." He waved me out of the bed. "C'mon. I'll help you master this."

I glanced around, staring at my bed. "That is a wonderful suggestion, truly, but I tend to practice right here. On my bed. So... why would we leave?"

... Eh... This kid is gonna make me drag another bed in here, isn't he? ...

Master Zelfree dismissively waved his hand. "Your eldrin searches dreams with you, correct? It's probably easier to travel together in these dreams if we're close." He walked to the door of my room and placed a hand on the handle. "I'll be back. Then we'll improve your dream-stepping together."

My room wasn't large.

Correction—only master arcanists had large bedrooms in the Frith Guild House. We had space limitations being atop the back of a giant atlas turtle, so it was logical, but that didn't change the fact. My bed was on one side of the room, and Zelfree had dragged a cot and placed it against the opposite wall. We were as far apart as we could get and there was still only about three feet between us.

We both lay back on our respective beds. I wasn't sure if Master Zelfree would intuitively know how to enter dreams, so I turned to face him. Once he went, I would follow.

Master Zelfree had his fingers laced and tucked behind his head like a pillow. He stared at the ceiling, his eyes unfocused. His forehead bore the arcanist mark of an ethereal whelk—I didn't know where Traces had gone to, but somewhere she had transformed into a floating magical sea snail just so Master Zelfree could aid me.

I appreciated her efforts.

... I wonder how Volke and Ryker are doing...

Zelfree's thoughts shifted from topic to topic with little rhyme or reason.

... Guildmaster has been acting strange... Am I missing the signs of infection, like I had with Ruma? ... No. She has a true form eldrin... She can't get infected... It has to be something else...

Zelfree scrunched his eyes shut and then opened them again.

... Focus, Everett... You're here to help the Venrover kid...

He glanced over at me and realized I had been staring at him this entire time. Zelfree exhaled, and to my curiosity, it somehow sounded sardonic.

I held my hands together on my chest. "Is this awkward for you?"

"You're the one making it awkward," Zelfree snapped. Then he returned his gaze to the ceiling. "Just... no more questions. We have things to do."

... How do I keep getting into situations like this? ...

"Like what?" I asked. "Surely you've never done *this* before."

Zelfree gritted his teeth loud enough for me to hear.

"My apologies," I muttered.

... Gotta watch what I think around him... Focus... C'mon, Everett...

"I do have a question I've wanted to ask you," I said.

"What is it?" Zelfree snapped.

"If the god-creatures are spawning in response to all the magical corruption brought about by the arcane plague, will they stop spawning now that we have a cure?"

Zelfree scoffed. "I doubt it. We can cure people of the plague once they catch it—but not after it corrupts them. Vethica has already tried."

"So, it'll linger in this world for a long while? Destroying mystical creature and arcanists, both their body and mind?"

Silence settled between us, but Zelfree's thoughts remained loud and active.

... Why is he so depressing? ... He concocts the worst scenarios for us to imagine...

"I don't want to be surprised," I muttered. "I like knowing the challenges we'll face. And the source of the arcane plague, as well as those still infected, will need to be dealt with. Well, by the god-arcanists, I suppose."

"Enough of this," Zelfree growled. "We're dream-diving now. No more questions. No more weird statements."

He closed his eyes and his borrowed ethereal whelk magic flared for just a second, sending his consciousness into the realm of dreams. I rested back on my bed and used my magic to join him—augmenting my wakefulness and manipulating the dreamscape so that I could control every detail.

Sure enough, both Felicity and Master Zelfree were waiting for me. Interestingly, the dream we had entered was an exact duplicate of my room in the Frith Guild—but whose dream was this? There was one bed, one cot, a bookshelf, and a dresser. Exactly like mine. It wasn't nighttime outside, however. A pinkish dawn, mixed with the vibrant color swirls of northern lights, illuminated the sky. It was glorious, but clearly a product of imagination.

"Did you create this?" I asked Felicity.

Her iridescent shell glittered as she twirled in the air. "*No, my arcanist. It wasn't me.*" Her telepathy sounded playful, and I wondered what had caused her to become so excited.

"I created it," Master Zelfree stated. "This is what I imagined as I used the ethereal whelk manipulation." He crossed his arms as he glanced around, one eyebrow lifted. "It wasn't as difficult as I imagined, but I haven't woven anything impressive yet. Or moving."

I examined the beauty of the sky a second time, taking note of the many colors. "Still. This is impressive. How did you produce something with so much detail on your first try?"

"I've been doing this for longer than I'd like to admit," Zelfree quipped, his tone dour.

... If I weren't quick at mastering new types of magic, I'd have been dead a long time ago...

"But whose dream are we in?" I asked.

Zelfree scratched the stubble on the underside of his chin. "Ryker's. I've been... helping him master his Mother of Shapeshifters's magic."

"He dreams of the guild?"

"I don't know. All I thought when I was using this magic was... *I hope his dreams are peaceful.*"

The tranquility of the sky, mixed with the stillness of the guild house, made for a calm dream. Zelfree had woven the perfect combination on his first go.

"So, you helped Ryker during the day?" I asked as I stepped closer.

Zelfree nodded.

"Are you're helping me at night?"

"It's rough for a mentor, Adelgis," he said.

"Maybe you shouldn't have taken on so many apprentices," I said. I had meant it as an honest comment, but even *I* felt it came out a bit sarcastic.

Zelfree scoffed. "You all turned out fine, didn't you?" When I didn't reply, he smirked. "Besides, everyone I took in was because they weren't wanted elsewhere. And Karna and I are the only shapeshifter arcanists here, so I had to be the one to train Ryker."

"So that puts you at eight people you're training?" I said —again, more sarcastic than I wanted.

... I swear he wants me to punch him... He even looks remarkably like his father...

I tensed, and Zelfree's whole demeanor changed that instant. "I'm sorry," he said. "That's not what I meant." He forced an exhale and gestured to the surroundings. "Just tell me how you're searching for people."

Felicity floated between us, but she didn't say a thing. Her tentacles waved in the air—I always enjoyed her odd mix of snail and octopus.

I relaxed and then placed my hand on his shoulder. It surprised me how much taller Zelfree was. I never thought of myself as short until I stood by men like him and Volke. It made me wonder if people would like me more if I had just a few more inches of height.

Then again, the people who admired Master Zelfree seemed to be fifty-fifty, so perhaps height would do nothing for me.

Zelfree stared at my hand on his shoulder. "I hear people calling you *Moonbeam*."

I lifted both eyebrows as I nodded once. "Uh, that's correct."

He gave me a sideways glance.

... You're acting like a moonbeam right now...

After a nervous chuckle, I said, "With apologies, I don't tend to have much company."

"*Ah-hem*," Felicity said, poking me in the thoughts.

"Well, except for my eldrin," I said. "I don't usually have much company. Plus, with the ability to hear thoughts, and to speak telepathically, I tend to forget that verbal words are preferred."

"I don't care if you speak or use telepathy," Zelfree said as he grabbed my arm. "Just explain the methods to your magic so I can test a few things."

After a long moment mulling over his question, I took a deep breath and said, "I search for something familiar. I found my sister hundreds of miles away, but I couldn't sense anyone else in my family home, not even the people I know. Gevnin, the gatekeeper, used to watch me and my sister out in the gardens... I've known him more than a decade. But I couldn't sense his dreams..."

"And you don't know why you can sense your sister's dreams and not Gevnin's?" Zelfree asked.

I sighed. "It vexes me." With a wave of my hand, I wove the dreams around us to create a hair tie. Then I pulled back my hair and secured it into a ponytail. "I've also found the abyssal leech that used to reside in me, but not my father... I understand the leech. It lived in me for many years. But my father? I should know him well enough. Wouldn't you agree?"

Master Zelfree stared at me, his eyes shifting focus from

me to the floor to the window. He pondered my question, though he said nothing as he slowly walked around the room. He grazed his fingers across the surface of the dresser, as if testing his sense of touch.

"But it's easier to manipulate dreams when you're closer to a sleeping person?" he finally asked.

"Oh, yes," I said, nodding with my own words. "I can enter nearby dreams without knowing a person."

"And in theory, it's easier for people you do know? Well, some people. Your sister. The leech."

"Yes." I held my hands together once again, trying to connect whatever dots Zelfree had formed. "Are you trying to suggest something?"

"Why don't we try going to Volke's dream?" Zelfree said. "I want to see how you do it."

"Very well."

I once again placed a hand on his shoulder, and Felicity floated close to me. Zelfree grumbled something, but he didn't object. With him being close, I concentrated on Volke and found his dreams in an instant—I knew Volke well, both his thoughts and his preferences. And his dreams had been interesting the few times I had helped him sleep through a restless night.

I hadn't done that in some time, however. Volke hadn't required my assistance since he had returned from the world serpent's lair.

Master Zelfree and I slipped out of Ryker's dream and entered Volke's without much trouble. The event jarred me a bit, however. The sensation of moving from one dreamscape to another had never felt so *electrical*. It was as if I had been momentarily shocked.

I shivered and then glanced around, confused as to our location. Felicity hovered around my head, while Master

Zelfree and I stood on a small island in the middle of a vast ocean. In the distance, a giant tree sprouted from the water —the world serpent's lair—and circling in the sky were birds of all kinds, from seagulls to vultures.

Most of the birds weren't even the type to be found near the ocean, yet here they were, creating dark clouds in the sky, their wingbeats a song of flight.

When I returned my attention to the ocean, I noticed the top of a castle jutting out above the waves. Half of it was still submerged, but the portion I could see glittered with marble, obsidian, and steel. I had never seen such a castle—was it something born of imagination? Or was it a real location, like the world serpent's lair?

"*There he is,*" Felicity said, pointing with a little tentacle.

Volke swam through the waves, heading for the mysterious castle in the distance.

"I've never seen Volke have a dream like this before," I muttered.

Zelfree rubbed at his arms. "Heh. This is a lot better than what it could've been."

... I remember being Volke's age...

"You seem wrapped up in remembering things from the past," I said, lifting an eyebrow. "Is everything all right?"

He narrowed his eyes. "What did I say about my past? *You discuss it with no one.* Not even me." Zelfree leaned his head from one side to the other, his neck popping with odd sounds. "The magic here is... odd."

I nodded. "I've never felt this before."

"Ever?"

"No. But I have a theory. This is the result of Volke's magic as a god-arcanist."

Master Zelfree placed both his hands on his hips and sighed. "*Everything* is the result of his new magic, apparently. He says the same damn thing. Just the other day he claimed his hair was growing faster, and that his eyesight had improved."

"When I see the dreams and memories of the abyssal leech, my father is instructing the arcanist on how to manipulate god-creature magic." I enjoyed the ocean breeze for a moment as I recalled every detail. Then I met Zelfree's gaze. "My father claims that the magic of the god-creatures is different from all other creatures and are in a league of their own. Who knows what kinds of effects that would have on their arcanists?"

"I'm not saying it's outside the realm of possibility," Zelfree said. "I'm just—" He cut himself off and held his breath for a moment. His eyes narrowed and his focus shifted to the castle in the distance. At some point during our conversation, it had risen higher above the waves. "Wait. The god-creatures have magic substantially different from all other mystical creatures?"

"That's right."

"But they have magic similar to each other?"

I shrugged. "My father seems to think so. The abyssal leech arcanist is working on manipulating the magic of the soul forge so that he can later manipulate enemy god-creatures. If my father is correct—and he usually is—that means the magic of one god-creature is sufficiently similar to the others as to be near identical. Or at least deriving from the same source, if that makes any sense."

"Like all the god-creatures were made from the same clay?" Zelfree asked.

"That's an apt analogy, though strange."

Again, Zelfree went quiet. He turned his attention to the castle in the distance. It had risen again—waves broke against the walls, and the more I saw, the more I realized it was a massive structure. Perhaps it was a fortress, rather than just a castle.

Volke continued to swim toward it, his head bobbing in the waves. Felicity watched with rapt fascination, unable to look away.

What was Volke searching for? Why dream of this?

A small part of me wanted to manipulate the dream so I could help him reach the submerged building, but I decided to wait. I had to use my magic for more important things in the meantime.

"Why don't you do the same thing the abyssal leech arcanist is doing?" Zelfree asked as he snapped his fingers.

I raised both eyebrows. "What now?"

"Become familiar with this magic. Watch the dreams of Volke and his world serpent, soaking in this *feeling* of being here. And then search the world for similar sorcery. If all the god-creatures share the same level and power of magic, that would help pinpoint them, right?"

I caught my breath, my excitement returning at the thought. "That's a clever idea," I muttered. "I had never considered it."

Would it work? I wouldn't know until I tried.

A crash of thunder drew my attention. The sky of Volke's dreamscape had shifted to a storm with the speed only a nightmare could bring. The ocean swirled, dragging Volke away from the castle and pulling him into the depths. He swam against it, but it wasn't enough. The violence of the ocean, and the crash of the waves, battered him again and again.

Master Zelfree and I shielded our eyes from the sudden downpour of rain, and I wondered where all this had come from. Was Volke feeling nervous or helpless in his new situation? No—it couldn't be. He was a god-arcanist now.

I waved my hand, hoping to weave his dream into something pleasant. My magic struggled to alter anything—it was like using a paint brush without having any paint on the bristles. I wasn't doing anything.

Determined not to be outdone, I took a deep breath and concentrated. With as much focus and power as I could muster, I tried again. I ripped at the fabric of the dream, unraveling the storm and replacing it with clear skies and gentle tides. I had never experienced something this difficult before—was it really the result of the god-creature's magic?

I exhaled and then gasped down breath, my body in the waking world dappled in sweat. I had altered the dream, but it had cost me. I pulled my hand close and rubbed at my knuckles. If Master Zelfree's theory was correct, I would have to become accustomed to this god-level magic so I could find the dreams of others, such as the soul forge.

If I could do that, perhaps I could physically locate them.

And that would be a boon beyond boons—we needed to know their location if we were going to stop the Second Ascension. The Occult Compass was useful, but without a piece of the god-creature, it was virtually useless.

"What was that?" Zelfree asked as he stared up at the clear sky. "A hiccup?"

"I think I know what I need to do," I said, ignoring his observation. "Thank you, Master Zelfree. You are, in fact, a talented mentor."

Six nights in a row, I entered Volke's dreams just to soak in the magic of the world serpent. He had the same dream every night. A castle in the ocean. A storm. Something drowning him. Each time I changed the dream so that he didn't have to suffer through the impossible, but occasionally I wondered what would happen if I allowed it to play out.

But Volke's dreams hadn't been my only priority. Tonight I had another dream with Biyu.

I wove together all her favorites, piecing together a puzzle of fantasy and whimsy. I thought I had done a decent job, but something was off.

Biyu danced around the room as a princess, but this time with no excitement or energy in her steps. Even when the dashing dragon arcanist prince arrived, she barely offered him a smile or a glance. Had my dreamweaving lost its luster?

Her thoughts seemed strange.

... This isn't right... I'm wasting time...

How could she think she was wasting time? She was asleep.

As Biyu danced near my location by the wall—dressed in shimmering pale pink, her hair up in an elegant bun—she looked at me with two eyes, no eyepatch. I smiled, but Biyu didn't smile back. She let go of her dancing partner and hurried over to me, holding the skirt of her dress as she moved. She hadn't interrupted the festivities. The dream continued without her—music playing in the ballroom, indistinct chatter and laughter from the guests.

"Are you all right?" I asked as Biyu approached. "Have I done something wrong?"

Biyu shook her head. When she reached my side, she took my hand and squeezed my palm. "Adelgis," she whispered, "I don't want these dreams anymore."

... They're not needed...

I furrowed my brow, my chest tight. "A-are you sure? I can always weave you something else. Or have some other narrative."

"No, thank you."

... It's just a waste...

"I don't think you're a waste," I said as I leaned down to get eye level with her. "You have no reason to think that way. I'll help you as long as you need."

Biyu tilted her head to the side. "I'm not a waste, Adelgis. I just thought... Using your powers for me was a waste. Shouldn't you be doing something else? I've had this dream many times already."

I forced the best smile that I could as I straightened my posture. "This is all my magic is good for, Biyu. You don't need to worry about wasting my time. This is how I'm useful."

... Useful... Like Captain Devlin said...

Biyu once again shook her head. "Captain Devlin told me something." While impersonating Devlin's voice, Biyu said, "*Stop thinking of yourself as useful or not useful, kid. Sometimes you will be. Other times, you won't. You can't base your happiness on that.*"

I chuckled. "Well, I suppose that's good advice?"

"Wait! He said more. Give me a second to remember it perfectly..." Biyu cleared her throat and held my hand close to her heart. She resumed imitating Devlin's voice as she said, "*Know the things and skills that make you happy and be the best at those. Not good at those. The best. You'll never work a day in your life if you do what you love, and you'll always be making your own happiness, no matter who you're with or where you go.*"

When I smiled this time, it was genuine. I knew Captain

Devlin to be an interesting man, but I wished I had spent more time with him when I was aboard the *Sun Chaser*.

"I'm really good at helping people," Biyu said, placing a hand on her heart. "And it makes me happy, which is why you should stop the dreams." She glanced over her shoulder, staring at the imaginary people I had woven for her stories. "All of this... I don't need this anymore. And I'm sure there are plenty of other people who need your magic now." When Biyu turned back to me, her smile went to her ears. "I want to help *you* now, Adelgis!"

... I help everyone... And then I'll be making my own happiness! ...

She kept hold of my hand, and I squeezed it in return.

"Discovering new things makes me happy," I said. It was a simplistic way of articulating my desires, but at its core, it was true. "And I have been using my magic to do more of that, as of late."

"You should keep going," Biyu said with a giggle. She tugged on my hand. "And if you think I can do anything to help, you just ask, okay? I need to pay you back for all the help you've given me."

"I think Devlin helped you the most this time."

Biyu half-frowned. "Well, I only spoke to him because of you, Adelgis. You told me he appreciated me and... and that's when I had the courage to ask him if I was useful." She resumed her radiant smiling.

... You're the nicest person I know... I want to be more like you...

"Uh, well, thank you," I said, unsure of how to respond to such a compliment. "I'm glad I helped, even if just a tiny bit."

"Now end this dream! You have things to discover, and I

don't want to stop you from doing the thing that'll make you happy."

When I returned to Volke's dream on the seventh night, I was prepared.

Felicity floated around my head, twirling as she went. Occasionally she tucked her tentacles into her shell, but other times she reached out and stroked the long locks of my black hair.

I knew the mistake I had been making. I had focused too much on Volke's dream, and not enough on the ambient magic. Instead of weaving the dream to end the storm, I stood on the tiny island in the middle of the storm-ridden ocean, and I closed my eyes. My goal wasn't to get to know Volke better, or to understand his thoughts—it was to soak in the unique feeling of the world serpent's magic.

If I could *feel* and *remember* this sensation, then perhaps I could use it to locate others.

It was electrifying—the magic hit like a lightning bolt whenever the dream shifted. Was the world serpent somehow inadvertently causing the dream? I couldn't be certain, but that was a mystery for another day. Instead, I held on to the electric feeling as I left Volke's dream.

With all my concentration and willpower, I searched beyond the Frith Guild and reached out to the surrounding territories. My mind stretched over the waters, land, and mountains—grasping in the darkness, hoping to stumble upon another familiar feeling.

"*You're doing it,*" Felicity telepathically said. "*Keep going, my arcanist.*"

Her encouragement pushed me forward. I reached out

as far as I could, and just as I was about to break, the edge of my awareness caught the same electrifying feeling.

It pulsed with power, like thunder in a dark cloud.

And as soon as I knew what it was, I focused on the location.

The north. Beyond the Isle of Ruma. Beyond the pirate city, Port Crown. Somewhere in the ice, where the wendigo roam. And its thoughts filtered into mine. The god-creature thought of life, and limbs, and renewal, and salvation... It thought of my father, Theasin Venrover, and how they had bonded in the depths of his lair. It thought about its importance in the world—it was the *soul forge*, a creature of life.

I jerked "awake" and sat upright, gasping for breath as my mind reeled with possibilities. It had worked! Master Zelfree's suggestion had worked! I felt the presence of a god-creature. Could I find the others through this same technique?

"I will," I muttered to myself as I slid off my bed and walked to the door on unsteady legs.

I had found my father.

Guildmaster Eventide had to know straight away.

12

THE FABLE OF THE STEEL THORN INQUISITOR

MATHIS WEAVERSONG

Before the events of Knightmare Arcanist *(Book 1)*

We were on the hunt for a man named *Kalroux.*

He was a pirate—first mate to Captain Calisto of the *Third Abyss*—and a wendigo arcanist. I didn't normally hunt individual pirates, but Kalroux was different. He left his ship every few months to venture to the cold northern territories beyond the sea. A town by the name of *Whitecrest* sent a message to the guild registry, asking for guild arcanist assistance in dealing with the rogue. Apparently, Kalroux had raided Whitecrest's supplies on more than one occasion. The Steel Thorn Inquisitor Guild accepted the assignment, despite how far it was from our guild house.

The Steel Thorn Inquisitors lived by a creed. We sought out injustice and defended those who couldn't defend themselves. Dread pirates—any pirate captain who had ransacked a minimum of five ships—were some of our top priorities. They were the type of villains who sowed distrust and chaos. They ruined more lives with their wanton destruction than most.

I stepped off the gangplank of our transport ship and onto the Whitecrest docks. They were a trade hub, and everywhere I turned, I noticed a merchant or supplier. Lots of coins changed hands here.

The shadow at my feet stirred, and I suspected my eldrin had grown restless on the long ride. Knightmares didn't sleep, and the journey had been uneventful.

"My arcanist," Luthair said, his voice dark and refined. "How would you like to proceed?"

I wandered down the pier, my gaze on the distant people and their wares. Silk from the southern islands, ore from the Argo Empire, star shards from New Norra, and spices from Port Akro all came through in large crates and barrels. It would be difficult to find an individual among all the bustle of commerce, but I had done this for years. I would manage.

"We should wait in town," I said, keeping my voice low. "Our information says Kalroux stops in this port every three to four months. Last known sighting was thirteen weeks ago. It's almost time for our wendigo arcanist to visit again."

I lifted my coat collar to half-hide my face. I wore no armor—I was a knightmare arcanist, after all—but I carried my sword and pistol out in the open for all to see. My arcanist mark, a seven-pointed star with a sword and a cape, was a rarity. I suspected most individuals wouldn't know what it represented, but if they did, they'd likely keep their distance.

"Will we confront this sea thief in town?" Luthair asked.

"We must. I don't want to risk him attacking anyone. Surely you agree?"

"Indeed."

I smiled to myself. While some mystical creatures were impulsive and foolhardy, knightmares were logical and stoic. I preferred the rational behavior.

The town of Whitecrest rose upward on a hill, the roofs of the many buildings dappled in fresh snow. Despite the cold weather, the dark bricks of the road were kept clear of ice thanks to the summer fairy arcanists. A court of fairies dwelled near the underground hot springs not far from this location, and I had heard plenty of stories of young men and women venturing into nearby caves to attempt their trial of worth.

Summer fairies weren't powerful mystical creatures, though. Much like will-o-wisps, they had weak, but useful, magic. Summer fairies created warmth, made flowers bloom, and their auras prevented terrible storms.

I stepped onto the main road of town, impressed with the wrought iron garden boxes and decorative signs. Someone in town had to be a creative blacksmith. Perhaps an arcanist.

Everyone in town wore heavy fur cloaks and rugged leather coats. I admired the white fur on their clothing, and I suspected it had come from the winter foxes that dwelled in the area. It had been a while since I visited these parts. The last time had been when I bonded with Luthair…

"Help! Thief!"

People stopped and glanced around. A few even ducked into nearby buildings.

I tensed and scanned the road. The person yelling sounded feminine, and once I spotted a woman by the entrance of a small cobbler's shop, I stepped into the shadows, moving through the darkness in a near instant. I rose out of the shadows near the woman, much to her shock. She flinched away, her hands up near the collar of her coat.

"Where is the thief?" I asked, my tone urgent.

The woman trembled for only a moment before turning and pointing. A young man ducked into a narrow alleyway between buildings, the haste of movement causing him to half-trip as he scrambled out of view.

The distance didn't concern me. I took a breath, calmed myself, and asked, "What did he steal?"

"My memento," she said. "He slid it right off my wrist." She held out her arm, and then motioned to her hands.

The north had some interesting traditions. They crafted *mementos* for all special occasions—woven bracelets of metal meant to be worn at all times. The special occasions could be anything. The birth of a child. A wedding union. A death in the family. Making a new friend. The more important or significant the event, the higher quality material was used in crafting the bracelet.

"It's made of winter silver," the woman said. "Please—it's the memento for my wedding."

"Wait right here," I said. Then I glanced at my shadow. "*Luthair.*"

Luthair chuckled. "Yes, my arcanist."

The darkness leapt up from the ground and surrounded me on all sides. The cold power of my knightmare soaked into my veins, invigorating me. Luthair's shadow full plate gave me all the armor I would need to confront a basic, non-magical thief.

The woman gasped as I plunged into the shadows once again. With Luthair's help, I navigated the street, turned down the alleyway, and darted toward the fleeing scoundrel. His footsteps echoed between the buildings as he ran toward a wrought iron fence. He used his momentum to leap halfway up, but it wasn't enough. He struggled to climb the fence—there were no easy footholds.

I exited the darkness in all my knightly glory. Luthair's cape billowed behind me, caught in the chilly northern winds.

"Stop, thief," I said, my voice and Luthair's speaking at the same time.

"I'm sorry," the young man said. He continued to struggle with the fence, half-climbing and half-slipping the entire time. He shoved a hand into his pocket and then withdrew the winter silver bracelet. "Have it back!" He tossed the memento to the ground.

Using the shadows, I snatched up the jewelry and brought it to my hand. Winter silver was unique. It felt cold to the touch, no matter the time of year or heat in the nearby area. The ambient magic of the mountains had soaked into the silver lode, forever changing the metal.

"*Are we letting him go?*" Luthair asked telepathically.

"No," we said aloud. Then I waved my hand and manipulated the shadows to yank the man from the fence. "You'll be taken to the local authorities to answer for your actions."

The man—he was no older than nineteen—screamed as shadow tentacles wrapped around his waist. He thrashed and flailed as though the darkness was going to eat him, but I never hurt the lad. Instead, I bound his hands and feet and dragged him along the ground as I walked back to the main road.

"Help," he shouted. "Someone, help!"

"I won't harm you," I said in my double voice. "Remain calm."

He blubbered something else, but then quieted down.

The moment I stepped onto the street, the woman hurried to my side. I held out her memento, and she took it from my shadow-gauntlets with shaky hands.

"Thank you," she whispered. "But... who are you?"

"My name is Mathis Weaversong," I said, Luthair's voice mixing with mine. "And I'm a knightmare arcanist with the Steel Thorn Inquisitor Guild."

It probably wasn't the smartest move to announce my presence in the town of Whitecrest. Word traveled fast, and soon *everyone* knew my name and face. While that didn't bother me, the constant requests of the populace did. It seemed the denizens of Whitecrest had a mountain of problems, though most were unimportant at best.

They didn't need a knightmare arcanist to fetch kittens from a chimney, or to help locate a goat that had gotten lost on the outskirts of town. I probably should've said *no* at some point—since I was still searching for Kalroux. But I couldn't bring myself to deny them.

And they did repay me for my efforts. I was given an inn room with a view. It wasn't much of a view—smokestacks from the local blacksmith created a near constant wall of darkness. And the tanner wasn't too far from our location, filling the block with a stench that made the hairs in my nose curl.

It was free, though. And I couldn't bring myself to deny their hospitality.

I stood in my inn room, admiring the brick work of the fireplace. The whole city was practically made of bricks. The roads, the buildings—even the town walls were thick structures held together by mortar.

Luthair stood in the corner of the room, next to the bed and a small reading table. He held still, imitating a decorative suit of armor found in most castles. When I moved, his empty helmet followed along, keeping watch. The windows were shut, and his cape never fluttered.

"You haven't rested since we've arrived," Luthair said, his voice echoing out of his empty suit of shadow armor.

"I'm not tired," I replied.

"If the Grandmaster Inquisitor had been here, you would've rested."

I shook my head. "But he's not, which means we have to work twice as hard."

Once upon a time, the Steel Thorn Inquisitor Guild had three times as many arcanists in their ranks. Now we barely had twenty. The number dwindled every day—the threats of the world were becoming more dangerous. The arcane plague, which had once been a faraway threat, was drawing closer to the Argo Empire, and pirates were using the diseased blood of mad arcanists to further their own lust for gold and star shards.

That was why the Grandmaster Inquisitor had accepted this assignment, even though it was far out of the way. He wanted me to investigate the arcane plague and stop any and all individuals or creatures who might be carrying it.

Normally we would've traveled in pairs to handle such threats, but that wasn't the case anymore. We had too many requests for aid, and not enough arcanists. It was the same with other guilds—even the Frith and Hunters Guild seemed bogged down in pirates and madmen. Luthair and I would have to deal with Kalroux and his wendigo on our own.

"We can't fail," I said as I turned my attention to the window. Smoke still wafted up from the nearby smith. "And once we're done here, we need to head off to the Isle of Landin. The Grandmaster Inquisitor has asked I handle a few more tasks before returning to Thronehold. Time is of the essence."

"We won't fail, nor will we waste if you simply rest for an evening," Luthair said.

I smirked. "You sound like my mother."

"Then your mother must've been a wise woman."

With a chuckle, I headed to my bed. White fur blankets covered the mattress, stacked nearly a foot tall. The pillows, on the other hand, looked flatter than paper. I stripped off my coat and belt, and then kicked off my boots.

"Do you miss this area?" I asked.

Luthair remained as still as a statue as he said, "Not particularly. Should I?"

"You were born from the murder of King Raulith, weren't you? He had ruled over these lands for a long while. Longer than most." I took a seat on the edge of the bed, trying to recall the length of his rule. "I thought knight-mares retained memories of the ruler who died?"

"You are mistaken," Luthair said. "Or if we do, I have long forgotten."

"I miss this area," I muttered.

"You weren't born here. Why would you miss it?"

"It was where we met," I said with a shrug. "Back when I thought I'd live my life as a silversmith." It had been chance that I found Luthair—a tiny knightmare, unbonded. I had traveled to the north to learn from the best silversmiths, but I had left an arcanist.

Luthair crossed his arms, his stance imposing. "I thank you for helping me track down King Raulith's killer."

"It was mostly the Grandmaster Inquisitor," I said. He had been summoned to deal with the situation, and he had taken me as an apprentice after witnessing my resolve to help Luthair. The memories swirled in my thoughts, causing me to smile. "Life can be unpredictable at times."

"Indeed."

I leaned back onto my bed, enjoying the softness of the fur. The flat pillows weren't as bad as I thought they would be, and I smiled as I stared at the ceiling. "King Raulith... Luthair... Your name is an anagram."

"All knightmares have names that are anagrams of the ruler they were spawned from," Luthair stated matter-of-factly.

"I never realized that."

"It is of little importance."

I lifted the blankets and threw them over my body. "I'm only going to sleep a few hours." I didn't want to lose too much time. We had things to accomplish.

"Yes, my arcanist."

"Wake me if I rest too long."

"You have my word."

A part of me felt he was being sarcastic. Luthair had a way with his words that amused me.

I enjoyed the warmth of the fur, surprised at how quickly it chased away the cold. Then I closed my eyes, and just as fast as I shadow-stepped, I fell asleep.

My dreams filled me with anxiety. They weren't nightmares, I just knew the haunting feeling that accompanied some of my memories. I knew I was dreaming, yet I didn't try to escape my slumber.

I dreamt of my time in Silverhaven, the capital in the north. We visited shops and silversmiths, examining the craftsmanship of world-famous jewelry and artificers. I had been more preoccupied with the knights roaming the streets, but the silverwork had been a glorious sight not worth missing.

I hadn't known at the time, but the knights had been searching for King Raulith's murderer. The knights were yeti arcanists, capable of great strength and sniffing out individuals, even in the snow.

My silversmith master had once been part of a large navy that helped the Argo Empire keep control of the island nations. The navy reduced in size as the islands regained their autonomy, but my master never stopped being a naval officer first and foremost. Even in his twilight years, he never saw himself as *old*, just *wiser and grayer*.

It caused problems. My dream went straight to the day that changed my life forever. A bandit had broken into our room in the dead of night. He had come for my master's silverwork—beautiful necklaces and bracelets made of high-quality silver. My master tried to fight the man off, but he was too old and frail. The man stabbed him.

I wasn't a fighter, even if I liked to imagine I was.

My dream warped my memory—the sky outside shifted to a scarlet red and snow billowed in through an open window. I fought the burglar, not because I wanted to protect the silverwork, but because I didn't want my master to die.

The criminal seemed desperate and deranged. He said he didn't want any witnesses. He would kill us both. I fought him in a panicked state, and my desperation got the better of me. I made mistakes, and the man stabbed me as well. Fortunately, I had the wits to grab his weapon and turn it around. We might've killed each other had it not been for Luthair...

He had been watching.

It was then that Luthair bonded with me, saving me from death. Apparently, a knightmare's trial of worth was the defense of another—especially those who were unable to defend themselves, for whatever reason. I had never imagined I would become a knightmare arcanist, but once my master died three days later, I was contacted by the Grandmaster Inquisitor and...

The dream did what all dreams do.

It melted away into something stranger and more bizarre.

<hr>

A banging on my door woke me from my slumber.

I opened my eyes. Night. My room, engulfed in darkness, would've been difficult to navigate, but I was a knightmare arcanist. I could see no matter the level of light. My first thought was to check on Luthair, but he had already gone to the door. He opened it up and stared down at a young woman in the hallway.

"Excuse me," she whispered. "Is the inquisitor in?"

"He is," Luthair said.

"May I speak with him? It's urgent."

Luthair glanced back at me, his empty helmet "staring" in my direction. I gave him a curt nod, and he returned his attention to the woman. "Come in."

The woman took small steps into my room, her eyes unfocused. I stood from the bed and manipulated the shadows to light the lantern hanging on the wall. There was enough oil that the flame sprang to life, brightening the area enough for a normal person to see.

She gave me an odd and hesitant once over, and I suspected I looked less than professional. My brown hair was disheveled, and my clothing wrinkled from tossing and turning. I suspected my eyes were adorned with heavy bags and my breath was none too pleasant.

"Are you the inquisitor?" she asked.

I nodded. "I'm Mathis Weaversong," I said. "And this is my knightmare, Luthair."

My eldrin shut the door, and the woman jumped. She watched Luthair walk to the edge of the room, his shadow boots clinking across the wood of the inn room.

"He won't harm you," I said.

"I've never seen a creature like that," the woman muttered.

"Knightmares are rather rare."

"They look evil."

I held back a laugh. With a smile, I said, "I assure you, they're creatures of justice."

The woman used both her hands to pat down her curly hair. She wore the same types of heavy white furs as most Whitecrest citizens, but she also had a pair of wool trousers covered in animal hair. The hair ranged in all colors—brown, black, rust, and gold.

"I assume you're a shepherd or a rancher?" I asked.

The woman's eyes went wide. Then she nodded. "Y-yes. I help tend a herd of goats with my mother and brother."

"And what's your name?"

"May Sun," she said in a quiet voice.

"And what can I do for you, May?"

She stepped closer to me, her posture rigid and her brow furrowed. "Inquisitor Mathis—I'd like to hire you to kill someone."

The request took me by surprise. Even Luthair was taken aback. He didn't have a face, but I could tell by the way he crossed his arms and then uncrossed them that he didn't know what to do with this bizarre request.

I forced a chuckle. "I'm sorry, but I'm not an assassin for hire."

"But I thought inquisitors killed evil men?" May asked. She got closer again, practically stepping on my bare feet. "The man I want you to kill is a murderer! He took my father from me. *Please*. He needs to be brought to justice."

She stared up at me with a round face, her eyes wide, and her eyebrows knitted. I didn't know what to say. I couldn't just go out of my way to kill a random individual when I had plans to hunt down a pirate.

"Did the man kill your father unprovoked?" I asked.

May shook her head. "My father and he had disagreements for years. They argued and argued. It went too far... And that's when it happened."

"It was an accident?"

"No!" May's shout startled me. She grabbed at the side of her head and frowned. "He planned it out. He came to the goat pass with a knife—far from town, and where he thought no one would see. *But I did*." She grabbed at her wrist and fidgeted with a bracelet made of onyx. A memento of death.

"Listen," I said. "I can't—"

"I have money," May interjected. "Do you take island coins? I have gold leafs." She dug around in the pocket of her trousers and withdrew a leather pouch.

Gold coins? Most people never saw that kind of money. Where had she acquired gold coins? Goat herding wasn't *that* lucrative. I shook my head and placed a hand on top of her pouch. "If your quest is just, I won't need payment. But I'm here in town for a specific reason. I can't abandon my assignment."

"But I've seen you helping others." May motioned to the windows. "Everyone in town is talking about it. Please. You have to help me."

"Those were simple tasks. I can't take the time to be judge, jury, and executioner for a man you claim is a murderer. I would have to investigate and—"

"But he is!" May stepped away from me, her hand clenched tightly on her pouch of coins. She shook her head as she backed up closer to the door. "I watched him kill the father. Right in front of my eyes. You have to help. No one else will!"

"No one? Why is that?"

"He's an arcanist! A summer fairy arcanist. He'll get away with everything because no one wants to bother the people who keep the weather in town calm."

Luthair turned to me, and I stared into his void-like helmet. He had no face or expression, but I could sense his concern. I felt the same, but I had to prioritize the worst threats first. Kalroux was still at large—he actively pirated and would harm again. Sometime soon. The murderer of May's father wasn't wantonly killing individuals left and right. I had to focus on the pirate.

When I turned back to the woman, I frowned. "I'm sorry. Perhaps you can submit a request for assistance to the guild registry in Fortuna. An arcanist from one of the nearby guilds will be sent to assist you. That's how I ended up here in the first place."

"But..." May placed her hand on the inn door, her lower lip quavering. "You're just as useless as the others."

Then she fled my room without another word. Luthair walked forward, but I grabbed his shoulder and held him back.

"We should've offered her assistance," Luthair muttered.

I slowly nodded. "I understand. But duty comes first. Inquisitors must maintain focus."

"It seems this town doesn't have many arcanists. She may be right. They could be getting away with crimes simply because they're using their magic to help the area. It's a simple form of corruption."

"I told you it was important to finish our assignment without delay," I said.

"That you did."

Luthair said nothing else as he melted into the ground and became my shadow once again. I stared at the darkness around my feet for a long time. It wasn't worth arguing about, I supposed.

Perhaps, once we were done with our assignment, we could help May solve her problem. But until then, I would remain true to my word and do as the Grandmaster Inquisitor wanted.

For ten days, I sent Luthair out in the town to listen for rumors. He could slither from shadow to shadow, hiding in plain sight as a puddle of darkness. Whitecrest was a trade town, which meant rumors changed hands as often as coins. Everyone had a tale to tell from their time at sea.

On the last day, Luthair returned to me with good news: Kalroux had returned.

If he had arrived aboard the *Third Abyss*, I would've seen it. Captain Calisto had crafted his vessel out of ghostwood— a type of lumber that created a thick fog. But Kalroux didn't come to port in a recognizable pirate ship, which was probably wiser on his part.

Unfortunately, wendigo arcanists had the ability to

become invisible. Unless Kalroux showed himself, I wouldn't be able to locate him just by wandering the town. I figured I wouldn't have to wait long—Kalroux raided the town each time he had returned. Sometimes food, sometimes iron work, and sometimes the trade goods brought by merchants—his focus didn't seem to be limited to one thing.

I walked the main street, keeping my attention on the sky. Flurries of snowflakes wafted down onto the town, but the summer fairy magic melted everything before it iced over the roads.

"Do we know Kalroux's real name?" Luthair asked from the shadows at my feet.

I shook my head. "No. All we have is his pirate name."

"*Kalroux* hardly sounds intimidating."

"It's the name of a prominent Death Lord," I said, my attention on the gray clouds. "Just like the name *Calisto*."

"I see."

"Kalroux is the Death Lord of Misery and Suffering. He resides in the abyssal hells, or so the legends say." I shrugged. "I'm not sure if it's intimidating or not, but it fits the theme Calisto established."

In order to blend in with the populace, I had purchased myself a fur cloak. I pulled it tight across my shoulders, using it as a shield from the chill. The crowds from the ports —people arriving from all kinds of locations—made it easier for me to appear as though I belonged.

Once the clouds separated, I returned my attention to the road. Carts full of barrels and crates clattered by at a consistent rate. Domesticated caribou pulled the carts, their large antlers a sight to see. I liked to imagine riding a caribou into battle—spooking my opponents with a mount just as frightening as my knightmare armor.

I stopped at a corner with a large four-story building. "This is the spot where you heard the rumor?"

Luthair shifted around my feet. "It is, my arcanist."

The sign hanging outside read, *Tagalong Tavern*. With a heavy sigh, I entered the establishment. Smoke and incense filled the establishment, and the moment I took a breath, I half-gagged.

The ground floor of the tavern was filled with square tables. A staircase led up to the higher floors, and I watched with mild amusement as a train of smoke floated upward, likely stinking up the rest of the building. The locals enjoyed their pipes, it seemed. And the locals were easy to distinguish—they wore their mementos on their wrists for all to see.

With watery eyes, I took a seat at an empty table. A barmaid sauntered over with a drink—it was the same drink that everyone had. A pale lager. The barmaid set it down on the table and offered me a tight smile.

"It'll be two bits," she said.

I didn't have the currency of the north cities, so I held out a few copper leafs.

The barmaid took the coins and then sauntered away to another table.

"Find Kalroux," I whispered. "And get me once you know his location."

"As you wish, my arcanist."

Luthair slithered away from my chair and headed for the staircase. I sat at the table, drinking my pale lager along with every other hard-working citizen of Whitecrest. Loud conversations filled the room, each table trying to talk over the other. Even the conversations upstairs seemed to roll down the stairwell and into our dining room.

I thought I'd been in here for some time, but half an

hour later, Luthair shifted back to the darkness under my table.

"My arcanist," he said, his gruff voice half-drowned by the boisterous arguments. "Kalroux was here yesterday morning."

"Where is he now?" I asked as I brought my drink to my lips.

"He spoke with a woman and then left with her."

"What kind of woman? A lady of the evening?"

"No, my arcanist. From what I heard, it was a young woman. She was quite distraught."

A distraught young woman? I clenched my jaw. "It wasn't... the same woman who had approached us a few weeks ago, was it? May?"

"One in the same."

"Curse the abyssal hells," I said as I slammed my mug on the table.

A couple patrons glanced my way. They lifted eyebrows and stared at the empty seats around my table, probably assuming I was touched in the head for talking to myself.

I stood. "Luthair, head out."

"Where, my arcanist? No one knew where they had gone. And the woman, May, never revealed the name of the murderer."

That didn't matter. May had already told us all the relevant details. Her father's murderer was a summer fairy arcanist. And not only that, but he was an arcanist who likely had dealings—or investments—in goat herds or goat herding property. It wouldn't take me long to discover who it was. The town wasn't large enough for a murder to go completely unnoticed.

What bothered me more than that was May's desperate need for revenge. She couldn't hire me, so she turned to a pirate instead? Perhaps I should've accepted her proposal and investigated this whole matter myself.

I quickened my pace as I exited the building.

Mallon Mencry.

He was the summer fairy arcanist who owned goat herding property. Apparently, he had attempted to purchase May's father's goat trails, but had failed to convince the man. After years of territory disputes, May's father ended up dead in a ditch, and now Mallon owned all the easy paths to and from town.

The citizens of Whitecrest said May's father had slipped off a steep hill, but I was coming to believe more of May's story with each passing moment.

After locating Mallon in town, I decided to head up the mountain to his home.

I shadow-stepped over the brick walls of Whitecrest and headed for the goat ranches. Goats were a main staple for the people of Whitecrest. They provided fur, meat, milk, and even companionship. I had never seen so many goats as pets as I had in Whitecrest.

The northern terrain wasn't like the island or even the Argo Empire. They had large mountains and deep forests that grew on the side of steep hills. Walking through the snow, uphill, while the winter winds rushed by, would be a terrible ordeal for anyone. Thankfully, I traveled through the shadows, slipping in and out with ease. I appeared in the middle of the forest, disappeared again, and then emerged on a rock overlooking the same grouping of trees.

I climbed higher and higher until I reached the location of the goat ranches—a peak with a flat enough plateau to allow for houses to be built. Three ranches, each complete with a barn and a sloped field, stood strong and proud. Instead of approaching the buildings, I motioned to the darkness.

"Let's merge," I whispered. "And we'll wait."

"Yes, my arcanist."

Luthair sprang out of the darkness and formed around me, his plate armor a comfort. With his power added to my own, I slipped into the shadows and hid among the mountain shrubs behind one of the ranches. The bleating of goats drifted into the sky, their incessant cries almost annoying, but I wouldn't be deterred.

If Kalroux *had* accepted May's offer, he'd be here eventually. I figured Kalroux wouldn't approach Mallon in town. Not because Kalroux was afraid of getting caught, but because May wouldn't want such a scene. Killing an arcanist was a heinous crime, no matter the city or territory. I was almost certain that she paid Kalroux to do it quietly—that way, she could say *he* fell down the side of a mountain slope.

"*I'm surprised Kalroux didn't just kill her and abscond with the coins,*" Luthair said telepathically.

"*Perhaps they know each other,*" I replied.

"*Perhaps.*"

"*Or perhaps he did kill her. But if that's the case, he'll be brought to justice for that crime as well.*"

Luthair's thoughts grew hot with anger. "*He cannot be allowed to live.*"

"*We're in agreement.*"

I waited in the darkness, my heart filled with conviction. We would confront Kalroux, defeat him in combat, and then question him about the Dread Pirate Calisto. Perhaps we would discover some of the man's secrets, and then we'd have an opening to defeat him as well.

It didn't take long before my patience was rewarded. As the bright reds and oranges of sunset rained down over the mountains, riders from town made their way up the road. There were four, all riding the caribou, each one with a heavy cloak and backpack. A single summer fairy—a tiny woman with pink dragonfly wings—fluttered behind the group, a trail of pollen left in her wake.

I remained in the shadows, out of sight, as the men on their mounts finally reached the plateau. They rode to one of the ranches, their steeds exhausted from the steep slopes. I would've followed them into their home, but that eventually became a moot point.

A blast of ice roared through the area, damaging a fence and part of a barn as thick rime manifested across everything. Wendigo magic was best used in the coldest of conditions. Their ice evocation built off existing chill, and the more there was, the worse it became.

The summer fairy evoked a wave of heat, but it didn't compare to the wendigo. The ice melted at a slow rate.

One of the four men was ripped from the saddle of their caribou. The invisible wendigo dragged him into the snow and then ravaged him. A second man was torn from his saddle, but this time by an invisible man.

The last two men kicked their mounts and spurred them to run—it didn't matter the direction. The caribou bounded away, even the two without riders.

I shadow-stepped out from my hiding place and headed straight for Mallon, the summer fairy arcanist. He shouted and flailed, unable to break free from his captor's grasp. To my surprise, the skin on his hands sloughed off, like a snake shedding its dead scales.

"Someone, help!" Mallon yelled.

I manipulated the shadows and stabbed at the area I

thought Kalroux would be hiding. Sure enough, the barbs of my darkness caught him off guard. Blood gushed out of nowhere, and Kalroux lost his concentration. He appeared out of thin air, his appearance just as described.

A tall man with dark hair, shaved on both sides. A tattoo on his neck made of three horizontal lines, " 三 ." A dark goatee. A scar on one eyebrow. Without a doubt, this was Kalroux. He didn't clothe himself in heavy winter clothing, like the locals. He simply wore a thin shirt, loose trousers, and three belts—one for a sword, one for a pistol, and one for a heavy pouch.

"Halt," I declared in my double voice. "I am Mathis Weaversong, a knightmare arcanist with the Steel Thorn Inquisitor Guild. You are charged with piracy, murder, and kidnapping."

Kalroux spit onto the ground near his boots, but he didn't release Mallon.

"Help me," Mallon cried. "He's a madman!"

His summer fairy buzzed her pink wings as she evoked more heat. It didn't matter much, but steam rose off the snowbanks on the sides of the road.

The invisible wendigo crunched the neck of the second man, and I cursed under my breath.

Furious, I manipulated the shadows and attempted to grab Mallon. But Kalroux was clever. He held up a hand and evoked more ice, destroying most of my shadows before they reached him. For whatever reason, the magically created ice prevented my shadows from taking hold—I couldn't shadow-step across them.

I withdrew my sword. I'd have to do this the old-fashioned way.

"By the authority vested in me," Luthair and I said, "I hereby sentence you to death."

"Guild dog," Kalroux said, disdain soaked in his words. "Come to meddle in affairs you know nothing about." He motioned me closer with a beckoning gesture of his hand. "Come at me, fool. I'll happily make your knightmare into trinkets."

I lifted my hand and evoked raw fear. The summer fairy fell from the sky and hit the bricks of the road. Mallon screamed and thrashed about. The invisible wendigo couldn't maintain its invisibility any longer. It became visible, its monster-like appearance enough to make me grimace. It had the body of an emaciated wolf, but it wore a skull over its face—a skull adorned with twisted antlers.

But Kalroux didn't succumb to my fear. Why? How was he immune? Did he have a magical item that protected him from the dread?

He evoked another wave of frost, catching my feet and locking me in place. I swung my sword at the ice, hacking away at the confinement. Kalroux lunged forward, drew his own sword, and slashed wide.

I lifted my sword just in time to deflect his blow, but I hadn't yet freed myself.

Kalroux pulled out his pistol and shot. The bullet slammed into Luthair's armor, and the sting of the blow hurt, but it didn't pierce through.

Instead of fighting him with my feet trapped in the ice, I unmerged from Luthair and leapt out of his armor. With all the speed of an expert combatant, and the surprise needed to catch Kalroux off guard, I lunged forward and stabbed. I caught Kalroux's pistol hand, puncturing his limb and nearly removing everything past the wrist.

Kalroux growled something I couldn't hear and then waved his hand. A blast of ice and mist filled the air, hurting my eyes.

Luthair slammed his gauntlets into the ice constraints until he was free. "My arcanist—what have I warned you about! Don't unmerge in the middle of combat!"

I ignored my eldrin and slashed at Kalroux again, despite the pain in my eyes. He leapt backward, narrowly avoiding my blow. Then he shimmered and disappeared, veiled by invisibility. I thought I had him on the run, but then the wendigo crunched its fangs down on my left arm.

I gritted my teeth, biting back a shout. Luthair manipulated the darkness of sunset and stabbed at the invisible wendigo. He cut the beast in the gut and throat, but it wasn't enough to kill. The wendigo released me, and I felt a tingle emanate from my new wound. Wendigo were diseased creatures. I didn't have much time before the sickness would take hold.

Luthair merged with me again, even though I hadn't commanded him to.

"*We fight together*," Luthair said telepathically.

I said nothing. Sometimes it was best to have two fighters, rather than one.

Kalroux evoked more ice, no doubt hoping to trap me again. But I wasn't having it. This had to end. I stepped backward, keeping light on my toes as I avoided most of the new frost coating the ground.

"Dastard," I muttered as I gripped my trinket sword close.

I evoked fear, and his wendigo became visible. Instead of hunting down Kalroux, I turned my attention to the wolf-monster. With as much power as I could muster, I chopped down on the wendigo, cleaving into the top of its neck. The wolf yawled, and I sliced at it again.

"*No!*" Kalroux shouted. He became visible as he leapt at me, his sword in his good hand.

With one final blow, I cut through the wendigo's neck, ending its life—and severing its magical connection with Kalroux. He yelled something and continued his charge at me. He brought the blade down on my shoulder, attempting to cut deep, but Luthair's armor was too powerful. Instead, I stabbed him in the gut, my blade still wet with his eldrin's blood.

Kalroux gasped and his body shuddered as he fell to his knees.

This was it. The fight had ended.

I yanked my sword from his body and took a step back. His ice melted at a rapid rate.

"You're scum," Kalroux said, pink spittle gushing from his mouth as he spoke. "I was all they had..." He collapsed backward, his death creeping up on him at a slow rate. "Why... Why now..."

I took a moment to catch my breath, but my throat tightened, and my arm throbbed in agony. The diseased bite of the wendigo would soon take its toll. "This is the consequence for a life poorly lived," I said in my double voice.

"Thibault," Kalroux muttered. "May... I'm so sorry..."

He sunk down into the snow, his breathing slower and shallower with each passing moment. Crimson wept from the injury in his cut, and it looked as though the skin had ripped at the edges of the sword strike.

"*No!* No!" The young woman, May, ran from one of the goat ranches, her fur cloak fluttering behind her. She dashed all the way to Kalroux's side, and then knelt next to his body. Her hands shook, and she tried to touch him, but she couldn't bring herself to do so. Instead, she pulled a memento from his wrist—winter silver. A memento for a happy occasion.

With tears streaming down her face, May turned to me. "How... How could you?"

"He's a pirate," I said, no hesitation in my voice, no doubt in my conviction. "Whitecrest had called for his death."

May pointed to Mallon. The man stood by the side of the road, his summer fairy in his arms, his eyes wide. *"He's the monster!"* May shrieked. "He's done so many terrible things! Kalroux was supposed to put an end to him, and now look at what you've done!"

Luthair and I unmerged. I understand why the woman was upset, but...

Mallon pointed at her. "She's a liar! Don't believe a word that comes out of her mouth!"

No part of me wanted to hear him speak. I shot a glare over my shoulder, and Mallon closed his mouth in an instant. When I turned my attention back to May, she had both her hands covering her face, her sobs audible and painful.

My arm tingled. My vision blurred.

"Luthair," I murmured. "Handle this. I think... I need... to rest."

Before I could hear him reply, I lost my balance and fell over. The last thing I remembered was hitting the snow.

I awoke in my inn room, my vision still blurry, even with my eyes fully open.

"Luthair?" I asked.

"Yes, my arcanist?"

Hearing his voice was a comfort. I wasn't in the hands of enemies—Luthair had gotten me to safety.

I groaned as I sat up in my bed. Bandages had been wrapped around my arm, but otherwise I wore nothing. I rubbed at my forehead, confused for a long while. Luthair was the only one in the room with me.

"Did you handle everything?" I asked in a quiet voice.

Luthair nodded his empty helmet. "You need not worry. Kalroux and his wendigo are dead. I brought their bodies to the authorities as proof."

"And the other problem?"

"Mallon will no longer trouble the other goat ranches. Or anyone else, for that matter."

He made the statements with a blasé tone, and I was almost tempted to ask him what he meant. But I decided against it. If Luthair said the issue was handled, it was handled.

"You wanted to investigate more of the arcane plague, correct?" Luthair asked.

I half-smiled. "As soon as my vision corrects itself."

"You should be fine in a few more hours. Until then, just rest. You need it."

"Such a fussy eldrin," I said with a chuckle.

Luthair's dark chortle joined my own.

"What about May?" I eventually asked.

Luthair brushed his cape aside and then turned his back to me. "I didn't know how to console her. I tried, but she wanted none of it."

"I see."

I regretted not being able to solve every dilemma and problem, but sometimes, there were no absolutely correct solutions. I had done what I came to do—rid the world of a villainous pirate. Perhaps he had family and loved ones—who didn't?—but that didn't make him immune to the laws of the world. If anything, he should've thought harder about his actions.

As a Steel Thorn Inquisitor, I had to do what was just.

"Rest, my arcanist," Luthair said. "We will take to the sea in the morning."

I nodded once and then rested back on my bed. "All right, Luthair. Let me know if anything changes."

"Indeed."

13

THE FABLE OF THE GARDEN OF
POISON

RHYS

Before the events of Warlord Arcanist *(Book 6)*

S ome people struggled to find their purpose in life. Not me. I had found my purpose while lying on my deathbed.

A terrible plague had swept through our village, killing everyone it managed to infect. When the hideous boils and lesions had appeared across *my* skin, I figured *I would be next.* I gave up and waited for death to whisk me away to the abyssal hells.

Fortunately, I didn't die right away. I suffered for a long while, unable to move or escape my home. The kirin arcanists of my village did everything in their power to heal me, but kirin weren't creatures of medicine.

That was when I met the man who changed my life. *Cane Helvetti.*

The Autarch.

He had healed my sickness, bonded with the rarest of all

mystical creatures—the golden kirin—and then he had led our tiny village into an era of prosperity. He was a man with vision and plans. A man of skill and talent. *A god among men.* He was worth dying for, perhaps ten times over!

It was an honor to help him achieve his goals, even if my body wasn't the strongest. Ever since the sickness, I had terrible shakes and jitteriness. I couldn't remain still, no matter how hard I tried.

Which was why it was difficult getting into the Garden of Poison. The key the Autarch had given me was a trinket that undid the magical lock on the main gate, but I often struggled to get the key into the hole. I poked it on the sides of the lock more than once.

Damn my useless body.

The moment I unlocked the gate, I smiled to myself. The garden was protected by nullstone—the walls and flowerbeds were all built with the anti-magic rock—otherwise, I would've teleported inside with my stolen rizzel magic.

I walked in, shut the gate, and promptly locked it back up.

Theasin Venrover was a particular man. He had rules and orders—*always lock the gate when you enter*—and I followed them without fail. Theasin wasn't as talented as the Autarch, but he had helped bring the Autarch's vision to life.

It had been Theasin's brilliant idea to take the diseased bodies of the kirin and use their corrupted magic to make the *arcane plague.* It had been Theasin's ingenuity that created the *decay dust*, nullstone powder that destroyed trinkets. And it had been Theasin's research that had allowed us to locate the soul forge so quickly.

Theasin was a useful servant—more useful than I—and that saddened me. I would have to improve myself. I wanted to show my worth to the Autarch. I wanted him to be proud he saved *my* life when he could've gone to the houses of so many others.

I shook the throught from my head as I entered the Garden of Poison. All sorts of plants grew in this twisted paradise, but each one was harmful or deadly. Snakeroot, hemlock, nightshade, and oleander—those were the only few I could name. Beautiful white ivy grew on the walls, and bright blue moss dappled several decorative boulders, but I knew not to touch anything.

The fumes left me faint, so I kept my breathing shallow.

Tucked deep in the back, beyond the bright flowers and thistles, was a magic lab used for crafting ointments, poisons, trinkets, and artifacts. We had star shards and pieces of all kinds of mystical creatures—the deadly plants kept the inquisitive at bay. Only unicorns and their arcanists could frolic throughout the garden without worry for their safety, and they were rare in these parts.

Once I had walked around a small bush covered in tiny white flowers—water hemlock—I spotted the short stairway underground. It led straight to the lab, and I hurried down without delay.

The gray brick walls, floor, and ceiling made the place seem small. It had all the welcoming warmth of a coffin, but that didn't bother me much. This was one of the Autarch's sanctuaries, and I loved it for what it was.

Several tables lined the walls, some covered in plants, others coated in star shard powder. Only one table had something of real interest. In the middle of the room was an arm from the soul forge—a piece Theasin had ripped off in order for us to experiment with god-level magics.

A single arcanist shuffled around the room. The mark on his forehead was a seven-pointed star with a leech wrapped around the edge. An abyssal leech arcanist—perhaps the last one in the entire world.

The man himself was less important to me. He wore thick robes to cover most of his body, and his black hair had been shaved short, leaving an even, short fuzz across his head. His arms were lanky and oddly proportioned. It was no wonder Theasin didn't speak of him often.

Yevin Venrover. One of Theasin's many children.

He stood next to the table with the soul forge arm, his expression half-bored. Dark rings lined his eyes, and I suspected he suffered from exhaustion. When he glanced up from his work, his face barely changed.

"Why are you here?" he asked in a monotone voice.

"I've come to collect your research," I said as I wrung my hands together. "It's ready, yes?"

"Almost."

Yevin moved around the room with the speed of a sleepy sloth. Didn't he understand that we had work to do? What if the Autarch saw us now? What would he think? Would he be disappointed in me? Would he regret saving my life over others?

"Quickly," I hissed. "I have more work to complete."

"Don't rush me," Yevin muttered. "This is dangerous. More than my father ever wanted."

"Your father said we would have the world serpent under our control! Desperate times call for desperate measures."

Yevin plucked a vial off the table with the plants and then ambled back over to me. He rubbed at his side, probably where the leech was writhing under his skin. It was lucky Yevin didn't have to feed the creature since birth—abyssal leeches could permanently alter the magic of creatures they infested as larvae.

"Be careful," Yevin said, straining his words to emphasize them. "This is a corruption that will affect the god-creatures. It's... something vile. It might be worse than the arcane plague. And it has its own will, just like the plague does."

He handed me the vial with a shaky hand. The liquid inside was a mix of gold and crimson. When I rolled it around on my palm, they mixed together to make a dark red. Something about it... spoke to me. Almost like the vial *wanted* to be taken from this lab and brought into the world.

Yevin cringed as I went to tuck the vial into one of my robe pockets.

"What did I just say?" Yevin barked, livelier than he had been a second ago. "*Don't be a fool.* If you break that vial, you'll never be the same. This whole city will never be the same. That was made with the blood from the soul forge and the bones of the apoch dragon."

I jerked and jittered, my body unable to remain still for long. I offered Yevin a sarcastic half-smile. "We'll just have to assume I won't smash the glass between here and my destination."

"You must be careful. *Must.*"

I nodded with his words, but even then, my head shook a bit. "What about the khepera arcanist? Will her magic reverse the effects of this new substance? Can she cure it like she can cure the arcane plague?"

"It's made with the magic of the god-creatures," Yevin stated. "It will only be affected by the magic of other god-creatures." He stepped away from me, his teeth gritted. "The Autarch wanted the world serpent eliminated... And now it'll be done."

14

THE LIST OF GOD-CREATURES & THEIR RUNESTONES

1—The World Serpent (The Jade Runestone)
2—The Soul Forge (The Rose Quartz Runestone)
3—The Fenris Wolf (The Shale Runestone)
4—The Sky Titan (The Marble Runestone)
5—The Garuda Bird (The Gypsum Runestone)
6—The Abyssal Kraken (The Amphibolite Runestone)
7—The Typhon Beast (The Red Jasper Runestone)
8—The Scylla Waters (The Lapis Lazuli Runestone)
9—The Tempest Coatl (The Opal Runestone)
10—The Progenitor Behemoth (The Sandstone Runestone)
11—The Corona Phoenix (The Bauxite Runestone)
12—The Endless Undead (The Obsidian Runestone)
13—The Apoch Dragon (No Runestone)

ALTERNATE SCENES & BLOOPERS

DURING KNIGHTMARE ARCANIST
(BOOK 1)

THE ENDLESS MIRE

I slowly turned around, my eyebrows knitted together until I caught sight of the speaker.

A mystical creature.

A giant snowy stag—a legendary white hart.

White harts were deer as large as a stallion, with gold antlers that curved up and around. All tales about them spoke of their stealth and ability to hide in plain sight, despite their massive size and power. The beast stood only ten feet from us, and I hadn't detected it at all. Invisibility? I didn't know. But it had clearly been close enough to hear our conversation.

"You're looking to bond... *aren't*... you?" the white hart asked.

His words were so unnatural, they were hard to understand.

And the white hart didn't open his eyes. They were tightly shut, almost sunken in. The beast hung his head as if he was going to drink from the mire water, but he never did.

"A white hart," Lyell whispered.

The beast coughed and snorted. "Pardon me," he said. "I had something in my throat." He lifted his head and opened his eyes.

"Are you okay?" I asked, my body tense.

"Oh, yes, very okay." The white hart sniffed the air. "Nice weather we're having."

I glanced around. "You're sure you're okay? Nothing strange has happened here?"

"Strange? Heavens no. Not here."

"You're not sick with a disease that causes madness?"

The white hart's ears shot straight up. "Goodness, I hope not. That would be a terrible experience."

Lyell chuckled and nodded along with his words. "Right? Who would want that?"

"No, it's been peaceful here for some time. Nothing wrong. I was just out for my morning walk and figured I'd take a new route." The white hart pointed with his golden antlers. "You two shouldn't be out here, though. You might get leeches or ticks. Wouldn't that be dreadful? I shudder just imagining it."

"Can we take your trial of worth?" I asked. "We were looking to bond."

"Well, he's too young." The white hart motioned to Lyell. "But you're the right age... And I *am* bored... Okay. We can bond."

"That's it?" I asked, caught up in my overwhelming disbelief. "You'll bond with me? No trial of worth?"

"I don't see why not? You're not secretly a villain, are you?" The white hart laughed at his own joke.

"No, I'm not..."

"Then it's a done deal. What's your name?"

I rubbed at the back of my neck. "Volke Savan."

The white hart held his head high, his antlers grazing the leaves of the mangrove trees. "Then from this moment forth, you'll be known as *Volke Savan the White Hart Arcanist.* That has a nice ring to it, right?"

Calisto whipped around and dashed at Illia. He pulled his cutlass with lightning speed, and I thought Illia would be sliced clean in half. She teleported the moment before he struck and appeared on top of another swing gun cannon farther down the deck. With her palm placed firmly on the cold iron, she glared.

"You've made the last mistake of your fucking life," Calisto drawled, his hatred evident in his slipping composure.

Illia gasped as she held a hand to her mouth. The fighting came to a standstill. Even Calisto's manticore, Hellion, turned to him with giant circles on his masked face.

"That's uncalled for," I said, my injuries preventing me from standing.

"What?" Calisto said, holding up both arms. "What's uncalled for?"

"The f-word." I shook my head. "Why would you ever say that?"

"Are you *serious*? I'm a pirate! I cut out a child's *eye*."

"That kind of language... is never necessary," Master

Zelfree groaned as he continued to bleed out across the deck. "There's no excuse."

Calisto frowned deeper than I had ever seen him before. "So, what? We're going to stop fighting because I cursed?"

"I think you should apologize," Illia said.

Nicholin hopped up and down on her shoulder. "Yeah. An apology is in order. Think of all the minds you've damaged with your *rude* language. This is a young adult story!" He swished his tail in anger.

"*Fine*," Calisto growled. "I'm sorry I used the f-word. Can we get back to the fighting now?"

Everyone glanced between each other and nodded— except for Master Zelfree, who could barely move and was about to die.

"Okay, then," Calisto said. "*Hellion!* Kill these wretches! I want their insides painted across my flag!"

My heart beat so loud I almost couldn't hear the crowds.

"Are we ready?" the announcer asked, laughter at the edge of his voice. "Then let's begin!"

Vercingetorix roared, signifying the start of the match.

"You handle the orthrus," Zaxis commanded.

He dashed forward, not bothering to hear my reply. Forsythe shot up and leapt into flight, his body glowing with an intense heat I hadn't seen before.

I turned to Luthair. We didn't need to speak. He merged with me in the next moment, his power invigorating. Wrapped in inky plate armor and with a cape fluttering at my back, I looked more like a true knight than even some of the Knights Draconic. With my shadow sword in one hand and the shield on my other arm, I faced Crevis and his orthrus, Grim.

The two heads of the orthrus flashed their fangs. Grim was a big dog, and when riled, his fur stood on end, poking through the thin leather armor secured to his chest and haunches.

Forsythe blasted fire from his body—flames erupted out past his feathers in a wave of extreme heat. Dart and his barghest shielded their eyes. Thousands in the crowd applauded.

"That attack was *super effective*," the announcer shouted.

While his opponents were effectively blinded, Zaxis lunged through the blaze. The metal on his knuckles heated, becoming reddish-white, and when he punched the bat-like face of the barghest, he seared away a layer of flesh. The black dog tumbled to the side, his screech painful.

"A critical hit!"

The cheering electrified my already restless body.

Crevis drew his sword and pointed. "Grim, use *quick attack*!" His voice, although boisterous, struggled to pierce through the excited cries.

Oh, no! Quick attack allowed Grim to attack out of speed order! Thankfully, he was a normal type, and I was a dark type, so there wouldn't be any extra damage taken. He struck me with a single hit and then returned to his side of the battle arena to dutifully wait for my turn to attack, for some reason.

"Someone better call Nurse Joy," the announcer said, still laughing. "Prepare for trouble and make it double, am I right? *Get it*? Because orthrus have two heads? *Double* trouble? Did you get it?"

DURING PLAGUE ARCANIST
(BOOK 4)
AFTER THE INCIDENT AT THE DIG SITE

I glanced past Hexa and held my breath. There it was. The *Sun Chaser* in all its glory. Winds swept around underneath it, disturbing the nearby trees and grass. Captain Devlin waited near the rope ladder, his arms crossed.

Master Zelfree stood next to him, his expression a lot more jovial than I had ever seen from him.

"Volke!" someone shouted. "It's really you!"

A girl ran toward me, her long white hair fluttering behind her. She never slowed her pace, and when she finally reached me, she collided with my chest, embracing me as though she couldn't believe I was real. Fortunately, she weighed much less than the others. Her impact on me was like a leaf on a brick wall.

I held her, half confused.

She was Princess Evianna, from the Argo Empire.

Her shadow swirled around her feet. "My arcanist," the darkness said. "You should give him time to recover."

Evianna's knightmare! Of course. Now I understood how

Illia had used her Occult Compass to find me. It all came together, and again, I couldn't help but smile.

"It's okay, Layshl," Evianna muttered as she pressed her face against my chest. "I know Volke missed me, too. And now that he's back, he can start training me."

"What?" Atty asked. She pushed her way through the crowd and then smoothed her white shirt and trousers. Somehow, she always seemed pure and bright. Her gold hair fell around her face in slight curls as she turned to face me. "Volke has to come with me to my family's home. I need his help."

Karna held up a hand, her doppelgänger magic somehow making her more beautiful than ever. "Excuse me? I already called dibs, thank you very much. No one is trying for Volke's attention and affection like *I* am."

As though anticipating some sort of interjection, Zaxis glanced over at Illia. The two of them stared at one another, having a silent conversation.

"I wasn't going to say anything," Illia muttered as she rolled her one eye.

Zaxis crossed his arms. "I just wanted to make sure."

"What's it called when there's a man in a relationship with multiple women?" Adelgis asked Fain. He rubbed at his chin. "I think there's a word for that."

"A divorce?" Fain quipped.

"No. It starts with an 'h' and ends in an angry fandom."

"*Enough*," I said, my face so red it put tomatoes to shame. I was blushing so hard that even my ears felt like they were on fire. "We aren't talking about this anymore!"

Master Zelfree—who had also gone red in the face—pushed Atty, Evianna, and Karna away. Then he shoved me toward the airship. "This is why I hate teenagers," he muttered under his breath. "Make up your damn mind already."

"Ya know, some of us don't even *have* love interests," Fain called out from the back of the group. "I'm just sayin'."

DURING WORLD SERPENT ARCANIST
(BOOK 5)

ON THE TREK TO THE WORLD SERPENT'S
LAIR

Although I should've been sleeping, I never found the ability to do so.

I waited out on the field of the atlas turtle, Luthair, my constant companion. Knightmares didn't need to sleep, after all, and he stayed out of the darkness the entire time. His inky-liquid armor was interesting to watch, but his cape caught everyone's attention. The twinkling stars in the lining of the material mimicked the night sky. I stared at it from time to time, remembering how the stars maintained their positions in the sky, even if they never received recognition.

That was what I needed to be.

As I watched the silhouette of a massive tree emerge through the fog of the horizon, I knew that this would be the time I had to stand strong. The tree was in front of us, but the ships of our enemies were on the opposite horizon, following us at a distance with their force of cutthroats and villains.

We couldn't allow anyone else to bond with the world

serpent. I would help take Ryker deep into the haven, and that would be when he bonded. Then we would have a god-arcanist on our side. We could win this war.

Hopefully.

"You needn't fret," Luthair said.

I inhaled deeply. "I'll try not to."

"No matter what happens, know that it is an honor fighting by your side."

My throat tightened with emotion as I glanced over at him. "Don't talk like that. Everyone will make it through this."

"Reality has a way of changing things."

Although I knew he was right, I didn't want to think about that. I wanted to focus on making it out of this *triumphant*. What would I do without Luthair? I couldn't even imagine.

Caught up in my memories, I exhaled. "When I was younger, the only people who had my back were Gravekeeper William and Illia. They believed in me when no one else would. Luthair... You were the first one outside of my family who thought I was worth something. Now lots of people depend on me and want my help, but it's... it's only because of you. I'm nothing without you by my side."

Luthair placed a gauntleted hand on my shoulder. "No, my arcanist. If we hadn't bonded, I would've spent my days sulking in the Endless Mire, hating myself for failing Mathis. It's only because of *you* that I'm even here at this momentous battle." He lowered his hand and stared at me with his full shadow helmet. "I won't let the same thing that happened to Mathis happen to you. I'll protect you because you're the type of man who changes the world with your passion, dedication, and honor."

I rubbed at my face, trying to keep my breathing steady. "Seriously—don't talk like that. We'll make it through this."

"*You'll* make it through this, my arcanist. I give you my word."

"Well, *that* doesn't sound like ominous foreshadowing."

ABOUT THE AUTHOR

Shami Stovall is a multi-award-winning author of fantasy and science fiction, with several best-selling novels under her belt. Before that, she taught history and criminal law at the college level and loved every second. When she's not reading fascinating articles and books about ancient China or the Byzantine Empire, Stovall can be found playing way too many video games, especially RPGs and tactics simulators.

If you want to contact her, you can do so at the following locations:

Website: https://sastovallauthor.com
Twitter: @GameOverStation
Facebook: www.facebook.com/SAStovall
Email: s.adelle.s@gmail.com

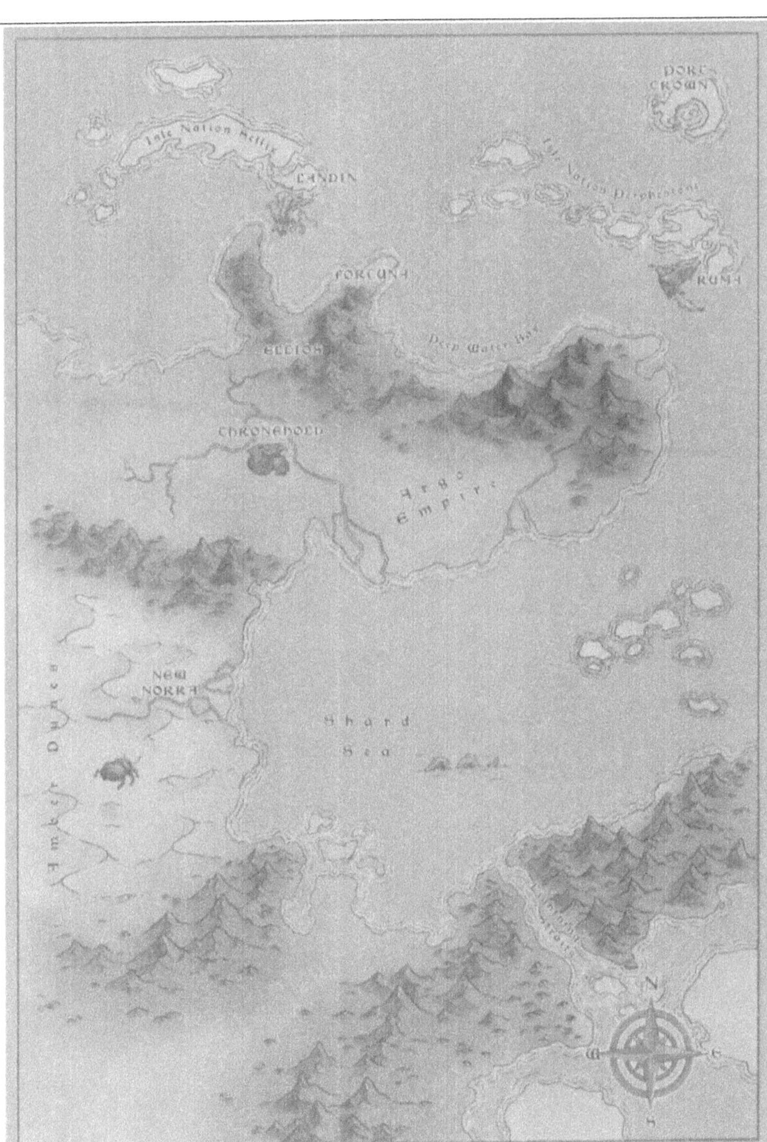

DORE-CROWN
Isle Nation Nellis
LANDIN
Isle Nation Prophecont
RUMI
FORTUNA
ELLIOS
Deep Water Bay
CHRONAHOLD
Argo Empire
NEW NORRA
Shard Sea
Amber Duchy
N
E
W
S